THE MIDNIGHT MAN

An Amos Walker Mystery

Loren D. Estleman

FAWCETT CREST • NEW YORK

A Fawcett Crest Book
Published by Ballantine Books
Copyright © 1982 by Loren D. Estleman

Library of Congress Catalog Card Number: 82-944

ISBN 0-449-21135-5

First published by Houghton Mifflin Company. Reprinted by permission
of Houghton Mifflin Company.

Manufactured in the United States of America

First Ballantine Books Edition: April 1987

To the Family Estleman
Four against the world

Now hast thou but one bare hour to live
And then thou must be damned perpetually.
Stand still, you ever-moving spheres of Heaven
That time may cease and midnight never come.

—CHRISTOPHER MARLOWE
Doctor Faustus

1

LOOK FOR US ON STARLESS NIGHTS WHEN THE MOON IS new. Look closely, because we're hard to see. We don't run in packs like wolves or feral dogs; we fear each other as much as we fear the light. The shadows are our home, and we know them as you know the staircase to your bedroom, the light switch on your bathroom wall. Look for us, but keep your distance. We're the Midnight Men, and the prey we're stalking could be you.

IT WAS ONE OF THOSE GUMMY MORNINGS WE GET ALL through July and August, when the warm wet towel on your face is the air you're breathing, and the headache you wake up with is the same one you took to bed the night before. Milk turns in the refrigerator. Doors swell. Flies clog the screens gasping for oxygen. Everything you touch sticks, including the receiver you pick up just to stop the bell from jangling loose your tender brain.

"Yeah?" If it's eloquence you seek, don't call me before breakfast.

The voice on the other end was female and very brisk. "Amos Walker? Please hold for Owen Mullett." After a muffled click, I was treated to the score of a hit musical I had managed to avoid when it played Detroit.

My eggs were making angry noises in the kitchen. Yawning bitterly, I carried the telephone in from the living room and propped the receiver under my chin while I diced part of a green pepper into pieces the size of pencil shavings and sprinkled them over the yolks and whites in the skillet. Next to cigarettes and whiskey, spices are my only serious addiction, courtesy of some gypsies on my mother's side. I let the eggs cook a while and then killed the gas. The music was still playing. I turned on the radio over the breakfast nook. It was tuned to the all-oldies station as usual. The telephone cord wouldn't let me sit down, so I placed the plate with the eggs on the edge of the table and ate standing up.

I was pouring a second cup of coffee when the telephone music stopped. I set down the pot and held the receiver out to the radio speaker. Little Richard was screaming "Lucille." I gave it five bars and then flipped it off and returned the instrument to my ear.

Someone was diddling the plunger. "Hello? Hello?" It was a harsh, impatient voice, the kind that comes with the key to the executive washroom. "Damn it, is anyone on this line?"

"This is Walker," I said. "I heard yours. What do you think of mine?"

"What are you talking about? I don't have time for kid games. Oh, to hell with it. This is Owen Mullett. Do you remember me?"

"I should say I do, Mr. Mullett. And even if I didn't, I'd remember your money." There was no reason I shouldn't. So far it had settled two alimony payments, overhauled my Cutlass, put new wallpaper in my office, replaced the venerable magazines in my reception room, and installed fresh lettering on the door.

Owen Mullet agreed. "Five hundred dollars a week just for staying available is hard to forget. Don't think Transcontinental Transport takes sums like that lightly in today's economic climate. We have investors to whom the notion of retaining a private detective—"

"What can I do for you, Mr. Mullett?"

He cleared his throat. It sounded like heavy static on the line. "Do you have any objections to going to the University of Michigan?"

"Think they'll take me?"

"Be serious, Walker. There's a load of bound newspapers due at the Ann Arbor campus this afternoon for microfilming. They're all from the last century. Some collectors would pay a bundle to have them, and they wouldn't ask too many questions about where they came from."

"All collectors are nuts," I said. "I tend to have not a lot to do with them, ever since a cop I know arrested one for collecting dead women's shoes."

"It's the driver we're interested in, not the collector."

"Talk away, Mr. Mullett."

Again he cleared his larynx. You can measure a company man's importance by the amount of presidential shoe polish lodged in his throat.

"As you know, we've been plagued by hijackings lately," he began. "A lot of hijackings. Far more than any of our competitors.

I ate my eggs and listened. I wish I hadn't.

LIKE EVERYTHING ELSE, TAILING A SUBJECT REQUIRES CERtain accessories: Water cooler. Dried foods. Portable electric razor. Binoculars. Paperbound books to help while away hours spent outside apartment buildings and motels. Complete change of clothing. Blankets. Gasoline credit cards. Change for parking meters and pay telephones. I had enough stuff jammed under the bucket seats of my little Cutlass to stock a bomb shelter. You never know how long you'll be out on one of these things. One time I picked up a salesman suspected of larceny from his employer Thursday afternoon and didn't get home until 3:00 A.M. Monday. Oh, and a large empty coffee can.

I had a full tank of gas and was parked in a loading zone across from a garage on Van Dyke, pretending to read the *Free Press* through a pair of sunglasses. The garage was a 1950s construction, white gloss enamel over cement block, with old-fashioned pumps out front, soon to be replaced by the kind that registers your purchase in liters, which was the Bureau of Weights and Measures' way of allowing merchants to charge more for less—as if they needed help. Enough die-cast letters had dropped out of the legend NORM'S SUPER SERVICE over the big doors to make it unintelligible.

A cabover Kenworth with trailer was parked next to the building facing the street, big as Judgment Day and bearing the company's red double-T logo on the front of the box. Its diesel was idling, belching round black smoke signals out of its chromed stack. The rig was waiting for a party named Dooley Bass, half owner of Norm's Super Service and sometime driver for Transcontinental Transport. He had been hijacked twice in three months and his employers were beginning to wonder.

I knew he was going to be sobering news when he emerged from the cool, dark interior of the garage, squinting into the sun and dragging a beefy brown forearm across his brow. He was all muscle and thick hard belly under a green work shirt stained dark under the armpits and down the front, and he wore his dirty blond hair in bangs the way Chuck Connors used to in *Branded*. He had a big, clean-shaven jaw and very pale blue eyes against the bronze of his face. He was younger than I. I hoped we could keep our relationship on a vehicle-to-vehicle basis.

He walked clear around the rig, kicking each of the outside tires with a square-toed cowboy boot that for a change looked as if it might have seen use west of Kalamazoo. His muscles bulged as he gripped the handbar and swung his six-feet-something up into the driver's seat. The door whammed shut, there was the plaintive *awharr* of a great transmission grinding reluctantly into grandpappy low, the engine throbbed louder, and when the traffic let up, sixteen tons of steel and rubber trundled, groaning and hissing, onto Van Dyke heading north. I let two cars go by and then pulled out behind. The corrugated steel trailer was easy to overlook, like a brontosaurus on a whole wheat roll.

I followed him up the ramp onto the westbound Edsel Ford Freeway and made myself comfortable, unsnapping the .38 in its police holster from my belt and laying it on the seat next to my hip. The air conditioner worked for two minutes and then quit, but with the vents open and my window down, the cool air coming in from outside felt good against my overheated skin. I got the radio going. Sarah Vaughan sang "It Ain't No Use." It was one I liked. If there was an omen in the refrain, it was wasted on me. I fired up a Winston and let the slipstream suck the smoke out the window.

Feeling a responsibility to my client now that I was on retainer, I had purchased fresh batteries for the paging device in my shirt pocket and was wearing it everywhere these days. It hadn't beeped once since. I hadn't really expected it to. Aside from the trucking firm, the only customer I'd had in a month was a kid who'd paid me a buck and a half to find his dog. I'm still looking for it, by the way.

There were worse assignments than this one, most of which I'd had. I'd heard rumors that trees and grass grew between here and Ann Arbor, and on a day like this coeds there were not known to wear very much while walking across campus. In Detroit they wore chain mail and carried mace in their handbags.

We hovered around the speed limit until we cleared the city, where Dooley shook the law out of his hair and opened the throttle. The trailer pulled away from me like the road-runner ditching the coyote. The Italians can brag all they want, but nothing without wings can catch a fully loaded semi when the driver chooses to slip the surly bonds of earth. I tried for a while, then fell back when the born-again Cadillac mill under my hood started shimmying.

I wondered if he'd made me. Just in case, I waited until he got hung up in traffic near Metropolitan Airport and passed him in the fast lane. After half a mile with the truck in my rearview mirror, I allowed myself to get bogged down behind a slow-moving van loaded with kids. By that time he was in the open, and the thunder of his engine drowned out the radio as he swept past on the right. I waited for a hole and crept out into his wake.

The brake lights of the cars that separated us flashed on in ragged order. He had slowed down suddenly. I had to pump my own brakes to avoid a pileup. The other vehicles started pulling around him, and when we dropped to forty-five it was either pass him again or yell my game plan out the window. I moved toward the outside lane. Abruptly he swung left. I yanked the wheel right to keep off his bumper, and drew abreast of his rear wheels.

Something big caught my eye in the rearview mirror, but

before I could react, a soot-blackened tanker labeled EX-PLOSIVE CHEMICALS rumbled alongside me in the far right lane. I looked up into the driver's shiny black face leering down at me through his open window. I was sandwiched but good. There was a third truck up ahead, and when I glanced up at Dooley on my left he was leaning as far out the cab window on the passenger's side as he could without surrendering his grip on the wheel. A long red cylinder spat and fizzled in his corded right hand. A live flare.

I finished cranking up my window just as he let fly. The flare struck the glass and bounced off, loosing orange sparks all over. I touched the brake pedal, but even as I dropped back a skull-rattling bellow drove my spine through my scalp. Behind me, a fourth truck with a grinning silver grille was closing fast, its air horn setting the pavement vibrating. Now I knew how a walnut felt.

I'd been stopped once behind a big Mercury at a red light when an eighteen-wheeler on its left made an illegal right turn, bumping one set of wheels up over the Merc's hood and damn near cutting it in two. The driver of the semi just kept going. He didn't know the car existed. I had four of them on me, and my car weighed barely half as much as that wrecked sedan. My nails dug holes in the steering wheel.

And then I was in the clear.

It was as if I'd realized suddenly that I was having a nightmare and consciously willed the situation to change. I was all alone in a stretch of open road. Up ahead, all four trucks were shrinking into distance as if a powerful spring that had been holding them back were suddenly released.

An automobile horn tooted behind me. My attention jerked to the mirror, where the driver of a blue Datsun was flashing his headlamps on and off and yanking his left index finger around in a short arc toward the apron. I couldn't make out his features.

I'd had enough of being scared for one day. I cruised across the right lane and rolled to a halt, sliding the Smith & Wesson from its holster even before the car stopped rocking. I left the driver's door open and was waiting on the other side with the revolver clasped in both hands, my arms stretched out across the vinyl roof, when he pulled up behind. A green Chevette slowed as it went past, then accelerated when the driver spotted the gun.

The man behind the wheel of the Japanese compact made no move to get out. I chugged a bullet into the pavement just ahead of the front axle. Pebbles and pieces of asphalt rattled against the underside of the fenders.

"Out, hands high!" I commanded. Some of my best stuff comes from B westerns.

He alighted, holding his hands at shoulder level. All six feet of him in a blue summerweight uniform with sergeant's stripes on the sleeves. Sunlight glared off his silver badge.

My stomach knotted. "Tell me you're going to a costume party."

"You're fresh out of luck, pal."

He might have been talking to a guy he'd stopped for busting a light. He was built heavy, not as flamboyantly muscular as Dooley Bass, but not as thick around the middle either. His rumpled black hair was shot with gray.

I said the sort of thing you'd expect me to say in that situation, laid the gun on top of the roof, and stepped back, raising my own hands.

He drew his side arm. "This side."

I came around the front and assumed the position, spread-eagled with my back to him and my hands braced against the roof. More cars slowed down to watch. I was this morning's gawkers' delight.

"Private heat, huh?" He divided his attention between the contents of my wallet and me. He had my .38 in his belt and his hands had been everyplace I might have been hiding another. "I'm on my way home. I hear these truckers yammering away over the CB about a hijacking and flag my ass across the service drive to here. I get on the horn and they're gone like butter on a hot sidewalk. Maybe you'd care to fill me in on the rest."

I cared. When I finished he made a disrespectful sound involving his lips and teeth.

"How long you been in practice?"

"Since about two years before I was born." I turned to face him. He'd holstered his revolver.

"Then you should know you don't tail one of these rigs unless you're in tandem. Once they make you you're meat for the grinder."

"I work solo."

"That's how they bury you."

"Are you holding me?"

"I could."

We watched each other. An empty haulaway stormed past along the inside lane, sucking at our clothes and hair. He handed back my wallet and gun.

"Permit's in order, which means no rap sheet. Anyway, I don't get the department band on my box and I'm damned if I'll go back to the station. Your driver's license expires next month. Happy birthday."

"Aren't you going to ask me if I want to press charges?"

"For what, littering? You must be kidding."

"Yeah. Thanks for mixing, Sergeant. A lot of off-duty cops would have directed their attention elsewhere. I owe you."

His face was built to grimace—square, much-lined, with tired eyes and a broad, humorous mouth. "Best way you can pay it back is if I don't see you or this bucket again."

I fingered out one of my cards. "If you ever need one."

He glanced at it, then unbuttoned one of his shirt pockets and poked it inside. His parting nod used up about a sixteenth of an inch of perfectly good space.

"What's your name?" I called out, as he was climbing under the wheel of the Datsun.

He strapped himself in. "Van Sturtevant. Van's my first name, not part of the last." He pulled his door shut with a cheesy *whang*.

I lit a fresh cigarette and lifted a hand as he pulled out into traffic, his engine cooking like grease on a cheap griddle.

POLICE SERGEANT SURVIVES TRIPLE SLAYING, read the headline in the next morning's *Free Press*.

2

I MISSED MY AIR CONDITIONER THAT MORNING. THE AIR swam inside the car and the seat burned my legs through my pants. The brittle brown husks of dead flies lined the dusty dash where it met the windshield. On my way to the office I made a mental note to give the interior a good cleaning, and forgot about it by the time I found a parking space.

My paper never showed up and I tuned in too late to catch the local news on my car radio. I picked up a copy at the stand down the street from my building. The banner caught my eye immediately. These days they only use that size type for notable murders and the odd nuclear holocaust.

One Detroit police officer was critically injured and two others killed in an apparent ambush on the city's northwest side early this morning, which also resulted in the death of one of the four suspects.

Sought in connection with the slayings are Alonzo Smith, 24, Luke David Turkel, 22, and Willie Lee Gross, 19. The three were wanted for questioning in an arson investigation at the time of the shooting. A fourth suspect, Roscoe

LaRue, 19, was wounded by return fire and reported dead on arrival at Detroit Receiving Hospital at 3:16 A.M.

Police said Sgt. Edward F. Maxson, 38, and Patrolman William Flynn, 22, were emerging from their squad car in front of a house belonging to Gross's father on Clarita near Mt. Hazel Cemetery when Maxson was killed instantly by fire from an upstairs window. A second shot missed Flynn, who returned fire and radioed for assistance, police said.

The call was answered by Sgt. Van Sturtevant, 43, who was patroling without a partner. Police said Sturtevant saw LaRue running from an alley behind the building and called for him to halt, shooting him when he failed to comply. Sturtevant was then wounded in the back and Flynn was slain as two guns opened fire from the cemetery. The sergeant, an 18-year veteran of the department, was reported in critical condition at Detroit Receiving Hospital later this morning.

One of the most intensive manhunts in the city's history . . .

And so it went, lousy with attributing phrases in a careful ballet around the libel laws, broken into fragments of columns and scattered throughout the first section so that I had to take it up to the office to finish it without being fined for littering. When I was done the place looked like Que Noc after Charlie's propaganda plane and then ours had passed over, jettisoning leaflets like bird droppings. I was tidying up when the telephone rang. It was the brisk voice from the secretarial pool, asking me to hold for Owen Mullett. I hung up almost gently.

It rang again half a minute later. I finished putting the mess back together, poured myself a slug from the office bottle, put it down in a lump, and lifted the instrument.

"Do you realize how much work I could get done in

the time it takes to get you back on the line, for chris-sake?''

"No," I said. "How much, Mr. Mullett?"

"How much what?"

"How much work could you get done in the time it takes to get me back on the line, for chrissake?''

"I don't know," he said confusedly. "A lot."

"Figure it out and call me back." I cut the connection.

I got one out and lit it, shaking the match the way a terrier destroys a rat in its jaws, and flipping it in the general direction of the glass souvenir ashtray on the desk. This time I answered on the third ring.

"What kind of shit are you trying to pull, Walker?''

"Your language is offensive, Mr. Mullett. Good-bye, Mr. Mullett."

"No! Wait! Don't hang—"

I nailed it on the first ring the next time. "I don't like your taste in music, either.''

"Don't hang up!" he pleaded. "Walker?''

"I'm here."

"Listen, I can't figure out what I did that put the bee on you, but don't you think I'm entitled to the report I paid for?''

I breathed some air. "You're right, Mr. Mullett. Hang on." I laid the handset down on the calendar pad and hiked around the desk three times, going faster each turn. I did sixty pushups. I boxed with my shadow and won on a technicality. I walked over to the original *Casablanca* poster in its imitation wood frame and sneered at Bogart. Flattened out in a forty-year-old, badly painted portrait, he still sneered better than I did. The bitterness out of my system, I went back to the desk and sat down and picked up the receiver and recounted yesterday's adventure, leaving out Van Sturtevant's name. He hadn't paid for that.

13

"Hm," he said. "Hm. Do you think Dooley Bass would recognize you again?"

"Only my car."

"What about the other drivers?"

"I don't know. I don't think it really matters. The way I see it, they were just helping out a fellow driver. He reported me as a hijacker. If they were in with him, their all being in the area just when they were needed stacks up to a pretty healthy coincidence. Unless the operation is a lot bigger than you think, in which case I'd call ICC. Not bloody likely, as Benny Hill says."

He cleared his throat. More shoe polish. "Are you still working for us, Walker?"

"That's up to you, Mr. Mullett. I was smarting off fairly heavily there. I guess I'm myself today."

"Don't give it another thought," he said expansively. I let him expand. People hear what they want to, and if he'd heard an apology on my end it wasn't my place to set him straight. "I've done business with all the car rental agencies in this area," he went on. "Give them my name and pick out something appropriate. Meaning inconspicuous."

That ruled out the red Jaguar with leopard-skin seats I'd had my eye on. "Dooley Bass again?"

"Yes. He's got a load of machine tools to Monroe Saturday. I'll call later with the particulars. The newspapers got to Ann Arbor, by the way. We're going to keep following him until he tries stealing from us again."

I wondered where Mullett was planning to ride. "He'll be wary now. Let's give him some slack."

"I'm not paying for slack. Trust me. This guy's got suicidal guts like the guy that killed Kitty Genovese. He'll tumble." He hung up on me this time.

I turned on the radio. There was nothing new on the

shooting, except that now the 22-year-old cop was the one who nailed LaRue on the fly. They were still milking the wire report they'd received hours ago. A rookie isn't likely to hit much of anything with all that lead screaming around his ears. It's hard enough when no one's shooting back. I turned it off and winched the city directory out of its drawer.

"Detroit Receiving." A woman's voice.

"This is Alex Wainwright at the *News*," I announced. "I'm checking on Sergeant Sturtevant's condition."

"One moment, sir."

A new voice came on. "Hello? Who is this?"

That was no nurse or doctor. That was Lieutenant John Alderdyce, childhood friend, adult nemesis, and Homicide detective in good standing. I shifted into my Sessue Hayakawa impression.

"Herro? Herro? This Fujiyama's Fine Libs?"

A pause. "No, it isn't. Who's speaking?"

"Ah. So solly. Call lestaurant. Long numbah. Goobye."

"Wait a minute. Who—"

I scowled at the receiver in its cradle. Department procedure would call for a man on duty at the hospital desk. The fact that he was from Homicide didn't necessarily mean the worst. But I was sorry I'd called.

MY SHIRT WAS ALREADY CLINGING TO MY BACK WHEN I reached the car, and as I pulled into the hospital parking lot the main building shimmered like the lost palace of Atlantis behind rising waves of heat. The pavement was tacky under my feet and the air was thick with the sweet smell of melting tar. I was gasping by the time I stepped from oven heat into the cool, muted atmosphere of the central lobby.

This was my first visit to the facility at its new location. I'd been wheeled into the old structure, nursing a bullet-splintered rib, shortly before the move. At the desk a fortyish nurse with a scrubbed look and the preoccupied air of a company commander in the midst of a bombardment directed me to the emergency room and promptly wiped out all memory of my existence. At least I think she was a nurse. She was wearing a pink pantsuit and nothing on her head. These days the whole world is in mufti.

Hieronymus Bosch might have taken inspiration from that emergency room. An old man in a crushed fedora and a fuzzy coat sweater—despite the heat—was sitting on an upholstered bench rocking back and forth, moaning loudly and cradling an obviously broken wrist in his other arm, while a dumpy, middle-aged woman seated next to him tried to comfort him with her arm around his skinny shoulders. At the other end, what looked like a ten-year-old kid sat sniffling with a bloody handkerchief to his eye, beside a woman whose overly made-up face was pale and contorted as she scolded him. To one side of the wide entrance, a teenaged nurse or something in a yellow shirt and designer jeans had a clipboard in one hand and was asking a young woman shivering on a gurney under a thin blanket if she was with Blue Cross. Men in white coats and women in pants hurried in and out through swinging doors, looking grim and efficient. Restaurants should do such business.

"I was wondering when you'd show up."

I resisted the impulse to hunch my shoulders at the sound of the voice behind me, and turned around. John Alderdyce—black, balding, and impeccably tailored as usual in a gabardine suit and gray silk sport shirt open at the neck—was entering on silent rubber heels through the door I'd just used. The whites of his eyes glistened malignantly un-

16

der heavy, blue-black brows. He was mopping his palms with a paper napkin like the kind you get in hospital commissaries.

"Was I that bad?" I started to place a cigarette between my lips, then put it back in the pack when the pubescent nurse or whatever with the clipboard glared at me.

"I've heard your Japanese accent before," John said. "Follow me." He turned and retraced his steps through the door and down a shallow corridor into a bite-size waiting room with pastel walls and some fruit salad hanging in frames. We had two short sofas and an ugly plant in an artificial wood stand all to ourselves. There were no ashtrays. That's how they save on NO SMOKING signs today. Neither of us sat down.

"How's Sturtevant?" I asked.

He looked grave, which meant nothing. He always did. "Still in surgery. The doctors say the bullet's lying against his spinal cord and they won't know how much damage it's done till it's out."

"I heard he was critical."

"You heard right. The best neurosurgeon in the place has been working on him for four hours." He paused. "There's about a ninety percent chance he won't walk again even if the operation's successful."

I didn't say anything.

"Why didn't you identify yourself over the phone?" he asked.

I moved my shoulders. "I didn't want you thinking I was mixing in your case. Lectures I don't need."

"Aren't you? I was just thinking of getting in touch with you when you called the hospital." He slid a pasteboard rectangle from an inside pocket and held it out. It was one of my cards. "This is a modern department, Walker. When someone gets shot and we want answers

17

we send his shirt down to the lab for tests. The pockets get checked first."

"That was personal," I said. "It has nothing to do with the shooting."

"Indulge a detective's curiosity."

I gave him a condensed version of the incident on the Edsel Ford. "I'm sure I can count on you to keep that off the books," I added. "Sturtevant probably didn't file a report, and a hole in the back is enough without Internal Affairs jumping up and down on it."

He nodded absently and looked as if he needed a smoke. As usual. I couldn't remember a time when he wasn't trying to quit. "I'll ask Sturtevant about it when and if he pulls through. I hope for your sake your stories mesh."

"So do I. You're ugly when you're mad."

"That's what my wife says. But we've got three kids, so I don't credit it."

"What you got on the shooters?"

The lines in his face deepened. "Everything but where they are right now. The usual stuff: Born in the ghetto of alcoholic parents, slashing tires at nine, in and out of juvenile hall at fourteen. Alonzo Smith's kind of an exception. He was a bad kid like the others, but when he turned eighteen he joined the marines for a three-year hitch. Most of them don't even bother to register for the draft, when there is one."

"How was his record?"

"Not as bad as you'd think. Black marks here and there, and once he did a week in the stockade for insubordination, but on the whole he seems to have taken to military discipline. That could be why he was so eager to join this neo-Black Panther group he and the others belonged to."

"Just them?"

He shook his head. "There are more, sad to say. Ass-holes all. They've been in and out of the slam so much their fingers are stained permanently with ink. We're rounding them up now. One of them knows something."

"I'm sure they can't wait to get to the tape recorder."

"Smith has a girlfriend. We'll work on her." His eyes darted toward the entrance and back to me. They were set deep and very bright. "Smith, Turkel, Gross. I never told this to anyone, but whenever I start an investigation I always write the suspects' names on a slip of paper and tape it to the bathroom mirror. That way I see them every morning when I'm shaving and I remember not to think about anything else for the rest of the day. But, you know? This is one time I won't have to do that. Smith, Turkel, Gross. Nope. No chance of me forgetting to think about them."

"How well did you know Sturtevant and the others?"

"Never met them. They whisked Sturtevant into surgery before I could question him. But I still won't forget. Maybe it's the names: Smith, Turkel, Gross. Tinker to Evers to Chance."

"It's not the names."

He shrugged. I got out my battered pack of Winstons and offered him one. He accepted it. I took one for myself and lit them both. To hell with hospital regulations. The match went into the phony wood pot.

Alderdyce drew the smoke in so deep that very little of it came back out. "What's your interest in this?" His eyes probed me like physician's fingers.

"Purely personal, like I said."

"Because he did you a good turn?" He looked skeptical.

"Not just that, although that would be plenty. I'm used to my neck and am apt to be very well disposed to anyone who saves it." I knocked some nonexistent ash into the pot. "When I was halfway through boot camp I saw a drill sergeant blown to pieces by a percussion grenade some wag had rigged to his footlocker. One second he was there and the next he was a bloody twist of hide in a shredded uniform. I didn't know him, but I was a while getting over it. When I read about what happened this morning I thought immediately of him. You never met Sturtevant; I only met him once. Does it make any sense?"

He looked at me strangely. "Don't mix in, Walker."

"Who, me?"

My guilelessness laid a large goose egg. "We dick around a lot about your work and my work and whether you should or shouldn't get involved in police business, but this time it's for real. There are going to be bodies on this one. Make an effort not to be one of them."

He screwed out his stub in the moist black earth in the pot and looked back at me. I was smoking in silence.

"Say it," he said.

"I'm just being grateful."

"For what?"

"For not having my name taped on your bathroom mirror."

He left. I finished my cigarette and went out a minute later. A small trim blonde was standing in the corridor, sniffling quietly into a sturdy handkerchief. She wore a tight black dress as if she were already in mourning, and her hair looked as if she had done it up in a hurry hours before and hadn't touched it since.

"Mrs. Sturtevant?" I asked gently.

She lifted a tear-swollen face from the hanky. "Y-yes?" Her eyes focused on a point halfway between us.

I wrote something on the back of the card Alderdyce had given me, placed it in one of her hands, and departed with a whispered inadequacy. At the end of the hall I turned to watch her mouthing the words I'd scribbled: "No charge."

That was my second mistake.

3

As I ENTERED THE LOBBY, A TALL OLD BIRD IN A GREEN surgical gown was chewing out a young orderly in a coarse stage whisper in front of a dozen nurses, patients, and visitors. He had a small, round head with a wild shock of snow-white hair mounted high on a skinny wattled neck and emphasized each imprecation with a downward slash of his thin right arm, like Hitler conducting Beethoven. The orderly took it without interrupting. When the older man finished the orderly clamped white-knuckled fingers around the handle of his empty gurney and pushed it and himself out of sight in the direction of the elevators. An embarrassed silence was soon shoved aside by the usual lobby sounds.

"He must have done something pretty terrible to rate all that," I said, approaching the old man.

He swung his face on me and gave me the once-over with sharp old eyes that weighed, analyzed, tagged, and catalogued all in one motion. Red spots the size of quarters glowed high on his otherwise sallow cheeks, but were already fading. "He's always hanging around the nurses' station when he should be working. This is a hospital, not a singles bar. Who are you, sir?'' His voice quivered on an iron core.

"My name's Walker. I'm investigating the Sturtevant case. Are you the surgeon who performed the operation?''

His parchment face shrank in on itself distastefully. "I just spoke with your Lieutenant Alderdyce. If the medical profession were run like your police department, we'd be trying to take out the same appendix three times. Don't you ever talk to each other?'' He started walking, eating up yards of tiled corridor with each lanky stride. I had to sprint to catch up.

"I'm not on Alderdyce's detail,'' I said truthfully. "How'd it go?''

"The operation went fine. The patient will never walk again, that's all.'' He spat the words. "I wish that were the worst of it.''

"What's the worst?'' My voice came from half an inch in back of my tongue.

He shucked the gown, stuffed it into a wheeled hamper under the supervision of a short jowly woman in a pebbled white uniform dress and black hairnet, muttered something pleasant in her direction, and went through a door marked STAFF ONLY with me on his heels. The woman's eyes followed his high thin back adoringly. He'd be the Robert Redford of the rubber-stocking set.

The doctors' lounge had more personality than the waiting room and no screwy paintings. A significant glance passed between the surgeon and a bearded youth in a turtleneck and shapeless white coat seated on a vinyl-upholstered sofa, and the beard put down his medical journal and left. The old man poured coffee from a glass pot.

"Off the record?'' He offered me some in a paper cone stuck in a plastic doohickey with a handle. I shook my head to the coffee but indicated that off the record was fine. He sipped. His chest and abdomen formed a perfect cylinder beneath his sweat-heavy T-shirt. His eyes nailed me to the wall.

"If you repeat it, I'll deny I said anything. Between us, the operation should never have taken place. Sturtevant's blood pressure is so high you'd need a master's degree in algebra to measure it. The anesthetic alone was enough to cause a stroke."

"Whose decision was it to operate?"

"Mine."

"I see," I said. "I think I will have some of that coffee."

"Help yourself."

I splashed steaming yellow liquid into a cone and doohickey. "So why'd you go ahead and cut?"

"I think you refer to it as a judgment call in your work," he explained, leaning his tailbone against a cafeteria table cluttered with papers and manuscripts in curled manila covers. "The bullet was lodged in the fibrocartilage between the third and fourth lumbar vertebrae, in such a way that a shift of a hundredth of an inch in any direction could cause paralysis, even death. We might have waited and tried to bring down his blood pressure before going in, but the risk was too great. A simple cough could have killed him. I judged his chances of survival to be greater with the operation than without it. Mrs. Sturtevant agreed when I explained the situation to her."

"Yet he is paralyzed."

He made a face and set his cup down on a clear space of table. It might have been the coffee. "There was too much nerve and tissue damage. What concerns me is what will happen if he suffers a series of strokes, which at this point is the only *if*. We can't administer anticoagulants to prevent them without the danger of starting him bleeding again. He's lost too much blood already. So he'll have at least one seizure. If he has more, they'll leave him either a vegetable or a corpse."

I listened to the hum of the air conditioner for a moment. "Does his wife know?"

"I watered it down for her. Anything else could result in a suit for malpractice." He watched me with hard yellow eyes, the color of the coffee. "That's the main difference between medicine and the law, Mr. Walker. The law is an exact science."

I drank up and ditched the cup. "You've been very candid and helpful. Thanks, Dr.—?"

"Praetorius." Straightening, he drove his surgeon's fingers deep into my fist to protect them from a gorilla like me. His palm was steel-belted and as dry as an AMA finding. "Alvin Praetorius."

I gave him a grin I didn't feel. "Praetorius? Wasn't that the name of the evil scientist in *The Bride of Frankenstein?*"

"I wouldn't know." He spoke coldly. "I don't watch children's pictures.

The humidity in the parking lot slapped me in the face like a mugger's glove, soggy-hot and smelling of air breathed and rejected. Still, I preferred it to the blander atmosphere inside. Out here they strangled you, shot you, slipped poison into your soup *d'jour*, knocked you in the head and sliced you up and mailed your remains all over the map, but at least when you died they didn't leave you lying there with your eyes and mouth gaping and tubes sticking out everywhere. Or slip you something questionable and cut into you on the assumption that life as a cabbage is better than no life at all. I like horror movies. In them the mad doctor always gets his before he goes too far.

THE HEAT WAVE DRAGGED ON THROUGH THE NEXT COU-ple of days, not really a wave at all but a motionless mass of breathless nothing squatting over all of southern lower Michigan and part of Ohio. I spent them in my undershirt catching up on my solitaire, waiting for the telephone to ring, and listening to the radio inform me that the dragnet was drawing tight around Smith, Turkel, and Gross. I'd believe that when they stopped telling me. Two days after the ambush, Sergeant Maxson was buried in full barbaric state. I caught the 11:00 P.M. recap and glimpsed John Alderdyce and one or two other cops I recognized among the plainclothes men following the casket down the church steps. The boys from the uniform division looked as alike in their dress blues as hairpins. Flynn's parents came from out West to take his body back home. No long blue lines or official eulogies for this rookie.

Owen Mullett called on Friday with the dope on Dooley Bass's trip to Monroe, and on Saturday, when everyone else was cooling off in the Upper Peninsula or boating on Lake St. Clair, I was breathing diesel exhaust on US-24 South with my knees in my chest behind the wheel of an inconspicuous rented AMC Spirit. I crapped out. Bass delivered his machine tools like a loyal trucker and returned to Detroit an hour ahead of schedule. At least this time he didn't notice me, for which I was grateful. He could have run over me and never felt a bump.

While I was in Monroe, Willie Lee Gross swung a stockless .30-caliber carbine out from under a long coat while being questioned by police on a street in Atlanta, Georgia, and was shot to pieces where he stood. That made one name gone from the mirror of John Alderdyce's bathroom.

I typed out a report of my Monroe excursion on the pre-Columbian Underwood in my office and delivered it in person to Mullett in his private thinking parlor on West Outer Drive Monday. He read it leaning back in a quilted leather chair behind a glass-topped desk you could have used for a skating rink, said something indelicate around the stem of his dead pipe, and filled me in on a load of Arrow shirts awaiting Dooley's attention in Flint.

"How long you want to keep this up?" I asked him, for what had to be the dozenth time. "What if Bass turns up clean?"

"Then you're free to meet with him and strike a deal for his biography. It should sell millions."

I liked that. I didn't care for Mullett and the brand of corporate bastard he represented, but somewhere under that two hundred and fifty pounds of executive luncheon there beat the heart of a born pain in the ass.

The next morning I was waiting at the warehouse in Flint when Dooley arrived to pick up the shirts. I ate a breakfast of dried dates washed down with stale cooler water while he was loading, and followed him down I-75 fifty miles north of where it becomes the Chrysler. This time I was driving a green Citation, a little more roomy than the Spirit but just as gutless. Nowadays you stick out like a bug on a butter knife if you drive anything you can get into without a shoehorn.

Things began to look interesting when Dooley made an unscheduled exit just above Pontiac. I stayed several car lengths behind him for ten miles along a two-lane blacktop until he ran out of pavement, where the traffic thinned out and I got right on his rear bumper to avoid being seen in his side mirrors. When he pulled into a driveway leading to a sagging farmhouse with a weather-battered barn, I kept going until there was a hill between us, parked as far off the roadway as I could get, and sneaked back on foot with my Nikon, screwing on the telephoto lens as I went. Birds squawked in the trees and gravel crunched under my shoes. I switched to the overgrown roadbank.

By the time I got there, my socks clotted with burrs, the barn door was open and three men in work clothes were carrying cartons inside from the big trailer. Dooley was smoking and watching beside a fifth party in faded jeans and a red-and-white-striped tank top over a skinny frame. The party was holding a sawed-off shotgun with the muzzle pointed at the ground. He didn't appear to be threatening anyone with it, least of all the driver. I clicked away.

I had exposed sixteen frames when one of the workers shouted and pointed to the big Edison pole I was crouching behind. He must have seen the sun glinting off the lens. I snapped one of him pointing for my trophy wall and took off at a gallop. There was shouting behind me, running footsteps, and then a hoarse roar that had no echo because it didn't need one. Shot rattled down through the trees in front of me at the base of the hill. A door slammed. A mighty engine growled over and over and caught with a racket like balloons exploding in close succession. Brakes let go with a whoosh, followed by the familiar groaning of the gear-change.

I reached the Citation just as the great truck lumbered into the road, jackknifing for the turn and bringing down a shower of leaves and branches from the trees on the other side. I got the little motor started and floored the pedal. The rear wheels spat gravel and grass. I pulled away just as Dooley's big square grille filled the rearview mirror.

Striped Shirt leaned out the passenger's window and his shotgun appeared in the mirror on the right side of the car, which had been what sold me on the midget machine in the first place. I threw myself sideways in the seat and the back window disappeared. When I straightened, the seat was covered with pebbles of glass. A couple of dozen black pellets studded the windshield, hairline cracks spreading out from them like strands in a web.

I gained ground on the hills—of which, fortunately, there were more than a few—but on long downward grades and the straightaway they struck sparks off my rear bumper. Then we went into a series of twisting turns that put me well out in front. I finally lost them by pulling around a circular driveway behind a farmer's house, waiting for them to thunder past, and piling back into the road going in the opposite direction. The last time I saw the rig, it was half obscured behind its own cloud of dust, turning a row of mailboxes into scrap metal and kindling as Dooley tried to swing around in a driveway too short for the purpose. The transmission whined and bellowed, the amplified baby's cry of an enraged grizzly.

WHEN THE MAN AT THE RENTAL AGENCY WAS THROUGH bewailing the loss of the rear window I gave him Owen Mullett's name and number. I smoked a cigarette in the sarcophagus the rental agent used for an office while he listened to music and then spoke with the man himself. After a minute he handed the instrument to me.

"Did you nail him?"

"In living color," I replied. "That's so you can see the red on his hands."

I gave the receiver back to the rental man behind the desk. He listened for thirty seconds and hung up, all smiles.

I took the film to a custom place for developing and slid the eight-by-tens and negatives into a folder with my typewritten report. During my drive to Mullett's office, police and helicopters cornered Luke David Turkel on the roof of a college dormitory in Raleigh, North Carolina. Half an hour later his broken body was taken to the Wake County Morgue, where pathologists dug out a slug from a Police .38 and another from a .357 magnum said to have been in Turkel's possession at the time of the attempted arrest. The fatal wound had been self-inflicted. Police said.

There was only one name left on John's mirror.

Mullett loved the pictures and authorized a thousand-dollar bonus on the spot. I didn't argue. I obtained his permission to use his firm's name as a reference and collected my check from his personal secretary, who had a brisk face to go with her voice. After banking the bonus, I ate that evening in a restaurant where, for the first time in a long while, I didn't have to place my order through an outside microphone. It didn't change my mood. My mind was miles away in the intensive care ward at Detroit Receiving.

THE MEDIA HAD A BALL WITH THE CONTINUING MANHUNT for Alonzo Smith. Network television crews and reporters from as far away as California camped out in front of Detroit Police Headquarters on Beaubien waiting for word that he'd been slain while resisting arrest. It was like the countdown to John Dillinger. Then on Friday, the fugitive spoiled everything by walking into the First Precinct and emptying his pockets before a bewildered desk sergeant, remanding himself into police custody. The out-of-state newspeople packed up and went home. Nothing spoils a good story like anticlimax.

At his arraignment three days later, Smith's girlfriend and two unidentified black male accomplices strolled into the courtroom on the fourth floor of the Frank Murphy Hall of Justice armed with M-16 assault rifles and strolled out with the defendant. No one saw them leave the building, but a search of the premises uncovered nothing.

That afternoon, Mrs. Van Sturtevant called me at my office.

4

IT WAS A TRACT HOME OFF LIVERNOIS, ALL ON ONE LEVEL
with lilac bushes out front and flagstones leading across a
nice lawn to a tiny porch with a black-enameled iron railing. It had been described to me in detail over the telephone, but I went past the place twice because every other
lot in the neighborhood was just like it. Why people wanted
to live like ants was a question for greater brains than mine.

I parked behind Sturtevant's blue Datsun and got out
under a blossoming locust where bees hummed somno-
lently like plantation darkies in an old musical. The sun
was hot on the back of my neck, the air heavy with that
scent you can't get too much of unless it comes from a
bottle. Kids' cheerful obscenities and the crack of wood on
artificial horsehide nearby testified to the existence of a
sandlot baseball diamond down the block. Another day
made for snoozing in a hammock with a portable radio
tuned in to the Tigers, and here I was in harness again,
and on the cuff to boot.

The doorbell was warm to the touch. I waited while
footsteps approached from inside, wondering how many
hours I had spent waiting for footsteps in front of how
many doors on how many days like this one. Down the

street there was another crack, louder this time, and a general tangle of shouted encouragement and shrieked insults. Extra bases at least.

"Thank you for coming, Mr. Walker. I'm Karen Sturtevant. We met the other day. My husband is in the living room."

I hadn't seen her at her best in the hospital. When she opened the door I probably still wasn't seeing it, but the improvement was more than satisfactory. She was a small blonde without seeming like one, that category having been swallowed up by the pert type with freckles and that air of good sportsmanship you can expect to find anywhere but in sports. She wore her hair in a modified page boy with a wave in front instead of bangs, framing a face that was just saved from being doll-like by a chin that came to a point. Her eyes were a cloudy green and she had a kewpie mouth. No lipstick.

"I thought he was still in the hospital." I stepped inside and she closed the door.

"So does the press. My brother and I smuggled him out under cover of darkness." She smiled tightly, just to be doing something with her mouth. "The doctors don't like it. He had a stroke, you know. They think he might have another. But I've spent time in hospitals, and if strokes can be carried those nurses are all potential Typhoid Marys." Her voice was rough-smooth, like velvet dragged over fine sandpaper. June Allyson was born with it, Lauren Bacall screamed herself hoarse to get it. That's how potent it is.

"I don't think they can be," I said. "Carried, I mean."

"What modern medicine doesn't know about the human body and its ailments would sink an ore carrier. The living room is this way."

She led me past a spotless kitchen into a living room with imitation wood paneling and a picture window looking

33

out on the picture window of the identical house next door. Today she was all in green, with a leaf-print blouse tucked neatly into a solid green skirt with a modest slit up the side. Her heels seemed high for ordinary house wear, but her legs didn't seem to mind. I decided I wouldn't either.

"Van?" She placed a hand on the shoulder of the man seated in a wheelchair in front of the big window. "Van, Mr. Walker's here."

He opened tired eyes to look at me. If not for them I wouldn't have recognized him. The strong, square face had fallen, its lines drawn deep by the weight of the grayish flesh and of the broad lower lip, pushed out in the bitter pout of the very old. His mouth wasn't humorous anymore. In two weeks his hair had turned the color of house dust. He had a blanket over his knees and a heavy sweater draped across his shoulders on the hottest day I had seen that season.

One side of his mouth twitched in a sign of recognition, and I knew then that the other side couldn't.

"He can't talk, but he'll understand everything we say." She half leaned on the arm of a houndstooth sofa next to his chair and waved me into the armchair opposite. "Can I get you something to drink?"

I shook my head. Somewhere in the house an electric fan whirred. I couldn't think who it was for. Mrs. Sturtevant appeared unaffected by the oppressive atmosphere in the room and the stirred air never reached me. Almost immediately I regretted turning down the drink.

"Okay if I smoke?" I tried to keep my eyes off her crossed ankles.

"Of course. There's an ashtray on the coffee table in front of you. What brand?"

I showed her the red-and-white pack.

"May I have one for my husband? The doctors say he

34

shouldn't, but he's put away a pack a day for twenty-five years and I can't think of anything that would do him more damage at this point than quitting cold."

I lit two, Hollywood fashion, and reached one over. She placed it between Sturtevant's lips on the good side. The tip reddened and one of his nostrils quivered.

"That last night, Van told me what happened on the Edsel Ford between you and those truckers," she said. "We were talking about it again today, and somehow I knew you were the man we wanted."

I must not have been wearing my poker face that day, because she explained: "We communicate. He can write a little with his good hand, but it's slow and he shouldn't exert himself. We've worked out a system. If he's holding my hand, he taps it with his finger. Once for no, twice for yes. If not, he blinks his eyes. You'd be surprised how refreshing a conversation can be without meaningless small talk."

"In that case," I said, "I'll spare you mine. I'm not an executioner. If you're looking for someone to kill Alonzo Smith, you're still looking. That much I don't owe your husband."

"That's exactly what we don't want. That's the reason I called you."

"You'd better go on. My brain molds up in muggy weather."

Half an inch of ash quivered on the end of Sturtevant's Winston. She took it gently from his mouth, flicked the dead matter into the copper ashtray on the coffee table, and put it back. Then she leaned forward with her hands pressed between her knees.

"If we wanted him dead, all we'd have to do is sit back and wait. The police will be more than happy to oblige. We're interested in justice, not revenge."

She had a tiny mole where the line between her breasts vanished into her blouse.

"Look at Van," she said. "He's forty-three, Mr. Walker. He could live thirty or forty more years in that chair—provided another stroke doesn't confine him to a bed or kill him. Do you really think a quick, antiseptic death would be appropriate for the man responsible? Even if Smith spends the rest of his life in a cell he'll never know this kind of imprisonment. But we'd settle for that."

I forgot about the mole and concentrated on her eyes. They weren't cloudy now. "How much of this does your husband want?"

She turned to him. "Van, do you agree with me so far?"

We watched his face. Slowly his eyelids moved down and up, down and up. She looked at me.

I said, "I gave you that card because I didn't know what else to do. I was flush and could have supplied cash for medical expenses, but that would get Internal Affairs on all our backs and besides, the department's insurance will cover the money end. You probably wouldn't have accepted it anyway. I didn't mean to make it sound as if I could succeed where the cops failed. I don't think you believe that either. So why did you call me?"

"I've been a policeman's wife a long time," she replied. "Some of it was bound to rub off. I went down to headquarters today and asked some of Van's associates about you. I was careful not to approach any of the officers investigating the shooting; I didn't want to get you in any trouble. Most of what I heard I liked, and when I repeated it to Van he liked it too."

I was smothering. It was that damn fan, whirring merrily in a place where no one could benefit from it. I loosened my tie and unbuttoned my jacket. The suit was new, bought out of Owen Mullett's bonus, and fit well even when I was wearing a gun, which I wasn't today. Not in a cop's house. I drew on what remained of my cigarette, which didn't help.

"Outside of John Alderdyce, who's up to his neck in the case," I said, "I can't think of any cops that would have much good to say about me. As a rule we get on like soap and dirt." I didn't say which I was. It varied with the telling.

Her tight smile returned, as automatic as a gesundheit. "One or two of them were polite. What swung us over was what the ones who don't like you said, and who said it. If *they* had recommended you, we'd have looked somewhere else."

"I think I know the ones you mean."

This time the expression was genuine. The cleft disappeared from between her brows and the shadows faded out under her eyes. I knocked five years off my estimate of her age. Then the humor evaporated and time rushed in to fill the vacuum. Her hand sought her husband's, lying motionless atop the blanket.

"It's a matter of attitude. With every police officer between here and Mexico hoping to send Smith to the morgue, one man willing to take him in alive might have a better chance of laying hands on him."

"Or getting dead." I blew some smoke. It hung in the thick air for a moment, then gathered its strength and started drifting toward the window. "What you say might have been true a week ago. Why didn't you call me before he turned himself in?"

"We were preoccupied." Her tone would chill champagne. "Maybe someone you cared about has never been shot and you don't know what it's like."

I did, but my biography wasn't part of the deal. I motioned for her to continue. Sturtevant's eyes slid from my face to hers and back. Cop's eyes. No bullet could change that.

"Something changed Smith's mind about facing the courts," his wife said. "Between Friday afternoon and this morning something happened that made him choose to risk death rather than life in prison. Find it, and maybe you'll find him."

"There might not be anything in that. Maybe he didn't want to leave custody, but you don't argue with an assault rifle. And if I corner him, what then? I'd have to call the cops. That citizen's arrest stuff is mainly a democratic myth."

She shrugged, deepening the hollow between her breasts for a breathless instant. "The moment of greatest danger comes just before the cuffs are applied, Van says—said. Subdue him before the law gets there, and they won't have an excuse to do anything but bring him in intact. All we ask is that you call us first. If you accept the job." Her face was as easy to read as a crooked optometrist's chart.

"I might have to farm it out," I said, thinking aloud. "There's no reason to expect him to still be in the city."

"We'll pay all expenses. Van has a pension coming."

"I'm not worrying about that. I told you, I'm flush. Let me get my tired old computer working."

While she waited, Karen Sturtevant tapped some more ash off her husband's cigarette. I watched it start growing all over again. Chimes bonged in the hallway.

"That's the nurse." She got up. "She's the condition under which the doctors agreed to release Van."

I killed my stub, stood. I felt as if I'd been sitting for a month. Then I felt guilty for feeling that way in Sturtevant's presence. "I'll give it a week. After that, you pay expenses. And arrange for my funeral if I screw up. I'll keep you posted on my progress, or lack thereof."

The doorbell sounded again. She looked at the man slumped in the wheelchair. He blinked once, twice. I almost heard his lids creak. "Fair enough. Excuse me," she said, and breezed past me trailing a faint scent of something half-remembered.

I studied Sturtevant. His weary cop's eyes remained on mine, one lid drooping as if frozen in the middle of a wry wink. "Sorry for talking around you like a footstool," I told him. I wanted to say more. He looked as if he was waiting for more. I didn't have anything more to say. On my way out, the nurse, a tall woman with a face like a stomach cramp, stared at me the way an antibiotic looks at a virus.

5

THE BASEBALL GAME HAD ENDED BY THE TIME I LEFT THE house. Boys of twelve and thirteen were walking down the street in pairs and groups, bats over their shoulders with mitts and gloves swinging from the ends, earth-colored and shiny in the palms. Somewhere in the neighborhood a power mower sputtered and started with an angry raspberry, and a private plane droned sadly through a blue hole in the smog over Detroit. The smell of cooking food floated out of open windows on both sides of the street. It was suppertime for everyone but me, the pilot, and the guy cutting his grass.

I hadn't wanted to admit it in her presence—professionals seldom do when an amateur makes a decent suggestion—but Karen Sturtevant was dead right about Alonzo Smith's reason for escaping being a good place to start. In criminal investigation it isn't so much the partial fingerprint or the lost button you concentrate on, but the inconsistencies in human behavior.

Philip R. Rasmussen had represented Smith at the aborted arraignment. He was one more of Detroit's shaky claims to fame, a trouble-shooting criminal lawyer with a flashy track record and one eye screwed to his next book contract. I opened both car doors to let the oven-air out and looked up the attorney's office number in last year's directory, dusty from bouncing around in the trunk for the past eight months. Committing it to memory, I started the engine and hunted for a telephone booth. The cool air rushing in through all four windows revived me like a shot of liquor.

At a service station on Chicago I told the attendant to fill the tank and headed on foot to one of three instruments on a pole next to the sidewalk. Twice I got a busy signal. On the third try I struck pay dirt.

"Rasmussen and Riley." A feminine voice, as individual as a gum ball. Typewriters made noise in the background, stuttering over briefs and requests for writs.

"Mr. Rasmussen, please."

"Whom shall I say is calling?"

I had been wondering where words like *whom* were living these days. "Amos Walker. I'm investigating the Mt. Hazel police shooting."

"Are you with the police, Mr. Walker?"

Well, I hadn't really expected it to work a second time. "No, I'm a private agent."

"I'll see if Mr. Rasmussen is in."

"What's he got, an escape tunnel?" I was speaking into a dead line. She'd put me on hold. It's a lonely place, hold. At least Owen Mullett's secretary played music.

She came back on. "I'm sorry, Mr. Walker, but Mr. Rasmussen is out."

"Bet you were surprised," I said dryly.

"I beg your pardon?"

"Did he leave a number where he can be reached?"

She gave it to me. I didn't have to write it down. It was the number of Detroit Police Headquarters. The extension was John Alderdyce's.

Detroit's center of law enforcement is a mammoth block structure designed by Albert Kahn and erected in 1922 at 1300 Beaubien, a street named after the French belle who is supposed to have warned the commander of Fort Detroit that Pontiac's warriors were planning to smuggle sawed-off muskets into the garrison under their blankets and take over. The story's probably a myth, but the building is real enough, severe and orderly looking with arched windows creating a dungeon effect along the ground floor. Just parking across from it made me feel like confessing.

A royal blue Continental Mark IV was parked in front of the entrance on the Beaubien side, in a slot designated for police use only. On the steps that led up to the door sat a sweating giant in a blue serge suit reading a comic book. He had a big head on a short neck, and you could have placed both your palms side by side between his eyes without touching either one. But you wouldn't have wanted to, for fear of getting your arms broken. A cap with a shiny visor lay bottomside up on one of his massive thighs, the sweatband turned inside out to dry.

"Nice crate," I observed, admiring my reflection in the deep finish on the hood. I decided that what looked like gray in my hair was an optical illusion.

"Yeah." He eyed me suspiciously over the top of the page he was reading.

The plate read SHYSTR. I pointed at it. "I know that. Didn't I read somewhere it belongs to Philip Rasmussen?"

"Yeah," he said again, and grunted. "Big joke. These lawyers got senses of humor. I know one's got a plate says CROOK-1."

"Bars or cars, I guess the truth's got to come out someplace."

He laughed. It sounded like the air horn on Dooley Bass's diesel. I joined him. When we were finished:

"How's chance me getting a word with your boss when he comes out?" I produced my wallet and flagged a five-spot.

He stared at it. His big jaw hung open, which it had to if he was going to breathe. His nose was flush to his face and bore the impression of its last fist. Then his mouth closed and he swallowed.

"I'd like to," he said. "I sure would. But I got orders. Nobody bothers Mr. Rasmussen outside of the office."

I poked down the fin and showed him the corner of a ten. Fresh drops of perspiration glittered along his hairline. He shook his head. The building hardly shivered when it moved. "Sorry, Bud."

"Suppose I staked you to plastic surgery," I offered.

He rose. The cap and comic book slid off his lap. His arms hung bowed, the hamlike hands dangling in front of his thighs after the fashion of weightlifters and certain primates.

I said, "I'm going."

"Wise choice."

He didn't sit down again until I was back in the driver's seat of the Cutlass. I smoked and drummed my fingers on the wheel. Thinking.

While I was doing that a lanky black youth in tank top and gym shorts came jogging around the corner, all arms and legs and glistening sinew. The bodyguard-chauffeur was immersed in his comic book across the street. I hailed the kid over. He obliged, and stood next to the car breathing in short athletic bursts and looking down at me suspiciously. He would have looked down at me if I were standing up. He was damn near seven feet tall.

"U of D?" I asked.

He shook his head. "Wayne State."

"This is a little out of your neighborhood."

"So's the next Olympics," he said. "But I'm going there anyway.

"Basketball, right?"

"Decathlon."

"Would five bucks spoil your amateur standing?"

A broad grin spread over his spare features. "Illegal?"

"A little."

"Make it ten. That's the world's biggest pigpen across the street, man."

Five minutes later we came out of an art supply store on Gratiot. I handed the Olympian the sack containing my purchase and a five-dollar bill. "Half now, the rest et cetera."

He nodded. We parted a block south of my car.

The Continental was still in front of police headquarters. Goliath had finished reading and appeared to be dozing with his big fingers laced across his stomach. I had time for another cigarette, and then Rasmussen appeared atop the steps.

He resembled his newspaper pictures, slight, bald in front, and wearing a suit of the same soft gray material they make clouds out of. He descended the steps with a nervous jerky gait, pumping his arms like a long-distance runner. The giant got to his feet hastily, dwarfing his employer as he tugged on his cap and lumbered down the steps to beat Rasmussen to the rear door of the sedan and hold it open, his comic book rolled and stashed in his hip pocket. It's surprising what a lot of money can do for a small man.

The chauffeur was just climbing under the wheel when the black youth sprinted around the corner, raised the small sack I had given him, and dashed it against the windshield of the Continental, all without stopping or even altering his pace. Bright red paint splattered over the glass, hood, and part of the roof.

Kong's roar shook the windows on my side of the street. The horn blatted as he clambered out, rocking the big car on its springs, and he took off running after the kid like a rearing bear, swaying from side to side with his arms extended over his head and the blue serge jacket bunched up around his chest. Meanwhile, the kid was doing everything short of falling on his face to keep from outdistancing his pursuer by more than two blocks.

I left the Cutlass, snapping away my butt, and crossed the street to the Continental. When I got the rear door open I found myself looking down the bore of a .32 automatic in Rasmussen's slender hand. I ignored it and shoved into the seat, swinging the door shut behind me.

"Put it up," I said, when he continued pointing the piece with his scrawny frame crowded into the corner opposite. "You aren't going to shoot anyone."

His eyes were wider than a sixteen-year-old virgin's, if there still are such creatures and if anything is capable of shocking them. He licked his lips with a pointed tongue. "You don't know that." He tried to make his voice tough. It sounded like gravel in a squeaky axle. The gun was steady but nothing else about him was, as if the weapon were shaking him.

I struck a match and touched it to the tip of a cigarette I didn't really need, just being casual. I didn't feel casual. If I have to have a firearm shoved up my nose, I'd rather the one doing the shoving be a professional, someone who knows how very little pressure is required to fire a bullet from an automatic.

"The trouble with you amateurs is you think a gun is charmed," I said, blowing out the match. "Wave it, and whoever's on the receiving end is your slave. You spend too much time in front of the tube.''

"We'll soon see which of us is the amateur. Who are you?" The barrel twitched.

"Relax, I'm not a kidnaper or an assassin. You should know that, having represented your share of them. Try not to shoot me while I go for my ID.''

His pistol hovered at waist level while I drew the wallet out slowly and opened it to the photostat of my license. He studied it as if it were the text of his next summation to a jury, then released his breath shudderingly, and fumbled the weapon into a clip under his left arm. He ran a quaking hand over his light brown hair, which started at his crown and grew in styled curls down to his collar.

"Two years ago, I was riding in a cab on Dequindre when a truck pulled out in front of the car and two men got out and shot the driver to death." He stared at the floor behind the front seat. "They were after me, and they'd have killed me too if the police hadn't arrived and scared them off. That's when I got a permit to carry a gun. This is the first time I've drawn it on anyone.''

"It's almost as bad as having one pointed at you.''

"It's worse." He raised his eyes to the red-smeared windshield, then glared at me. "Do you realize what it's going to cost to have that stuff removed?''

Now he was all outraged lawyer. I said, "It's just poster paint. You can wipe it off with a handkerchief and spit. You do spit.''

He was still looking at me. "When the occasion warrants.''

"Let's talk about Alonzo Smith.''

"I've talked about him all I care to for one day, thank you. What do you think I was doing in police headquarters, fixing a parking ticket? And why should I talk to you at all when I should be breaking you for what you just did?''

"Even if you could link me to it, you'd just be handing the review board a laugh. Besides, we have time to kill. Your chauffeur is going to be busy for a while.''

He started. His face was narrow and small-boned, as delicate as a woman's. "If you've had something done to him—!''

"I couldn't have anything done to him with a four-inch shell. The kid'll take him around the Grand Circle once or twice and have him back here in time to take you home for martinis. Who hired you to defend Smith?''

"That's privileged," he said automatically.

I mashed out my butt in the armrest ashtray and shifted in the seat to face him. I needed binoculars to see him clearly. It was a big car. "That's lawyer talk. Fine in a court of law, but how's it stand when some cop corners your client in a blind alley with a gun in his paw and no witness for blocks? I'm not out to kill him. I'm probably the only one looking for him who isn't. If he comes in soles up I've failed. What good are ethics that won't bend to save a life?''

"He deserves to die.''

I stared at him stupidly. Two women stopped to gape at the stained windshield and walked away asking what the city was coming to if a person couldn't park his car safely in front of a police station. My ears were all right, all right.

"Maybe we'd better back up," I suggested.

Rasmussen held up a thumb and forefinger. "I was that far from winning acquittal on a plea of insanity. The commissioner himself laid the groundwork for me by calling Smith, Turkel, and Gross mad-dog killers at the time of the shooting. Then my client's spaced-out girlfriend showed up at the arraignment with two storm troopers and threw my case into the shithole. Whatever they get, they asked for it."

"You took on the case gratis, didn't you?" I said. "What's in it for you, a book?"

"Movie of the Week. ABC called me Saturday and made an offer for my account of the trial. Provided, of course, I got him off."

"Incentive."

"It takes more than dedication to be a good attorney these days. Perry Mason didn't have to contend with these assholes."

"That's show biz. Who besides you had access to Smith between the time he gave himself up and the arraignment?"

"No one, except the police. That Lieutenant Alderdyce and the men assigned to him."

"How did Smith act during your conferences? I'm not asking you to repeat content.

He smiled bitterly, without parting his thin lips. "He called me honky and a few other names less delicate. He thought I'd sell him out to my lily-white buddies in the system. What you might expect."

"If he felt that way, why didn't he demand a black to represent him?"

"Because the price was right, and he didn't mean what he said. Because when you come down to it, his type of black is just as bigoted as they claim we are, and believes that only a white man has a chance pleading a black man's case before court, even if the judge and jurors are as black as he is. Because he wanted to win."

"What changed his mind?"

"So far as I know, nothing." He met my gaze. "I consider myself a fair judge of what goes on behind a person's expression. I have to be; it's my stock in trade. When those

48

people invaded that room with automatic weapons, Smith was just as surprised and frightened as the rest of us. He wasn't any less so when he left with them. I think he thought he was going to be killed.''

I was still digesting that when something moved between me and the sun, and the door on my side was torn open, almost spilling me into the street. The monolithic chauffeur, red-faced and heaving, growled and closed a hand like a car crusher on my shoulder. It was a bad time not to be armed.

"It's all right, Herbert," said Rasmussen. "Mr. Walker was just leaving. We won't see him again. Will we?" He looked at me as if he had just grown a yard.

"Not until after Herbert's had his shots." I got out. I felt the chauffeur's eyes on my back until I reached my car, when he turned his attention to the paint on the windshield of the Continental.

Tomorrow's answer to Bruce Jenner was sitting on the passenger's side of the Cutlass, sweating but breathing about as heavily as a somnambulist. I gave him the rest of what I'd promised him and watched his narrow back loping away. When I was a kid, no black would have dared to be seen running near police headquarters. Times change both ways.

6

Square One found me reading the late edition of the *News* between bites of roast beef sliced not too thin in a little supper place across from what used to be the Kern block on Woodward. The headwaitress was built like Cass Elliott, with arms like Arnold Schwarzenegger, and kept up a running patter of good-natured insults with the regulars as she went around freshening everyone's coffee without being asked. The music was subdued, and though the lights were low you could see what was on your plate without having to set fire to a napkin. They ought to declare those places national treasures while there are still a few left. For all I knew this was the last one.

There were no fresh details on the courtroom raid beyond those released that morning, but that didn't keep the reporters from padding the front section with speculation. Alonzo Smith had been seen crossing the Ambassador Bridge to Windsor in a yellow van with California plates, sucking a Coke at a service station on Chalmers, bagging groceries in a market down by the river. An Ohio woman swore it was he who snatched her purse while she was waiting for a bus in Toledo. On the strength of the bridge story, the Governor of California was calling for an investigation to learn if the fugitive had indeed spent time in that state. It wasn't even an election year.

As if the cops didn't have enough screwy leads to follow, the Detroit Police Officers Association was offering five thousand dollars for information leading to Smith's arrest and conviction. Next to that item was a piece about a professional bounty hunter from Oklahoma named Munnis "Bum" Bassett, a six-foot-five former bail bondsman with more magnum-powered weaponry than it was safe to shake a stick at, who vowed, so help me, "to bring that critter in alive—or dead." How he planned to collect on a corpse was something he either didn't want to go into or the reporter didn't think was worth asking.

That raised my spirits. A cowboy in town was just what the doctor ordered to keep the boys with badges off this peeper's back. I was a criminological genius next to Bum, who came out of the interview sounding slightly to the right of Caligula.

The inside pages carried background on Smith's outlaw girlfriend, which interested me more. She was a twenty-year-old white woman named Laura Gaye, a native New Yorker and a born-again Christian who had come out to enroll in pre-med at the University of Michigan, then left after six months for a job at the Ford River Rouge plant. Until the blowup at Mt. Hazel Cemetery, she had been living for some time with Smith in a commune frequented by drug peddlers, black revolutionaries, and hippies still coming down from the sixties on McDougall. She had a widowed father in New York who couldn't be reached for comment. A picture lifted from her high school yearbook showed a pretty, serious-looking girl with bangs on her forehead, a far cry from the frizzy-headed scarecrow described by witnesses to the incident at the Frank Murphy Hall of Justice. Hitler's baby picture was cute, too.

It seemed like a good enough place to start. I circled the McDougall address in pencil, left a buck for the waitress with the ready pot and Rickles' best routines, and paid at the cash register, wondering if I had enough time to buy a bulletproof vest before penetrating the inner city at night.

It was eight-thirty and still light out, although the sun was below the skyline, sucking red and purple streamers down with it. West of the city you could read a newspaper by natural light until ten, one of the advantages—if you could call it that—of living on the extreme western edge of the Eastern Time Zone, with a little help from Uncle Sam turning back the hands on the clock like a small boy trying to finagle an extra hour before bedtime. On the horizon the cylindrical towers of the Renaissance Center were lit up like a whorehouse on Saturday night. I'd had some trouble a while back over a man whose office was on the top floor of one of those towers, and I wondered idly if he was still working at this hour.

Most of the street lamps on the lower east side were broken, which was a blessing aesthetically. Warehouses and tenements wallowed in the mulch of decades, their windows boarded up as if in an effort to shut out the world around them. Yellow mortar oozed out of brick walls covered with obscenities sprayed in black and candy-apple green; slat-sided mutts with glistening sores and eyes bright with the madness of hunger rooted among the offal spilled out of overturned trash cans; heaps of stale laundry shaped vaguely like human beings snored in doorways with their heads leaning against the jambs and their open mouths scooping black, toothless holes out of their stubbled faces. As I swung onto McDougall the beam from my headlamps transfixed a bloated rat perched atop a mound of shredded plastic garbage bags, twin beads of red phosphorescence glowing from its eyes. Entering my intended block, I realized suddenly that I'd been breathing through my mouth for the past five minutes and closed it.

Many of the numbers had worn off the buildings, if there had been any to begin with. I parked under a functioning street lamp that might discourage the more timid vandals, got a flash out of the glove compartment, and climbed out to search for the place on foot. Twenty yards from the car I turned back and drew the unregistered Luger from its hiding place in the trunk. I made sure there was a cartridge in the chamber and shoved the works under the waistband of my pants. I'd left the Smith & Wesson in the office safe.

The air was the temperature of human saliva, the street solid black beyond the circle of lamplight except where the still-climbing moon made right triangles the color of milk-water through gaps between buildings. I felt clammy under my clothes—hardly an uncommon reaction for a white man abroad in Blacktown that late. The tiniest noise brought the automatic out of my pocket, the beam of the flash bounding toward the source of the disturbance. Terror grows in the dark like mushrooms.

When I located the number, it was a faint outline in what was left of the darker paint on the front door, the metal numerals having fallen or rusted off in someone's grand-father's time and never been replaced. The brick structure had been a gymnasium the year the Marquis of Queens-berry took First Communion. Anemic early moonlight lay on the few remaining stippled glass panes in the eight-foot windows near the roof, and the earth had begun to reclaim the broken concrete stoop under my feet. PIGS KEEP OUT, demanded the penciled legend on a square of paper nearly as old as the building, taped above the crusted doorknob. That didn't apply to me, so I twisted the knob and went in. Two barrels of a sawed-off shotgun were waiting for me in the darkened entrance.

"What's the matter, pig? Can't you read signs?"

It was a girl asking the questions, in that twangy drawl some blacks can't get rid of after several generations up North. In the icy light of my flash the weapon looked no longer than some pistols, stockless and supported in two dark slender hands with ragged nails. If it went off at this range I was ground meat.

I shifted the beam higher, but not too high or I'd have missed her entirely. Lashless eyes blinked in a flat face surrounded by a halo of frizzed black hair. "If you know what's good for you, you'll turn that fucking thing off. *Now*, man." The gun jumped.

I switched off the beam. A shaft of moonlight fell on two bare feet on the other side of the threshold. "I'm not a pig," I explained. "You have the wrong barnyard animal."

"That's your opinion, fuzz. Buzz off, fuzz." The rhyme amused her. She repeated it, giggling. It was not a reassuring giggle.

"I'm not with the police, I'm private."

"Same difference. You want to leave or you want me to call someone to help you leave?"

"Neither." I tromped on her toes and knocked aside the barrels of the shotgun with my elbow. For good measure I brought the flashlight down hard on the carpus in her wrist. She shrieked, and while she was shrieking I wrenched the weapon out of her grasp. I stiff-armed her away from me and groped for a light switch on the right side of the door. In this building it was on the left side. Light trickled down from neon tubes in two ceiling troughs. Three more remained dark, and one of the two flickered and buzzed like a June bug trapped between screens.

I put away the flash and stepped inside, kicking the door shut behind me. She was bent over, holding her injured wrist between bare knees. Her ensemble consisted of severely cutoff jeans and a dirty sweatshirt with no sleeves. Loose threads hung down everywhere. If she was fifteen, I was twenty-one and still in college.

"Jesus Christ, you busted my wrist!" she moaned.

"No, I didn't. Next time don't shove a gun in someone's face unless you don't want him to have a face. I smelled the bluff when you threatened to call someone instead of shoot me. Besides, I've stared down enough muzzles for one day. Where is everybody?"

I felt as if I'd passed through a time warp and been catapulted back fifteen years. The old gym floor, which made tiny snapping sounds as I lifted my soles from its gummy surface, was strewn with rumpled sleeping bags, knapsacks, furniture out of *Home and Orange Crate*, and olive-drab blankets stenciled U.S. ARMY. Revolutionary slogans from another era were scrawled in chalk on the gnawed wainscoting, down to and including FREE HUEY. I seriously doubted that any of the current inhabitants was old enough to know that Huey wasn't one of three ducks. There was even a poster of Che Guevara, the one that makes him look like the Messiah and not a greasy little bandit, killed eating grubs from trees in South America.

A loft of sorts added in recent years ran the length of the rear wall, joined to the floor by a wooden ladder and murky with shadows beyond the reach of the ceiling fixtures. That gave me an uneasy moment, but the junior-size gun moll laid my fears to rest by answering my question.

"There's two guys with guns trained on you upstairs," she said, testing her wrist for breaks. "I was you, I'd give back the shotgun and split."

"Just as well you're not." I broke it, drew out two 16-gauge shells to keep from blowing off my foot, and tossed them across the room. One bounced and rolled, the other stuck fast where it fell. The gun was short enough to hide in a shoe. "If there was anyone up there you wouldn't be telling me, and if they were armed I'd be a carcass now. What are they doing, making a score?"

"What's it to you?"

"Who writes your dialogue, Spillane? Any more guns around?"

She shook her head. It was a pretty head, just like a bottlebrush. "Pigs confis—confiscated them after Laura busted Smitty out of the slam. They got no right. They's all registered."

"This too?" I held up the abbreviated fowling piece. "It's about two feet short of legal."

"That wasn't here when they come. I wasn't neither."

"What do they call you?"

"Puddin' 'n' Tame." She giggled again.

I peered at her. Her pupils were shrunken to pinpoints. Coke, probably, or maybe just plain angel dust. There were no needle tracks in her arms or legs and she hadn't yelled loud enough when I stepped on her toes to be shooting between them. Not on that foot, anyway. She appeared to have forgotten all about her wrist. I flipped the shotgun's release catch, separating the barrels from the action, set the former down atop a broken packing case, and pitched the firing assembly up over the railing into the loft. The girl glared.

"Temptation's a dangerous thing," I explained. "Where did Laura stay when she lived here?"

She closed her mouth so tight it bulged, the way kids do when medicine's coming. But her eyes wandered past my shoulder. I followed them to a door in the wall behind me and grinned. "Thanks, Puddin'."

It had been a locker room once. The nozzles in the gray-stalled showers were coated with orange rust and there was mold in the corners. Forty-year-old sweat soured the air. The toilet, sequestered in its own alcove, was an old-fashioned affair of white porcelain with a chain. The Pony Express man had given it a quick wipe with a rag when he delivered it and no one had cleaned it since. The smell in there would have revived a corpse.

The lockers had been moved out of the main room and plasterboard partitions erected, forming a rats' maze of eight-by-eight cells containing old exercise mats for sleeping and various personal items from clothing to coke spoons. There was graffiti here too, of the OFF THE PIGS variety, along with similar artifacts of the Kerouac-cum-Hoffman era that until tonight I had thought was as dead as John Lennon.

I knew which stall was Laura Gaye's the moment I saw it, even though it surprised me. A couple of pairs of jeans and some T- and sweatshirts had been flung into a heap in one corner, next to a small stack of hymnals and an army surplus footlocker with a sprung lock. A large crucifix carved from a single piece of wood was mounted on a nail in one of the partitions. But for the clothes, the place was as neat and clean and pious as a monk's cell, and I'd have bet the clothes were too before the cops got to them. The footlocker was empty, which didn't disappoint me. The cops would have been through it too, with tweezers.

"They didn't find nothing neither."

I hadn't heard her approaching on bare feet. When I turned, Puddin' 'n' Tame was leaning against a partition looking into the cell. Her eyes glittered. She'd just had another snort or pop.

"I thought you said you weren't here when the cops came."

"Some of the others was." Her voice was dreamy. "Pigs

didn't find nothing on account of there wasn't nothing to find. Deak ain't nobody's trained nigger.''

"Deak?'' I seized the name. So far no one had identified either of the men who had accompanied Laura Gaye into the courtroom.

Her hand drifted to her mouth. I suppose that in her mind it flew, but when you do dope your reactions go first. Something like terror stirred her sluggish features. Then she giggled.

"I'm a teensy bit high,'' she said, exaggerating the dreaminess. "I don't think—''

"Tallulah?''

The name echoed in the big room outside. A man's voice, deep and resonant. The whites of her eyes leaped out of the gray gloom.

"Child, where the hell you at?''

Another voice mumbled something unintelligible. My nerves did a wild tango. I sidled toward the door, Luger in hand. It started to open on complaining hinges.

"Look out!'' Tallulah lunged for the gun. I jerked it away. My arm collided with the door and the automatic clattered across the concrete floor. When I dived after it, a mortar shell burst at the base of my brain. I kept going, the Luger forgotten.

For a euphoric moment I felt better than I ever had in my life, but that was the siren song of the unconscious. I rolled just in time to avoid another kick to the head. A hobnailed boot glanced painfully off my shoulder. I grabbed at the ankle, but a toe from an unexpected quarter caught me hard in the ribs and pain splintered up my side.

"Get her out of here,'' snarled the deep voice. The door opened again and swung shut.

A boot like the one that had struck my shoulder—maybe the same one—left the floor aimed at my face. This time I got hold of it, flailed my legs until I had a heel braced against its mate and shoved upward. There was a splitting sound and a hoarse scream of agony. Then steel flashed in the corner of my eye. I ducked and something swished shrilly past my ear. Not quite past. A large fat drop plopped to my shoulder. The lobe stung.

"No blades." It was the first voice, though less deep, made shallow by rage and pain and lost wind. "We'll bust up this white motherfucker without help."

There were more than two, maybe as many as six. A hundred wouldn't have made much difference. I glimpsed faces in the stark locker-room light, shining black faces, distorted with fury. But mostly I just saw legs and boots. I kicked back and grabbed and tried to get up, but there were too many legs, too many flying boots. They got me in the stomach and groin and neck and head, in the elbows and knees, and all the time that deep black voice kept repeating, "White motherfucking son of a bitch white motherfucking son of a bitch white motherfucking son of a bitch," until the litany merged with the roaring in my head and then the roaring stopped and then there was silence and then there wasn't even that. There wasn't anything, least of all me.

7

SOMEONE WAS STANDING ON MY EYELIDS.

He had spurs on and the rowels made my eyes ache. I decided to try to open them anyway. The effort squirted fresh pain into a hundred and one tender spots in my anatomy and gained me nothing beyond a dull headache. I lay there gathering strength for the next attempt while my stomach rocked itself still and sweat trickled down noisily from my forehead into my ears. Meanwhile I watched the pyrotechnics going on inside those stubborn lids. They were corpuscle red and spleen green and arterial blue, with here and there a dash of bile yellow to give the whole thing balance. There were tubas too, but I didn't much like them because every toot reminded me of the pounding in my head.

Time for another try. No, it wasn't. Yes, it was. I conjured up a crowbar and pried. I knew if I got one loose the other would break free on its own, as with stuck windshield wipers. Something gave. I cast the crowbar back to the limbo whence it came and grated open the lids.

I'd been cheating myself on fireworks. They were outside, not in, and with the veil gone they leaped into naked brilliance, whirling and plummeting and exploding into colors I couldn't identify. My stomach lurched. I rolled hurriedly onto my throbbing right shoulder and said good-bye to the roast beef I'd eaten in the little place on Woodward.

I dry-heaved for a full minute after there was nothing left, then turned laboriously over onto my hands and knees and remained like that for a minute or an hour, my head hanging, body burning, and the cold clamminess in which I had lain seeping deeper into my bones. It was pitch dark, but I knew from the gritty wet feel of the surface under my hands that I was in some alley, a location in which my work has occasionally dropped me, not always standing up. It smelled of vomit and motor oil and damp and drunk's urine and the dry musk of rats. So did the alley, but my work was worse. Traffic hummed in the distance. Except for Vietnam I had never been in a place where I couldn't hear traffic humming.

I went through the routine. *What's your name?* A fairly simple question, but there might be a trick to it. What the hell, take a chance. Walker? *First name?* Amos, but don't spread it around. *Height?* Around six feet, or it was before tonight. *Weight?* One eighty-five. *Eyes?* Two. Brown, if you're particular. *Hair?* Also brown. Some gray. *Next of kin?* None, unless you count my once-wife, living in California with an out-of-work artist on my alimony. *Interests?* Old movies, jazz and early rock, good Scotch, staying alive. Not necessarily in that order. *Reason for present predicament?* My mother's fault. She dropped me on my head when I was eighteen months old and broke my common sense.

You're hurt, Walker. Maybe more hurt than you've ever been, even in Nam. Breathing is agony. Get help. You know so much about it, where do I go? No answer. There's nothing more useless than an unreliable Id.

61

Odds are you've never been in total darkness. Few have. When you are, all bets are off. I knew where the ground was because I was kneeling on it, and the thread of logic to which I was clinging with my teeth and all four limbs told me that the sky was opposite. That gave me only four directions to choose from. I selected one and started crawling that way. My injured knees hurled white-hot barbs at my brain every time I put weight on them, but if I tried to stand without support they'd buckle.

At length I put out a hand and touched a cold brick. My fingers curled around it, and then the fingers of the other hand curled around one six inches higher, and so on until I ran out of reach. Good old wall. I leaned against it, listening to my lungs creak as they filled and released, filled and released. With every breath I felt the pinch of a damaged rib, or maybe two. Thank God it wasn't the one the doctors had pinned together. My face ached and my eyes were swollen almost shut. I was in no shape for the big game, or even to reach the end of the alley alone, wherever that was.

Then a light pierced my world of darkness.

It sprang toward me, then away, playing games. Damn childish, that light. I started pulling my way toward it. Hand over hand, wobbling on round heels. Whoever had been holding down my eyelids before was now standing on my feet, and he'd brought a friend. I dragged them along. The light didn't look any closer. It was like that nightmare in which something you want, something you have to have, is always just out of reach, and the harder you work the slower you move. I started to cry.

"Hold on there, hoss. You drunk or what?"

I stopped crying and started laughing. The line, and its guttural delivery, were strictly Randolph Scott. Instead of the end of the alley, I had reached that point in the nightmare where since nothing made sense anyway, I had no trouble accepting the presence under a city street lamp of a bearded giant in a ten-gallon hat and checked shirt, grinning at me over a .44 magnum that would have knocked all three Earps and Doc Holliday out of their high-topped boots at the OK Corral before they had a chance to draw.

And like all nightmares, this one ended before my face hit the pavement.

"DRINK THIS HERE."

I had been suspended for some time in that phantom world between light and dark, aware of my surroundings, of activity going on around me, of the unfamiliar sensation of something soft and wet dragging itself over my face like a big dog's tongue, and yet unaware of what it all meant or what it had to do with me. My first realization was that I was lying naked to the waist under a sheet, and I wondered if all the corpses were this alert on the slab. When my eyes focused on a big seamed face with a shaggy red beard, it struck me that the Wayne County Morgue was looking pretty far afield for its personnel. The owner of the face and beard was dressed in a red-and-black-checked shirt, and his big cowboy hat was hanging on the back of his chair beside the bed. I was still having that same wacky dream.

"This here" was a pungent brew in an insulated mug held under my nose, steaming hot and reeking of childhood remedy and a familiar, acrid something that stood for everything that was right about America.

"What is it?" My vocal cords squeaked against each other, and the lips I was using had been donated by someone else. I hadn't got the hang of them. They were a couple of sizes too large, for one thing.

"Chicken soup and Kentucky sippin' whiskey," said Redbeard, in a southwestern drawl gone gravelly around the edges. "The soup part's got something to do with one or two sheenies skulking around amongst the Irish and Cherokees in my family tree. The whiskey part comes from just plain livin'. Beats all hell out of that there brandy they're always bringing folks around with in movies."

He was supporting the back of my head in a horned palm. It was either drink or drown in the steam. I drank. It tasted like boiled rags, but as the warmth spread outward from my stomach and settled into my bruised muscles and joints, the pain and stiffness subsided. It wasn't a permanent cure, but then neither is anything else short of time or death. I took two more sips and waved the concoction away. It was curling the hairs in my nose. He lowered my head to a pillow.

"Who the hell are you," I asked, "besides the world's biggest Saint Bernard?"

It took him a second to get it. Then his ragged moustache turned upward and the cracks deepened in his sunbeaten face, making it look like a mask carved out of old barnwood. His eyes were blue marbles pushed back almost out of sight under a heavy shelf, and his beard had begun to bleed gray. Pink scalp showed through the dozen or so hairs in his widow's peak.

He chortled. I'd never heard anyone chortle in my life, but I recognized it right off. "That's good," he said. "I guess I sort of do look like one at that. And I did scrape you out of a tough spot and give you spirits, and folks have been known to liken me to a dog's relative. My wife in Oklahoma calls me Munnis, but mostly I'm just plain Bum."

I shook the coffee grounds and egg shells off the newspaper item encountered in a healthier time and stuffed away in my memory. He fit the description. I looked around. I occupied a studio couch unfolded into a bed, at one side of a long narrow room with sliding windows and a tiled kitchen area at the far end equipped with a small steel sink, a refrigerator scarcely large enough to contain a six-pack and cold cuts, and a two-burner stove. A lot of blond veneer suggested a room in a cheap motel or a small house trailer. The dimensions were wrong for a motel room. Daylight was leaking in through the windows.

Two things made it different from most trailers. The first was a unique feature located halfway between the bed and the sink, made up of steel bars running from floor to ceiling and enclosing an area four feet square with a locked door. It looked as if it had been built to cage a gorilla. Beyond that, a child's-size table with a Formica top supported a number of handguns and a stack of cartridge boxes. A pump shotgun and a rifle with scope leaned against the wall on the other side. I inclined my head in that direction.

"You travel around with those loaded? There's a law against that in this state."

"Not if they're in a house trailer, which constitutes a home," he said. "Little trick I picked up when I was a bail bondsman. We got the same law where I come from."

"The cell optional or does it come with the trailer?"

"You like it?" He reached over and shook one of the bars. The trailer swayed. "Had it built special. Before, I had to take a partner along to keep an eye on the meal ticket. Now I just stick 'em in here and forget about them, and there's no splitting the bounty. No one's busted out of it yet."

"Cozy," I said. "If you're the Bum Bassett I read about in the paper, you're six-five. What keeps your feet from sticking out past the end of this bed?'' My own came right to the edge.

"Nothing. Wintertime I wear hunting socks. So you know me.'' It was a statement of fact, not of pride. People who have been famous a long time have nothing to prove.

"We don't get a lot of bounty hunters up here these days." "Nor buffalo neither, I expect. There ain't a lot of us still around.''

I struggled into a sitting position. The effort undid the anesthetic effect of the broth and whiskey and awakened the stitch in my side. I put a hand to it and felt tape. It girdled my abdomen like a cummerbund.

"I've taped enough of my own to know a cracked rib,'' Bassett explained. "I was you, I'd have that X-rayed. Move around all you care to meanwhile, but don't blame me when you put a sharp end through a lung.''

I leaned back against the wall, breathing carefully and waiting for the pain to diminish. When it did: "Where's this thing parked?''

"Damn!" He cuffed a treelike thigh with his hand.

"What's the matter?''

"I bet myself you'd ask how long you was out first.''

"Okay, how long was I out?''

"Too late. We're in a K-Mart lot in Warren. I know, it's one hell of a hike from where I found you. But them newspaper bloodsuckers will never think of looking for me here. It's getting so I can't take a crap without finding one of them in the tank. Also, it's the only place I could find where I didn't have to trade two mules to pay for a spot. And I thought inflation was bad in Tulsa.''

"Where *did* you find me?''

He blinked. "Don't you know?''

"Give me time. I only just found out where I am now."

"I reckon you was kind of out of it at that." He scratched his head. He didn't make near as much noise doing it as a Rotomill tearing up pavement. "I was coming away from that communist place on McDougall where the niggers and freaks hang out when I see you in the alley next to the building. I was that close to smoking you. Last time some-one came at me out of the dark that way, I blew the son-of-a-bitch redskin in half."

He'd maligned about four different racial and social groups in that snatch of conversation, but I didn't belong to any of them so I let it dangle. "How long ago was that?"

"I knew you'd get around to that for real sooner or later. Eleven, twelve hours. It's coming on noon now." He paused. "You wouldn't want to let me in on what you was doing there."

"Same as you, I suppose. That true what they said in the paper about you promising to bring Smith in dead or alive?"

He winked, a gesture that involved a simultaneous side-ways jerk of his head, like Buffalo Bob being conspiratorial with the peanut gallery. "You got to put on a show for them reporter fellows. In this business it's important no one takes you seriously. Hell, you should know that. You're a P.I."

"You've been through my wallet. Where is it, by the way? Not that I don't trust you, but I don't know you from the King of Ruritania. And my clothes? And my car, as long as I'm asking. Just for future reference. I don't feel like dressing or driving or spending money again this year."

"I don't know nothing about a car. Wasn't no keys in

your pockets, so I figured you didn't have one. Your clothes are in that closet, your wallet too. You're wearing your pants and socks. I didn't want you getting the wrong idea about me."

He gestured at a knob on a section of wall next to the bed. No seam showed to indicate a door. I took his word for it that it opened and that there was a closet behind it containing my shoes, shirt, and jacket.

"Got a smoke?"

"Figured you'd ask." He dug a sorry pack of Winstons from a flap shirt pocket and handed it to me. It looked familiar. "They're yours. I gave it up years back. You should, too."

I took one out and let him light it with one of my matches. "You saved my life and I'm grateful," I said, blowing smoke. "That doesn't make it yours. How come my friends at the commune didn't greet you the way they did me?" I knew it was a stupid question even as I was asking it. He looked about as easy to knock down and kick apart as Rushmore.

He nodded. "So that's what happened. I thought so. No one greeted me *any* way. I knocked, but nobody answered. I didn't go in."

"Sticky wicket," I said.

"Huh? Oh, yeah." His teeth flashed insincerely in his beard.

"If it's not too personal, why'd you pull me out of that alley?"

His forehead broke into a mass of inverted V's, one on top of another. "Where I grew up a man didn't ask questions like that. He knew the answer."

"Code of the West, huh?"

"I reckon it sounds sort of funny, put like that. But there's sense behind it. Women don't get raped and murdered out on the plains because somebody's scared to dial a phone. One scream and the whole neighborhood's out with Winchesters and lynch ropes.''

"As long as the right person gets lynched.''

"Maybe not always. But for every innocent that swings there are ten less women raped and murdered.'' He paused. "Question now is, what do I do with you?''

"What's the matter, you run out of closets?''

"I got to go places, but someone's got to stay here and look after you.'' He stood, and suddenly the trailer was crowded. There must have been three hundred pounds stuffed into his flannel shirt and brown-faded jeans, but though his waist was leagues from narrow there wasn't enough fat on him to fry an onion. He had to stoop to avoid putting his head through the roof.

"I won't swipe anything I can't pocket.'' I put some ashes in a coffee can reeking of tobacco juice on the floor between the bed and the wall. No wonder he didn't smoke; he could stink up a room without striking a match.

"It ain't that. I know where you live in case anything comes up missing, and Bum's righteous wrath is a terrible thing to behold. I just don't cotton coming back here to find you on the floor choking in your own blood. That's not what I scraped you out of that alley for. I'll send back a doctor, but I need a tough nurse to hold you down meanwhile.''

"I know one,'' I said, and gave him a name and number.

He wrote it down with a pencil stub in a pad with bent corners, both taken from a hip pocket. "I'll call her from a booth. Ain't got no telephone hookup to this trailer. Sometimes I got to move out fast.'' He demonstrated what he meant by reaching the door in half a stride, cowboy hat in hand. He scooped the big .44 off the table into a snap holster inside his waistband.

"Got a lead?"

He looked back disapprovingly. "Did I ask you that?"

"Sorry," I said. "Occupational hazard. Good hunting."

His departure left a very large empty.

8

I SLEPT; I DON'T KNOW FOR HOW LONG. THE CRYSTAL ON my watch was shattered, the hands frozen at 9:37, recording for posterity the exact moment when I gave up membership in the human race and became a soccer ball.

Suddenly I was ravenous. Last night's dinner was coagulating in the alley off McDougall, and but for the soup Bassett had supplied, now ice-cold on the lamp table next to the bed, I hadn't eaten anything else in twenty-four hours. I tore aside the sheet, rested, lowered one foot to the floor, rested, lowered the other, clenching my teeth against the pain in my side. My knees didn't like the idea of having to bend. I had a stiff neck, and the pattern of bruises on my leaden arms made them look tattooed. I still didn't have any feeling in the fingers of my left hand.

A dizzy spell struck when I got up. I braced myself on the lamp table, waiting for my center of gravity to catch up. Then I started walking. I only bounded off two walls on my way to a wash basin and chemical toilet behind a folding screen at the rear of the trailer. A bloody cloth was crumpled in the basin, which explained the soft wet thing on my face earlier.

There was a shaving mirror screwed to the wall above

the basin. My face didn't look too bad for chopped beef. About the only thing that wasn't swollen was my nose—a relief, because I'd broken it once boxing in college and the septum hadn't been the same since. The water jug was three-quarters full. After filling the basin, I splashed tepid water over the wreckage, fumbled a towel off a plastic rack, and patted it dry. Naked air stung the lacerated flesh.

The activity was loosening my cramped muscles, but the Russian saber dance was definitely out of the question. At the closet I climbed into my shoes and shirt and got my wallet out of the jacket. Nothing was missing inside. I put it back, leaving the jacket hanging. The flashlight protruded from a pocket. I didn't bother to look for the Luger; my assailants were low on weapons after yesterday's police visit.

The refrigerator yielded a half-gallon of milk and a package of bacon, open but with only a few slices gone. I turned on the gas and drank milk from a glass found in a cupboard above the sink while I buttered a skillet and laid four fatty strips sizzling in the bottom.

While they cooked I nosed around a little. It was good practice. The guns on the table included two .38-caliber revolvers, one a Smith & Wesson like my own, the other a .357 magnum, and a .45 Colt Army automatic. The shotgun leaning against the wall was an Ithaca 12-gauge pump, pre—World War II, the rifle next to it a Remington 30-06 automatic. All were well oiled, fully loaded, and shared that spotless, pampered look only the true firearms fanatic can achieve. It was damn trusting of him to leave them lying around with a stranger on the premises, but as he'd said, he knew who I was and where I lived.

The drawers built into the wall were full of cowboy stuff—checked shirts, sun-bleached jeans as soft as chamois leather, a dozen or so paperback books with titles like

Showdown at Cimarron and *Jake Lomax—Town Tamer*, the covers loose and curled from much handling. Pots, pans, and canned goods filled the cupboards. The doors of one cabinet were padlocked. More guns, probably. The *News* piece said he had one of the largest collections of firearms in the Southwest, not that I expected him to cart the whole thing up here. A thick manila folder on top of the cabinet contained syndicated press clippings on Alonzo Smith, Luke David Turkel, and Willie Lee Gross, going back to the Mt. Hazel shooting. Someone had drawn a fat felt-tipped marker through everything dealing with Turkel and Gross.

The only genuinely personal items in the trailer were a few snapshots buried in a drawer: Bum in a white T-shirt as broad as a board fence, standing in someone's back yard with one huge arm flung around a washed-out-looking woman half his size in a print dress; a young, beardless Bum, laughing and standing up a tiny version of himself in his lap in a shabby easy chair; Bum, still clean-shaven, towering over a family group in a different yard, including a younger woman closer to his height and two boys, the one from the earlier picture and the other, older and more serious-looking.

The others were more of the same. I put them away feeling like a peeping Tom—hardly a new sensation for me. I made it back to the stove just in time to turn over the bacon before it caught fire. The smell of frying fat started my stomach working. I had flipped off the burner and gone for bread to make a sandwich when the trailer creaked under someone's weight on the step-plate outside the door.

There was no reason to suspect that one of my various enemies had traced me here, but I hadn't taken so many kicks to the head I was ready to believe none of them could. I loped to the table on the balls of my feet and snatched up the magnum. When in doubt choose the weapon with the greatest stopping power.

The door opened outward and she stuck her profile square in front of the muzzle. She heard the hammer drawing back and turned. A medium dark face, like antique gold under a black light. Even features arranged in a heart shape, the *V* of the chin repeated in the sardonic dip of the unpainted mouth, slanted nostrils, and almost Oriental eyes, large and dark and full of history. Tightly curled hair cropped very close to the head. A long neck. Nefertiti in a flame-colored blouse, white shorts, and sandals. Her eyes lifted from the gun to my face.

"Nigger season already? My, how time flies."

I let down the hammer gently and returned the piece to the table. "You're being coarse again, Iris," I admonished. "Who said it became you?"

Sparks flew from her eyes. "Who the hell are you to lecture me? I don't hear from you for six months—"

"Five and a half."

She ignored the interruption. "—and when I do, it comes through some other white dude who sounds like Matt Dillon over the phone, saying you been banged around again and you need a nurse. Do I look like a nurse?"

"No, but then you don't look much like a hooker, either." Her open hand struck the only part of my face that didn't hurt. A second later she was all over me and halfway down my throat, all silken arms and sinuous legs and darting tongue and nipples as hard as bullets. Her lips burned.

When we came up for air she said, "What is it with you and trailers?" Her voice now was a purr, with few of the crisp West Indian overtones that came out when she was angry.

I didn't answer. We'd once spent some very nice moments in a mobile home in a park west of Detroit. I had just been beaten up that time too, and with brass knuckles, but with nothing like last night's success. She leaned all her weight on my supporting arm so that I had to hold tight to keep her head off the floor, and ran gentle fingertips over my contusions and abrasions.

"If I didn't know better, I'd swear you were still swoll up from the last time. What happened?"

"Just a little message from the other side. If they'd meant business I'd be this week's unidentified stiff on the Eleven O'Clock Report. Say, you've lost weight."

"Don't change the subject." The accent was back. She lifted the burden from my arm and pushed out of my embrace. "Is it going to happen again?"

"Not if I stop what I've been doing. How about some bacon? There's enough for two, if you don't mind splitting a sandwich." I stepped back over to the stove. The meat continued to crackle even with the fire off.

"Bacon? I'd rather eat a tarantula. That stuff will kill you." She unslung a white leather bag from her shoulder and put it down on top of the guns on the table. I remembered another bag of similar design she used to carry, for practical reasons. She hardly glanced at the arsenal; in her line the trick was to avoid tripping over them. The cell was something else.

"What the hell is that? What kind of place is this?"

"Down in Oklahoma they used to call it the Tumbleweed Wagon back when Hanging Judge Parker was in practice," I said. "A couple of federal marshals would haul it around the Indian nations, picking up fugitives and strays for trial back in Fort Smith. The principle's the same. Our host just updated the transportation."

"How come you know so much about it?"

"I owe it all to a lifetime watching B westerns. Sure you won't have any?" I held up the bacon on a spatula.

She made a face and shook her head. I shrugged, moistened two slices of bread in the grease of the skillet, and went through the ritual, lining the slices up with the crusts like cards in a deck. She watched, fascinated and appalled. "You're really going to eat that, aren't you?"

"I wasn't at first. I'd planned to mail it to my foster child in Albania, but I can't find a stamp." I leaned against the refrigerator and took a bite. It tasted as good as you can expect a bacon sandwich to taste under those circumstances, which is merely terrific.

"When you finally succumb to cholesterol poisoning," she advised, "don't count on cremation. You'd just melt into a puddle of grease on the undertaker's floor and they'd have to bury the mop." She closed her mouth, then opened it again. "Are you going to?"

"Be cremated?"

"Don't be difficult. Are you going to stop what you been doing before they kill you?"

I shook my head, chewing. "I'd like to say it's because I owe a guy, but it's gone past that. Now I'm mad."

"Well, the hell with you." She reached for her bag.

"What'd I say?"

"I can't be mixed up with a guy who wants to be dead before he's forty." She thrust her arm through the strap and hoisted the heavy-looking satchel effortlessly up onto her shoulder. The streets made them strong or they chewed them up and spit them out. "Besides, I can't watch you eat that sandwich."

I put it down and went after her. I almost didn't catch her; a charley horse rendered my right leg useless. She had the door open when I laid a hand on her shoulder. She pulled away, glaring.

"Why'd you call me, anyway? You need a keeper, not a nurse."

"I don't need either. I need information."

The fire in her eyes cooled too far. They grew frosty. "You mean a snitch."

"This trailer belongs to a cowboy named Bassett," I explained. "He and I happen to be working on the same case from different ends, which is how he came to pull me out of the Twilight Zone after a bunch of black militants finished playing kick-the-can with my cranium. When he asked me who I wanted to take care of me until the doctor gets here, I thought of you right off. Partly it's because I think you might have what I need to get back on target. Mostly it's because you're the only one in town who seems to care whether I die from poor diet or a knife in the kidney."

"What's the matter, you lose your friend in the cops?"

"A cop's the last thing I need. If Alderdyce finds out I'm in on this one despite his warning, he'll put on his seven-league boots and make what happened to me last night look like a game of girl's high school volleyball."

Her expression sobered. "Alonzo Smith, right?"

"How'd you guess?"

"Bassett. I read about a Bassett in yesterday's paper. He's after Smith for the reward. You said you were both working on the same case. Well, I don't know where Smith is. Every one of us niggers don't know what all the others is doing all the time. Would you believe I never even met Lou Rawls?" Her voice had a blue edge.

"You're a working girl," I said. "Customers have a way of opening up when the lights go off. Also, you know the dope scene. The people I'm dealing with are into cocaine, and probably some of the hard stuff as well."

"Well, I'm not anymore. I copped the cure."

I studied her closely. As long as I'd been in the racket.I could never tell when some people were giving it to me straight. She held out her arms. "Look. No tracks. Would I be wearing short sleeves if I was shooting up? Or short pants?"

"As I recall, you shot between your toes." I slid the leather strap off her shoulder. She met my gaze defiantly, but made no resistance.

"It's not that I don't trust you." I went through the bag. "I get lied to a lot, often by the best people." It was full of purse stuff, no syringes or rubber hoses or cellophane packets stitched into the lining. I gave it back.

"Deak," I said. "That name mean anything to you?"

Her expression didn't change. I braced myself for another slap. The imprint of her hand was still hot on my face from the last one. Then she grew thoughtful.

"Deak could be short for Deacon. I know a lot of those. Anything else?"

"I think he hangs out, or did once, at the commune where Smith and Laura Gaye lived on McDougall. I got his name from a girl there named Tallulah. Black. Jail bait. Nice hair, if you like sponges. A doper. You know her, don't you?" I'd been watching her color bleed gray.

She nodded, not as if she'd been looking forward to it. "Tallulah Ridder." I almost didn't hear it. "We used to shop in some of the same stores, and I don't mean the kind with fairy floorwalkers and end-of-season discounts. She's Deak Ridder's kid sister." She fell silent, then: "He's bad; Amos."

"That's okay. I'm good enough for both of us. Know anything else about him?"

"If I said I did you'd make me tell you, so I'm not saying. If you want to commit suicide that's your lookout, but don't ask me to hand you the gun."

We played stare-me-down for a while, but that soon made as much sense as urban renewal. Someone started collecting shopping carts in the parking lot outside. We listened to the jingling rattle. I said, "I'll just get it from someone else, someone who may not bother to let me know how deep a hole I'm climbing into. Maybe I won't know Ridder when I see him. But he'll know me. You want to give him that edge?"

"Oh, hell." She folded her arms and glowered at the base of the refrigerator. "He's tall, about your height, but skinnier. Bald in front, fluffs his hair up in back. Wears a Fu Manchu moustache. I heard he worked out at the Rouge plant when he wasn't pimping, but that was a couple of years back. I don't know where or on what shift, or even if he's still there."

"Laura Gaye worked at Rouge. Could be she met Smith through him." The description didn't match anyone I remembered from last night, but then I'd been preoccupied. "Ever hear his voice? Was it deep?"

"He never said anything where I could hear it. He used to pimp for some girls I knew. But I heard plenty about him." She looked at me. "Stay clear of him. Smith's a killer, but Ridder is Grade A fanatical black militant. With him every white man is fair game, not just cops. I mean it. When you see him coming, cross the street."

"I'll keep the advice in mind."

"But you won't take it, will you?" You could cut the West Indies in her speech with a cricket bat.

"Not taking it and ignoring it are two different things." I changed the subject. "How long you been off poppies?"

She counted on her fingers. "Three months, two weeks, six days"—a glance at her watch—"forty-four minutes. It's getting better. I don't count the seconds anymore. And you wondered how come I've lost weight."

"Is it as rough as I said it'd be?"

"Does the mayor think he's Jesus Christ?"

I laughed, and it really did hurt, just like they say. "You'll clear the post with room to spare." I took her wrist gently and turned it so I could read her watch. 1:56. "Got a car?"

"I took a cab. What happened to that bomb of yours?"

"That's what I mean to find out. I lost the keys, probably while I was getting the bejesus booted out of me, but I've got a spare set under the hood. If I still have a hood. Hail us a hack and I'll drop you off on the way." I got my jacket out of the closet, put a hand under her elbow, and opened the door. The fresh air made me realize how stuffy it was inside the trailer.

"What about the doctor?"

"He can sue me for malpractice. Just a second." I left her and went back for the sandwich. "Okay, let's go."

She dug in her heels. "With that poison?"

"With alacrity." I pushed her out ahead of me and snapped the lock on the door on my way through.

9

"YOU ALL RIGHT, MISTER? YOU DON'T LOOK SO GOOD."
The hack was a squat black with a bald head, glasses, and
an unlit cigar screwed into the center of his face. There
wasn't much concern in his eyes as I paid the fare and
tipped him a buck; so long as I didn't die in his cab, his
world turned well enough. I told him I always looked like
this, and he sped out of my life. If he'd stayed I might
have explained that the effects of a night's sleep and Bum
Bassett's surefire cure for everything had worn off and that
I was beginning to feel like something forgotten in the back
of the refrigerator.

Daylight did for McDougall what a bare electric bulb
does for a mutilated corpse. Today the street was in the
possession of a gang of dirty kids roller-skating over the
broken sidewalk in their fathers' cut-down pants. They always seem to be able to afford things like roller skates, for
some reason. One of them ran into an old black woman
stumping along with a shopping bag in one hand, bounded
off, and rolled around her, shouting quaint obscenities at
her as she sought her balance. It was the kind of neighborhood that couples in their mid-fifties dream of retiring
to someday.

I'd spotted my car among the other abandoned heaps along the curb. The wheel covers were gone, and someone had loosened the lugs on the right rear wheel preparatory to making off with that too, only to be interrupted or to lose interest in the face of something a little more flashy. I opened the hood. Everything was there, including the case containing my other set of keys, fixed with electrical tape to an unlikely spot, never mind which one. I undid the tape and slammed down the hood, anxious to be out of there and away from the smell of rotting garbage. The stench grew worse as I neared the trunk in quest of the lug wrench to tighten those nuts.

The spare tire had been removed to make room for her. At her age the fetal curl seemed natural, except that the head was all wrong. It was turned too far around on the neck and was looking straight up at me, the eyes flat and without luster in the brilliant sunlight. She was still wearing the sweatshirt and cutoffs.

I lowered the lid slowly and leaned on it until the lock caught. A swell of hot air thick with putridity and snarling flies struck me full in the face. I didn't know how I could have missed seeing the flies. There were hundreds of them, fat and slick and drunk from the stink. My mouth filled with bile. I started walking, only dimly conscious of my destination, holding my back stiff like a souse with dignity. Anything to get clear of that smell.

Two blocks down stood a corner party store with its faded awning in ribbons and a square of cardboard taped over a hole in the plate-glass window. The counterman, a lean old black with hair like dirty cotton, hesitated suspiciously when I asked to use his telephone for a local call, but pointed it out at the end of the counter. I thanked him very politely, dialed police headquarters, and asked for John Alderdyce's extension. The voice I got wasn't his.

"Hornet." From the sound of it, the guy on the far end was up to his eyes in boredom and sinking fast.

"You want me to hold on while you swat it?" My wit's sharpest when I'm in mild shock. You ought to have caught me the day my mother died. "Let me have the lieutenant."

"He's in the can, wiseass. What you got that's too hot for a sergeant?" He didn't sound any more enthusiastic than he had when he answered the telephone. I told him, aware of the counterman staring at me with eyes suddenly too big for his corrective lenses. Sergeant Hornet listened without interrupting. When I wound down:

"You kill her?"

"Yeah," I said. "I broke her neck, dumped the body into the trunk of my own car, and called you up just to confess. That's how I hang on to my license, by always confessing my murders right away, thus saving the taxpayers a lot of money. I'm a conscientious child-killer. The TV news people keep asking me to appear as their Good Guy of the Week, but I keep turning them down on account of I'm self-effacing. I'm a self-effacing, conscientious child-killer. So it's more realistic to leave the corpses where they fall and let you guys waste time chalking and dusting and photographing and analyzing; so call me sentimental. I'm a sentimental, self-effacing—"

"Enough already!" He wasn't bored now. "You drunk or what?"

"I'm loony, but not from drinking. It isn't every day I find a stiff where my jack should be."

"We'll be there in ten minutes."

"Sergeant?"

"Yeah."

"Is it all right if I don't go anywhere meanwhile?"

"Ten minutes, wiseass." The line went dead.

Hanging up, I felt better. A couple of one-liners off a good straight man and Wiseass Walker was good as new, or at least new-used, never mind how bloody his trail. I smiled and thanked the counterman again, paused to turn the brilliants on a young black woman who had entered the store in time to hear the last part of my telephone conversation, and went out. I glimpsed my reflection in the glass door on my way through and realized then why they had backed away when I looked at them. I was grinning like a Death's-head.

Ten minutes came and went with no sign of cops, time enough to determine that the door to the old gymnasium was unlocked and wander through, eyes skinned for the odd button or sign of a struggle. There were plenty of both, but in that rat's-nest to find neither would have been suspect. Laura Gaye's cell in the locker room was the only neat corner in the place. Someone had even bothered to fold away her clothes. In the light of that discovery a pale blossom opened briefly in the detecting part of my brain, then closed.

I was still prodding at the petals as I scaled the ladder to the loft in the main room, holding my side and pausing after every step to wait for my sore legs to stop trembling. There was no one up there either, just more partitioned-off cubicles full of dirty laundry and hate literature.

When the first blue-and-white showed, I was standing on the shattered front stoop, fishing out the last of my Winstons that hadn't got in the way of someone's flying toe. They came Code 3, which made sense. Had the killer still been in the neighborhood, those red and blue lights and out-of-sync sirens would have put him in Trinidad before they braked to a stop. That's why some uniforms stay uniforms; they can't keep their mitts off those buttons and switches.

The "keener" was still grinding down when the doors popped open simultaneously. The first cop out was the driver, a trim kid in crisp blue without a wrinkle, his big eyes browless under a shiny black visor adjusted with a carpenter's level. His partner, red-haired and freckled, looked like a very young thirty but could pass for eighteen. As he came around the front of the unit his eyes swept the street from end to end and came to rest on me. In that brief moment he had counted every crack in the pavement, priced my new suit, and generally come to the same conclusions about me that I had about him. No slack. Their hands rested on their side arms.

"ID," said the older cop, stopping short of the stoop so he didn't have to raise his head to look at me, which was the reason I'd waited for him there instead of stepping down. They like it best when they can stand over you and make you squirm while they fumble out their pocket pads. It's all a game, like kids throwing each other down a hill to stand on top, or gunfighters maneuvering around to get the sun in their opponents' eyes.

I produced the photostat of my license. He inspected it and gave it back. "You been used some." He was smiling the way cops smile at motorists they're going to ticket.

I didn't say anything. The senior man, whose pocket tag identified him as R. L. Fearing, quit smiling. "We got to be careful these days. It's no fun being a target for a nut."

"Someone pinch me," I said. "I just heard a police officer explain himself."

"Yeah, the watch commander calls me down for that all the time. Where's the dead one?"

"Walk this way." I stepped down and limped toward the Cutlass.

"Funny guy," he said, following.

The stench seemed worse. Breathing through my mouth, I unlocked the trunk and flung it up. Fearing said, "Phew!" and moved back a step. His partner, slower to react, gaped, sucked in a lungful of tainted air, and left us. He trotted quickly across the street to a vacant lot overgrown with weeds. We heard him retching.

"Rookie," said Fearing. "You want to bring us up to date?"

"I can't see the percentage in it," I replied. "In a little while you and the kid will be back out chasing speeders. Homicide's for cops with pensions to risk, not their necks."

"Ain't it the truth? If they turned over investigation to us uniforms, we could rename this town Fantasy Island inside of a year. Eight Mile Road would be jammed with crooks getting out of the city."

"Run for office. Make that your platform."

"Not in this town, brother. Not unless I threw in two welfare checks a week for every vote."

He dropped his voice on the last part. An all-black crowd had begun to gather, lured by the bubblegum machine still revolving atop the blue-and-white, but the smell was keeping them back. I lowered the trunk lid without locking it and lit up. The smoke tasted like decayed flesh. Things would for the next day or so.

"You always have him drive?" I was watching the kid weaving back this way, wiping his mouth with a white handkerchief. His face was gray.

Fearing nodded. "That's where Maxson and Flynn went wrong. Smith and the others know it's usually the experienced officer behind the wheel, so who gets it first? Maxson. Flynn was the rookie, slower on the uptake. The second bullet was meant for him but it missed. If the older one had been in that spot, he'd have nailed the shooter while the kid was still falling. But he wasn't, so they're both dead. That's not going to happen with us."

"Makes it kind of rough on the kid."

"Rookies are like baby turtles," he said. "As soon as they hatch out they make a run for the water. Them that make it without getting eaten by birds grow up to be big turtles. Them that don't—don't. An officer's first responsibility is to stay alive."

Twenty-six minutes after I called headquarters an unmarked unit pulled up and Alderdyce piled out, followed closely by a fat plainclothes man whose maroon jacket and orange plaid pants made him look exactly like an insurance salesman. By this time two more scout cars had arrived. I had cops coming out of my pockets.

John was all in brown today: brown suit, brown vest, brown shirt, brown tie darker than the shirt but not as dark as the suit or the shoes, gleaming like beer bottles on his narrow feet. His mood was even darker. I glanced past him at the insurance salesman.

"Sergeant Wasp, I presume."

"Hornet, wiseass. So you're the guy that called." He'd had his high for the day and was bored again. He had a nice head of dusky blond hair combed in thick waves, and a heat rash on both cheeks that made him look jolly. It was an illusion.

"Let's see her," rapped Alderdyce.

He was looking anywhere but at me, a bad sign. I obliged. His sour expression didn't change as his eyes flicked over the remains in the trunk. Hornet whistled. I started to say something, but the lieutenant cut me off.

"Shut up. Where can we talk?"

There was a paradox there, but I didn't comment on it.

I nodded toward the gymnasium. He told Hornet to wait there for the lab crew and followed me into the building. I felt like I hadn't since the last time my high school principal entertained me in his office.

10

INSIDE, ALDERDYCE KICKED THE DOOR SHUT WITH A HEEL, snatched hold of my lapels, and rode me into the wall on the other side. I outweighed him by fifteen pounds, but he worked out every day and I was caught by surprise.

"You son of a bitch, I'd yank your ticket and make you eat it if I thought you'd have teeth after I'm through with you."

He didn't shout or scream. He seldom did. His hoarse whisper said it all. His eyes were bloodshot and he was breathing hard through his nose, like a boxer psyching himself up for a bout.

"You've changed brands of mouthwash," I said. "I think I liked the old one better."

He let go of one lapel and backhanded me across the mouth. I tasted blood. "Watch your lip or lose it! When I tell you to back away from something I'm not just testing my tonsils. How can I pound it into that thick peeper's gourd of yours that *Alonzo Smith is mine*?"

His last words banged around among the rafters and were swallowed up in the vastness of the room. I said nothing. We stared at each other for a space, and then he pushed me away and paced to the center of the room, where he turned and faced me again. I worked on the fresh wrinkles in my suit, which wasn't looking so new anymore. By the time he spoke again he had himself in check.

"Feed it to me."

I touched my handkerchief to my lip, but the blood was all inside. I used it instead on my forehead, neck, and the backs of my hands. It was close in the room. "I came here last night to see if I could get a line on Smith. A little girl stuck a baby shotgun in my face and I took it away from her. She was on something at the time; for all I know she never came off. We were talking when five or six of her friends showed up. We had words."

"Hard words, from the looks of you."

"I'm learning to adjust," I said. "When I get so I look forward to getting the crap beat out of me, this job will be one long free ride. Anyway, I went away from here for a while, and when I came back I was stretched out in the alley next to the building with the rest of the refuse. A fellow named Bassett collected me and I spent the rest of the night and half of today in his trailer in Warren."

"Bassett?" John repeated. "Munnis Bassett? Bum?"

"The world hardly seems big enough for two. He left to get a doctor and to follow some lead he had, and I caught a cab back here for my car. The keys must have dropped out of my pocket during last night's dance, so I got out an extra set. That's when I found the little shotgun rider in the trunk."

"Know who she is?"

"She called herself Puddin' 'n' Tame, if that's any help." The reply came without hesitation. I'd been rehearsing it ever since I got off the telephone with Hornet.

"Who's your client?"

"We've had this conversation before, John. Play back my answer from the last time."

He sucked in a long draft of stale air.

"You've never been involved in a cop-killing. The rules aren't the same. Do a fan dance with the facts and you'll have so many badges up your ass you'll clank when you sit down."

He didn't sound as if he disapproved of the idea entirely.

"It's got nothing to do with the official investigation," I said. "How long do you think I'd last in this business if I went around violating confidences? My whole reason for existing is an unusual ability to take my mouth out of gear when it counts."

"You could use practice." His scowl lightened. "I won't press it. I've got a pretty good idea who did the hiring, and shame on her. A police officer's wife should know better. What'd the girl tell you before the lights went out?"

Among cops there are two styles of interrogation. Some try to dazzle you with footwork and trip you up by rambling on about something innocuous like baseball or their sex lives, then firing hard questions out of nowhere. It's pretty effective, especially when you're tired, which you'll be because there's nothing in the police manual about giving a suspect breathing space. Others, like Alderdyce, just plod along, one question after another, slugging away until they find a soft spot. If they're not satisfied with an answer they just go on to the next question and return to that one later to see if you've changed your mind. If you have, God help you, because they'll grin and lick their lips and go back to the beginning and start all over again. The success level is about the same, unless you're a cagey P.I. with something to hide.

"Mostly she giggled," I said. "She might as well have been in Cleveland for all the good she did me."

He studied me a long time before speaking. "I hope you're not holding back. Your license won't take the heat."

I let that one die on its own.

The door opened and Hornet poked his head inside. "White coats here, John."

"Okay. Step in here a minute. Once again, Walker. For the sergeant."

Actually it was twice, once to determine if the details varied too much and again to see if they didn't vary enough. Science really ought to study a policeman's brain if they can ever get one untangled. I could hear cops yelling outside as I talked. The crowd was growing.

"Busted neck was enough to kill her, the M.E. says," put in the sergeant afterward. "From a blow to the face, if that makes any sense. Spun her head around farther than it's supposed to go. I had to drag that much out of him. He won't say for sure till the autopsy."

Alderdyce grunted. "The medical examiners' lament. Time we had another conversation with Mr. Bassett."

" 'Another'?" I echoed.

Hornet flashed capped teeth in a quick grin. "He stopped in at headquarters when he hit town. Just like the old bounty men used to do at the marshal's office. Horsey as hell, ain't he?"

"You said Warren?" The lieutenant got his note pad from an inside pocket.

I nodded. "At least, that's where his trailer was earlier this afternoon. The K-Mart parking lot. I guess he likes to save his money for ammunition."

He wrote it down, tore out the page and gave it to the sergeant. "Get on the horn to the Warren Police and have them send a couple of men out there. I want that cowboy in my office today." To me: "Stick close. I want you there, too, to look at pictures."

Hornet was first out the door. There was a lot of shouting going on now, only part of it by cops. The street looked like the overflow from Cobo Hall during an Aretha Franklin concert. Black faces everywhere. On his way through, Alderdyce half-turned and said, "About that cuffing. I was out of bounds. That doesn't mean you didn't have it coming."

I waited for the kicker. Some of the spectators had begun chanting civil rights slogans from the sixties.

"You in a mood for advice?" He raised his voice above the din.

"Everyone's Judge Hardy today," I said loudly. "Do I have a choice?"

"No."

"Then I guess I'm in a mood to listen."

He scrutinized me, his eyes white slashes in his shiny black face. Then he nodded a nod that if I had blinked I would have missed completely. "I guess that's as much as I'll ever be able to expect from you. If I remember right you were raised Catholic."

"Episcopalian. Now I'm an agnostic. Atheists don't ask questions I can't answer and believers don't answer questions I don't ask. They both think there's hope for me."

"Who cares? Just light a candle, if that's what Episcopalians do, and pray that your playmates from last night chilled that girl. Because if they didn't, guess who's got the best motive in their eyes. There's no appeal from the court of instant reprisal."

"Catchy," I said. "Any line on Smith yet?"

He said something unworthy of him and plunged into the sea of surging bodies.

The boys from the Tactical Mobile Unit had drawn a broken line of sawhorses around the area where my car was parked and stationed officers in the spaces between. They were young, and held absolute faith in the varnished brown nightsticks in their hands. No one had told them during training that more officers had been beaten with their own sticks than had beaten others, or that at the first sign of riot the experienced cop's instinctive reaction was to hurl his stick as far away from him as he could. Alderdyce got out his folder and stuck it in his outer breast pocket with the badge showing. I had a badge too, from the Wayne County Sheriffs Department, but it was honorary and wouldn't have gotten me past the ticket window at a Don Knotts film festival. The lieutenant instructed the uniforms to let me through. The clamor of voices was terrific.

A group of strangers in suits and sport jackets were gathered around the open trunk, badges twinkling in the slanted afternoon sunlight. One, a slim youth straight out of a 1955 high school yearbook—complete with crewcut hair and horn-rimmed glasses—was putting instruments away in a shiny black metal case balanced atop the Cutlass's rear bumper. Medical examiners were getting younger too. The whole world was under thirty and I was Genghis Khan's saddle.

Another lad, black, with a modified afro and a leather case of different design under one arm, stepped forward to greet Alderdyce.

"Two or three clear prints, Lieutenant. Looks like we got a match on the driver's door handle and steering wheel. Want me to run 'em through the computer, or what?"

"First check them against Walker, Amos," John growled. "Way things have been going, you probably won't have to do anything else. And dust the gym. That shapes up to be the murder scene."

The other's grin was broad and blinding against his coffee-colored skin. "Got a suspect already, huh? Gee, that's great work.

"Meet Walker, Amos." The lieutenant jerked a thumb at me.

The smile fell. Fingerprint experts aren't used to dealing with suspects face to face. I picked up his grin and tried it on for size.

"I don't bite," I told him. "Hard."

"Well—" he said, and stood there gazing at a point halfway between John and me. Then he turned and strode purposefully away. Alderdyce watched the retreat, shaking his head.

"Babies."

I said, "Don't be intolerant. You were one once."

"I wish you could convince my kids of that." A piece of asphalt the size of a softball glanced off his shoulder and landed on the pavement with a clatter. He spun on the crowd, glaring. No one stepped out to confess.

"Getting ugly, John." This from Hornet, who had just finished speaking over the radio in the unmarked unit. "It's all that shit about police vengeance—Turkel and Gross. They're saying the department offed the girl to try and smoke Smith out. That race thing, same as always."

"Why pick on me? Do I look white in this light?"

The sergeant looked embarrassed. "Aw, hell, John. You know how they feel about black cops."

"No." Alderdyce pushed his face close to Hornet's. "How do they feel about black cops?"

He shuffled around some. "Christ you've heard them. Turncoat. Traitor."

"Uncle Tom?"

Hornet hesitated, then met his superior's gaze. "Yeah." It was barely audible. Then he spoke up. "Maybe we need more uniforms."

"No." Now the lieutenant was shuffling. He brushed asphalt dust off his brown coatsleeve, avoiding the other's eyes. "Not yet, anyway. It'd be like waving a red flag in front of a bull.'' Turning to walk around the sergeant, he saw me.

''What are you gaping at?''

I reached up and pushed my mouth shut.

He made his way to the car, where the medical examiner was charging a new-looking briar pipe. Since he looked pretty new himself, the impression was of a kid playing Sherlock Holmes in a school play.

''When'd it happen, Doc?'' Alderdyce asked.

The M.E. struck a match and applied it to the bowl. Speaking between puffs: ''Beats (chug-chug) me. Leave a body (chug-chug) in a trunk (chug-chug) on a day like this (chug-chug), it's anybody's guess.''

John stretched out an arm and took the pipe from the other's mouth. ''Guess.''

The youth stiffened indignantly, then adjusted his glasses. ''Not later than sunrise. Body temperature won't tell me anything; it must have been a hundred and fifty degrees in that trunk. Rigor mortis is complete, but there's a six-hour margin for error in figuring that. I'll have to get inside and determine how far putrefaction has advanced before I can say anything definite.''

''Early this morning, then.''

''Or late last night. You wanted a guess. I won't stand by it in court.''

''That's the D.A.'s headache. Thanks, Doc. Sorry about the chimney.'' He gave back the pipe.

''These things aren't as easy to light as they show on TV.'' He ignited a fresh match. ''I'd appreciate it if you didn't call me Doc. I don't call you fuzz.''

''Okay, kid.''

The sergeant was standing where we had left him. Alderdyce directed him to take the photographer and check out the gymnasium, then escorted me to the unmarked car. As I climbed in:

"You were kind of rough on Sergeant Honeybee back there."

"That's Hornet." He started the engine. "Worry about yourself. And plan on doing without wheels for tonight. You're getting a free vacuuming, courtesy of the lab." He executed a neat three-point turn inside the sawhorses, waited for the morgue wagon to pass on its way in, and started crawling through the simmering crowd. Something struck the rear window with a crack and bounded off the trunk. He ignored it and kept rolling.

11

IT WAS NEARLY SIX WHEN I LEFT HEADQUARTERS. THE AIR smelled of hot metal and monoxide. Even the hydrants were sweating. My stiff neck was worse, and if someone had come along smoking a cigarette while I stood stretching on the bottom step I'd have mugged him for it.

Under questioning, I had repeated my story yet again, this time to a tape recorder, and squinted at mugs from the department's file on black militants. Deak Ridder had been among them, but I didn't point him out. He didn't look like one of the group that had tap-danced on my skull, and since the cops weren't tipping their hand neither was I. If any of the others were pictured I didn't recognize them. Maybe if someone had held up a boot in front of each face—

I took a cab to my office. It was a new crate with clean carpeting and no burn holes in the leatherette upholstery, but the driver had a blind spot for potholes and tried twice to put my head through the roof. "Sorry," he said after the second near-concussion.

"That's okay," I replied. "You'll make it next time."

I had him wait in front of a drugstore while I went in and bought a carton of Winstons. The rest of the trip I smoked and watched the scenery hurtle past. Figuring how to square things with Alderdyce when he found out I was sitting on vital information. Because he would find out, and when it got around that Walker wasn't playing by the rules I'd have to find somewhere else to ply my trade. Lansing? Too many politicians in those capital towns. I'd spend half my time following husbands and other husbands' wives to cheesy motels and the other half trying to collect my fee. Flint? Nothing interesting ever happens in Flint. Another state? I'd be forty before I had the geography down to where I could operate, and a private investigator at forty I didn't want to be. Not that I had the kind of skills that would be useful in any other line except police work—and a forty-year-old cop is even sadder.

At my building the driver stared at my fifty-cent tip as if it were radioactive. "Invest in a helmet," I advised him. He tried to leave tread marks on my toe. Cabbies have no sense of humor.

I had customers in my outer office the way I had six figures in my savings account. The new magazines on the coffee table dated even as I glanced in their direction. Go try and show consideration for the clientele.

The sanctum sanctorum smelled like a refrigerator in need of a cleaning. I opened the window to let in fresh smog and switched on the circular fan they'd found left over from a previous civilization when they dug the foundation for the building. It wasn't noisy at all when there was demolition going on across the street. Dust stirred on the desk and a corner of the cheesecake calendar on the wall opposite lifted, offering a tantalizing glimpse of Miss September.

Sitting behind the desk I killed some time staring at the new wallpaper. Stylized brown butterflies on a shade of amber that didn't show dirt, reminiscent of the pattern in

my folks' dining room when I was a kid. I wondered if
they were still designing houses with dining rooms. All I
knew for sure was that the wallpaper made the rest of the
room look that much seedier.

Holding out on the cops is a double-edged sword. I
couldn't count on them for simple information like Ridder's current address. Just for the pure hell of it I looked
him up in the city directory. He wasn't listed. Then I got
a brainstorm and dialed Barry Stackpole's private number
at the *News*.

"Rumor mill." He sounded alert and youthful. I hated
him when he was like that, which was most of the time.

"Walker," I said. "How's the gangster beat?"

"Amos the shamus. Hell, there's no glamor in it anymore. Tony and Vito Jack are in and out of the slam and
Tony Z's up to his ears in indictments. You heard Mor-
ningstar's dead."

"I heard." I'd done a job for the old man a while back.
"Listen, this might be out of your ballpark. Black militants."

"What do you want to know?"

"Whatever I can about a party named Deak Ridder." I
spelled it. "I'm told he fronted for a while out at Rouge,
but that's not current. I would be ever so grateful if you
can come up with an address."

"How grateful?"

"A fifth of McMaster's. Two if you can have it for me
in an hour. I'm at the office."

"Fifths, remember," he said after a pause. "None of
that half-liter shit."

"Do I sound like a Canuck?" Barry was born in Mon-
treal.

"You'd never pass the literacy test. Later." He cut the
connection.

It was time to report. I gave the Sturtevants a try, but the line was busy. It still was five minutes later. Suddenly I was very hungry. I got the beeper out of the desk and clipped it inside my jacket just in case Barry called early, and hotfooted it down to the counter on the corner. Oscar of the Waldorf would have denied parentage of the tuna fish sandwich I got, but at least it came before I took a bite out of the waitress. At the register I bought a package of English walnuts. I was cracking the first one in my lap at the desk with the stapler I'd broken cracking the last batch when my door opened and a black man walked in.

"You're quiet," I observed. I hadn't heard him coming through the outer door.

"I practice." He had an effortless voice, drawly with a hint of a whine on the *i*'s and *a*'s. He was considerably over six feet tall and weighed about a hundred and forty pounds. His beanpole frame was draped in a shapeless paisley shirt, tail out, and stiff jeans with patches on patches. He had sandals on his feet. His lean face was all planes and hollows, with deepset gray eyes and a mouth as broad as an airstrip. I didn't know him from George Washington Carver.

"Quiet men don't usually require my services," I said. "How can I make your life easier?"

"You can start by putting your hands on top of the desk." He swung a long leg over the customer's chair as if mounting a horse and sat. In the same movement he whipped a big automatic out of his hip pocket and pointed it at my breastbone.

I looked at him rather than at the gun. Its expression never told anyone anything.

"I don't think so."

His eyes smoldered in their sockets, and for a moment he looked ready to squeeze the trigger. Then he flicked the gun nonchalantly in an armed man's shrug. "Maybe you got jock itch. Anyway, I don't think you sit with a piece in your lap day after day just waiting for someone like me to come in and stick one in your face, so have it your way. But wind your watch and you're a mural on the wall."

"Colorful."

He grinned self-consciously. "I got it from *Police Story.*"

I waited.

"I hear the FBI is offering to help the local pigs look for Alonzo Smith," he said.

"I couldn't say. I haven't seen a paper since yesterday."

"Take my word for it, then. So why don't you just park yourself somewhere till the traffic passes?"

"Somewhere like where?"

"The Upper Peninsula, maybe. I hear it's peaceful out on Mackinac Island. They don't allow cars there. A man can get run over in this town just standing on the corner."

"Move on to the threat," I said wearily. "I get paid by the day." The gun was very big and the room was very small. One shot would kick me backward on the swivel's casters and through the window. When it hit the papers— not very hard, I was strictly third section—the news would sadden very few and brighten the day for a few more, not many. In two days it would be shelf liner. I didn't want anyone standing a can of beets on my face, but that didn't mean I'd sit still for much more Warner Brothers dialogue.

"I'm a friend of a friend," he explained. "This friend don't care for private noses sniffing around his sandbox. He's a friend, but he can get to be an enemy. People he's an enemy of have a habit of not sticking around long enough to take off their hats. Or am I being too circumspect?"

"Your vocabulary's patchy. *Circumspect* stands out in

that kind of speech like French cologne at a cockfight.'' I pulled a curtain down between my face and my brain. ''This friend—his initials wouldn't by any chance be Deak Ridder, by any chance?''

Something came into his gray eyes, but he poked it out of sight before I could latch on to it. The gun was steady in a hand so thin the bones showed through the dark flesh. ''You ain't scared enough,'' he said calmly. ''Maybe I should ice you right here and save a friend some trouble.''

''Maybe you could.'' It sounded like someone else using my voice. ''If you were the Kaiser and that was Big Bertha in your paw.''

''Big who? What's that supposed to mean?''

''That's supposed to mean there's a Colt magnum in a holster screwed to the left side of the kneehole in this desk, pointing at your belly. Don't look for it; it's behind the modesty panel. I admit your belly's not much of a target, but we both know at this range a bullet from a magnum doesn't have to come very close.''

The dangerous look returned, chased by the toothy smile. On him it looked like the grille of a '57 Buick. ''You're bluffing.'' He sang the words.

I grinned into the glare of his pearly whites. ''Move your chair.''

That didn't get much reaction. We'd been kicking around so much clever parlance he was probably trying to translate the directive into English. I clarified.

''Go ahead, try to move it. Bet you can't.''

A second slid past, and then he shifted his weight to the balls of his feet and pushed back with his rump, eyes and gun still on me. The chair didn't budge. His brow knitted. The chair was vinyl and chromium and not that heavy.

''Bolted down,'' I said. ''I prefer my targets stationary.''

This time the smile lacked conviction. "I still think you're running one past me."

The brittle crunch of a hammer drawing back took up all the available space in the office. "Fade, Raskolnikov."

He faded. Backing out, automatic in hand, he didn't even brush the door casing. Oh, he was a pro.

I waited until the outer office door closed, and then I took my hands out of my lap and put the damaged stapler and pieces of crushed walnut on top of the desk. My hands weren't shaking any worse than a drunk's on the fourth day of a seven-day cure.

You see a lot of salesmen in the private-eye business whether you want to or not, and they all drink too much coffee. That's why I'd fixed the customer chair so that they couldn't move in too close. That caffeine breath is too much for me.

12

THE TELEPHONE SHRILLED. I'D HEARD LOUDER NOISES, BUT not just after playing chicken with a hired killer. When I came down from the ceiling Barry Stackpole was on the line.

"Fifths, remember," he said.

"Yeah, yeah. Just a second." I laid down the receiver, fired a match and grasped that wrist in my other hand to bring the burning end to the cigarette in my mouth. When I let go, the flame shook itself out. I retrieved the instrument.

"Okay, what you got?"

"Deacon Aloysius Ridder," intoned the reporter. "Pipe those initials, will you? Booked once for armed robbery and twice for assault with intent to kill. None of them took. The witnesses experienced a sudden change of heart. Suspected former Black Panther, well-known pimp, and all-around prick with a chip on his racially downtrodden shoulder the size of a city councilman's ego. Believed still to have relations with black revolutionaries. Shrinks have him down as paranoiac, possibly homicidal. Your common everyday garden-variety maniac."

I whistled. "Any address?"

"Last known, an apartment on Mt. Elliott, across from the cemetery. Building burned to the ground a couple of months ago. Guess what three local notables, two deceased, are suspected of torching the place?"

"Smith, Turkel, Gross." I sounded like Alderdyce had at the hospital.

There was a brief silence before he spoke again. "It's no fun playing guess with a detective. Anyway, this wouldn't be the first time disgruntled minority members matched a slum tenement to get back at the landlord. Say, you're not after Smith, are you?"

"I promised you Scotch, not a story. Keep unwinding."

"The hell with you," he said cheerfully. "I called a friend in personnel at the Rouge plant, never mind her name, and asked her to run Ridder through the computer and find out if he's still employed there." He paused again, milking the moment.

"Spill it, Hitchcock."

"Day shift, eight-thirty to five. Final assembly." He sounded smug. Reporters always do when the routine clicks, which it doesn't that often.

"Security's tight down there. Any idea how I can get in short of storming the front gate?"

"I've got a police pass I could let you have for an exclusive."

I filled that one with water and tested it for leaks. "Keep my name out of it," I said finally. "I'll have a hard enough time getting the cops to eat this one without grabbing a curtain call to boot."

"I'll just make myself the hero."

"You've had plenty of practice. As one pro to another, how'd you get all this?"

"That's privileged," he purred. "First Amendment and

all that. But if a certain policewoman in records asks you to be best man at our wedding, you don't know me.''

I laughed. ''How many betrothals does that make, Barry?''

''I'll leave numbers to the boys in Circulation. Is there a dead alligator in your office?''

''Let me check. Nope. Why?''

''You sound as if you just finished wrestling one.''

''Wrong. But I did just chase out a gorilla with a walnut. What do you know about a black trigger—tall, skinny, gray eyes, Southern accent?''

''That description covers about a hundred in this town. Gun?''

''Forty-five automatic.''

''That narrows it down to seventy,'' he said. ''Now tell me about the walnut.''

''That's privileged. Much obliged, newshawk.'' I hung up. A little mystery is healthy in every relationship.

The Sturtevants' telephone was still tied up. Well, I had nothing else to do before eight-thirty tomorrow morning, when Ridder's shift came on. I pulled my sore muscles down three flights to the street, flagged a cab, and gave the driver the address off Livernois.

This time I had a sane driver. I settled back in the seat and skimmed the copy of the *News* I'd bought from the rack near my building. There was nothing in it about the dead girl on McDougall, but there was an early, unsubstantiated report of a near-riot in that neighborhood. The cops wouldn't be able to sit on it much longer.

Police in Ecorse had arrested a black man that morning as he was launching a rowboat onto the Detroit River. He looked a little like Alonzo Smith and they were convinced he was making a getaway for Canada. They released him two hours later when a local physician identified him as his retarded son, and explained that this was his third runaway fishing trip on the polluted waterway. Three men had turned themselves in at Detroit Police Headquarters claiming to be Smith, but they were shown the door on account of two were old enough to be his father and the third wasn't even black. Some poor schnook from Alderdyce's detail was in Toledo checking out that purse-snatching report on the off chance that the woman who made it wasn't daffy. And General Motors didn't build Chevies.

I had trouble concentrating on the words. I kept going over the confrontation in my office and coming up with more questions I didn't need. If the gunsel had come from Ridder, he must not have heard about his sister's death or he would have sent him in shooting. On the other hand, the look I got from the errand boy when I mentioned Ridder's name made me wonder if he was the one behind the visit after all. On the *other* hand, if Ridder hadn't sent him, who had? That was three hands, too much for one man. I made my mind blank and concentrated on the pavement slipping under the cab, trying to hypnotize myself into believing I was Sherlock Holmes. I couldn't even manage Dr. Watson. It had been a long day, and it wasn't over yet.

I was too late for the baseball game. There was a golden light over the Sturtevants' subdivision that made each house look a little different, something the developers hadn't counted on or they'd have had the sun rezoned. This time the nurse answered the bell. She was almost my height, and her dyed-black hair skinned back into a knot at the nape of her neck gave her already severe face the look of a diamond in the rough, hard and homely. She didn't like my face either, or maybe it was just the bruises.

"My name's Walker," I said. "We met yesterday, sort of. Is Mrs. Sturtevant in?"

"No, she's not. You'll have to come back later." She started to put the door in my face. I braced a hand against the panel.

"Can I wait for her? We have kind of an appointment."

"I don't know. Mr. Sturtevant shouldn't be disturbed. It's time for his speech therapy."

"In his place I'd welcome a little disturbance now and then." I showed her the county buzzer. She made a show of reading the embossed legend as if it meant something. At length she backed up a step and opened the door just enough for me to squeeze my shoulders through one at a time. If the Japanese had been that obstinate we'd still be busy in the Pacific.

On the way into the living room I saw that the telephone was off the hook. The recorded message that instructs you over and over to hang up and the peevish alarm that follows it had recognized their match in the nurse and given up a long time ago.

My client was in his wheelchair facing the window. The sunlight took on a coppery tinge coming through the glass and lent his features the look of rosy health. It was the veneer of veneers. He was as dead as a man could be and still be breathing. His eyes were in the shadow of his brows and I couldn't tell if he was watching me or the television that was going in the window across the way or the pictures in his brain. He had a bathrobe on over striped pajamas and his bare feet were thrust into backless slippers. A paperback copy of one of Wambaugh's police novels lay open face down on the arm of the chair I had occupied on my last visit. She'd been reading to him when the doorbell interrupted.

Somewhere in the house the fan was still whirring, still with no effect upon the shut-up room.

The nurse drew the drapes, and the illusion of health was gone. He looked grayer than he had the day before. Maybe everything did, and it was just me. I got out a cigarette and tapped it against the back of my other hand.

"Could I have a few minutes alone with him? It's a private matter."

She pressed her lips tight. They were painted scarlet, which was a mistake. They made a raw slash against her pale skin. "Five minutes," she said. "He must be under my close observation. And no smoking."

I made a thing of putting the weed away. When she had withdrawn into another room, I held up the pack for Sturtevant to see. His eyes were visible with the drapes shut. The lids moved down and up twice. Yes. I lit two and placed one between his lips.

I didn't sit for fear my joints would seize up. Standing with my hands in my pockets, I filled him in, beginning with my ill-timed visit to the commune on McDougall and continuing through my recovery in Bum Bassett's trailer, the corpse in my trunk, and that bit of pulp that had taken place in the office that evening. "Right now Ridder's the only handle I've got," I wound up. "I don't usually tip my leads to clients, but I've got a funny feeling about this one. I'd like someone to know where I'll be tomorrow morning. Which is why I'm waiting for your wife."

I paused. I don't know why, maybe from force of habit. I like to talk, and I have to kick myself every few minutes to give others a chance to comment. Sturtevant didn't, of course. He just sat there without moving while the ash grew on his cigarette. I continued.

"What I can't shake is the feeling that there's purpose in all this. Laura Gaye and her friends didn't bust Smith

110

out just because they wanted to stick it to the white establishment. The raid was too well organized for aimless fanatics, the escape too well planned. No one even saw them leave. Then there's the girl's murder. If that was the work of militants, it was to shut her up. She was a doper and inclined to let things slip. For the sake of my faith in human nature I'd like to believe that Ridder had nothing to do with his sister's death. And I'm still trying to fit the joker in my office into the deck. Everything swings on the conviction that the group needed Alonzo Smith for something specific. My theory is that whoever took the trouble to tidy up Laura Gaye's cell after I left the place last night knows what it is.''

Sturtevant's exhausted eyes were looking right through me. His left hand came up slowly from the padded arm of his chair to the cigarette, took it from his mouth, tapped ash onto the carpet, returned it, and lowered back to the arm. I started at the movement. It was as if the Lincoln Memorial had scratched its nose. I'd forgotten he wasn't totally paralyzed.

''I'm a little worried about Bassett.'' I spoke faster. My five minutes was up. ''He gave the newspapers a statement about bringing Smith in alive or dead. When I asked him about it he said it was just showmanship, but I'm not so sure. The reward is for arrest and conviction, so I can't see what he's got to gain from knocking him down. That doesn't keep me from wondering about his motives. Character and motive, that's what my work comes down to. Just like a writer.''

The nurse came back into the room. If she'd overheard any of the monologue it had no effect on her. She spotted the cigarettes and gave me a withering look.

''Sorry.'' I took one last drag and killed my stub in the ashtray on the coffee table.

"You'll have time enough to be sorry when Mr. Sturtevant's in his grave and you realize you put him there." She rapped out the words.

I was fresh out of snappy retorts. I watched her pluck the half-smoked Winston from her patient's mouth and crush it out with the no-nonsense movement of someone experienced in extinguishing other people's smokes. Then she turned his chair around and wheeled him through an open door into a bedroom. Most of the plaster held when she pulled the door shut behind her.

The front door opened and closed a few minutes later and Karen Sturtevant walked into the living room. She stopped when she saw me. She was wearing a lime-colored cotton blouse open at the neck and another of those longish skirts with a slit up one side, in the shade of green the pansy decorators call chartreuse. Her platform sandals were a darker green. When your eyes are that color you can't wear much else. Her face was shiny, and the faint scent she wore was made slightly acrid by perspiration. On her it was like musk.

"I didn't see your car in the driveway. Where's Van?" She clutched her pocketbook—also green—in white-knuckled hands, bracing herself.

"Relax," I said. "He's being tucked in by Erich von Stroheim in drag."

She smiled in relief, but tension haunted the tiny cracks at the corners of her eyes. "I smell tobacco. I've gone a few rounds with Nadine on that subject myself." She put the purse down on the telephone stand. Noticing that the receiver was off the hook, she replaced it. "What happened to your face?"

"I box on the side. Been shopping?"

She shook her head. "Seeing our lawyer. He wants to draw up Van's will."

"Does a policeman have much to bequeath?"

"The lawyer seems to think so. I don't know whether I agree with him yet. It seems silly. Van's brother died two years ago and his parents are long gone. We don't have children. Have you made any progress?" She indicated the sofa. I accepted. She sat down beside me, crossing her legs. The slit fell open and I had to speak slowly to get the words to come out in the right order.

"This Iris," she said, when I had brought her up to date. "Is she a detective?"

"She's a hooker. Sometimes that's better."

"I see. I think. Can I get you a drink?"

I said Scotch rocks would do. She got up with a scissoring movement of her slim legs and went into the kitchen. The refrigerator door closed, ice rattled against glass. At the end of three minutes she reappeared carrying a small barrel glass in each hand.

"Are you in love with her?" She handed me a glass, tucked a leg under and sat down.

"In love with who?" I had to change hands to drink. She was that close. The musk was stronger.

"Your face looks awful."

"I've been told that."

"You know what I mean. I feel responsible."

"Don't. I warned you about the possibility of screwing up. I'm the type that doesn't benefit from experience. I have to learn how to be a detective all over again every time I go out. Sometimes I don't learn fast enough. It isn't your fault, and maybe it isn't even mine. It's just something that happens, like green eyes."

I'm dumb. I hadn't seen it coming, not that fast. She took my glass from me and leaned forward to set it down next to hers on the coffee table, and as she came up she twisted a little and tried to devour the lower half of my face. Her body pressed hard against mine from breast to thigh. There wasn't anything under her blouse but her. I responded. She was quivering all over.

"God, it's been weeks," she murmured between writhing lips. Her nails dug into my biceps. I was getting her into a reclining position when the nurse came in.

13

I TRIED TO DISENTANGLE MYSELF, BUT MRS. STURTEVANT hadn't seen the newcomer and it was like wrestling a nest of pythons. The nurse paused in mid-step, then continued past briskly and picked up the police novel from the arm of the easy chair. She didn't look at us on her way back to the bedroom.

I got loose, seized my glass, and emptied it in one installment. That was a shame, because it was good Scotch. "I'll have a typewritten report in the mail tomorrow," I said, standing. "As of now I'm a free agent."

She remained as I had left her, looking up at me from the cushions on the end of the sofa and breathing like a marathon loser. "If you're worried about Nadine, forget her. She's the soul of discretion."

"It's not her I'm worried about. There are a lot of things I'd do for your husband, because I owe him. Assuming his matrimonial duties isn't one of them."

"St. Amos the Incorruptible," she said acidly. "I wasn't exactly alone on this couch."

"I didn't say you were, Mrs. Sturtevant. But when a man's on the wagon it's not a good idea to hang around liquor stores. I know a couple of good local P.I.s who might be persuaded to take an interest in this case; I'll include their names in the report.'' I started out.

''Wait! Please.''

I waited. She struggled into a sitting position, grabbed her purse off the coffee table, and clawed a cigarette out of a fresh pack. I was right there with a match, but she set fire to it herself with a table lighter. I'm not fast enough for today's woman. She drew the smoke deep, then lifted a hand and swept back a lock of blond hair with that gesture no one ever has to teach them.

''I don't want you going away thinking what a whore I am,'' she said. ''In six years of marriage that's the closest I've come to cheating on Van—not that there weren't plenty of opportunities in our crowd. And it isn't even that, really. You can't cheat a man out of something he can't have anymore. You don't know what it's been like this past— how long has it been since the shooting?''

''A little over two weeks.''

''My God, it seems like two years. I'm not trying to excuse my behavior, just explaining my position. For a few moments there I wasn't an invalid cop's wife. It felt damn good.''

''You don't owe me any explanations, Mrs. Sturtevant.''

''I owe myself one. Oh hell, this is beginning to sound like *Ryan's Hope*.'' She mashed out the smoke after only a couple of drags. Then she looked at me. ''Don't abandon the investigation. You can report by telephone if you like. I'll put it on a paying basis.''

''How much?''

Her mouth fell open a little. Then she drew it shut, and there were hard lines at the corners. ''How much will it take?'' Her voice was cold.

''You tell me,'' I said. ''What's a little girl's life worth?

What's the sticker on a private agent's relationship with the police that he's worked years to build? How much will you bid on each bone that gets broken before this thing is wrapped up?"

She was staring at me. "I don't understand."

"I didn't expect you to. I'm not making a lot of sense tonight. That's how much I owe Van. When I have something I'll call."

"Just call?" She sounded smug.

"I said I was on the wagon."

I HOPPED A CAB TO MY HAMTRAMCK ABODE, WHICH looked the way I felt. The air inside was hot and stale and little curls of dust twitched and danced on the living room rug when I opened the windows. I got out the sweeper and did what I could with it, then emptied the contraption into the kitchen wastebasket and dragged into the bathroom for a hot and then a cold shower. The icy water pricked at my various cuts and bruises like dentists' needles. The thick tape around my abdomen felt like a suit of armor.

I toweled off carefully and stepped into a fresh pair of shorts. If I had a wife, she might have had a drink waiting for me when I emerged from the bathroom, but I didn't anymore, and the one I'd had never had been home anyway. Three years married to her had put me in fine shape for bachelorhood. I mined out a bottle of Haig & Haig I'd given myself for Christmas, poured some of its contents over ice in a glass, and went into the living room carrying the glass and the bottle.

The TV listing had Robert Mitchum starring in *Thunder Road* at ten o'clock. I made a note to see it again, but nothing came of that. I passed out in my chair halfway through a rerun of a situation comedy, which considering the program was just as well. But I hated missing *Thunder Road*.

I woke up with my head doubled under me and a stiff back to go with my neck. I felt chilled. Daylight bled feeble gray through the windows, but the wall clock my grandfather had bought for my great-grandmother when he was nine years old said it was already 7:45. I stood and stretched, my bones cracking. The carpet was damp where I stood barefoot looking out one of the open windows. According to the thermometer on the back porch, the temperature had dropped eighteen degrees since last night. I sneezed. That figured.

There was nothing to eat in the house, but I didn't cry over it. My head was echoing from all that Scotch, and half the Third World had tramped through my mouth overnight without anyone pausing to wipe his feet. I fixed up the coffeemaker and left it gurgling while I shaved and dressed. Studying my reflection in the mirror above the bathroom sink, I decided that the swelling had gone down some. Then I decided it hadn't. But I didn't feel as sore as I had the day before.

An hour later, coffeed up and sporting a comparatively fresh suit, I finished putting another hack's son through college and presented myself at police headquarters, where a glowering Lieutenant Alderdyce gave me a voucher for my car. In pinstripe shirtsleeves with the cuffs turned back and his tie at half-mast, he still looked sportier than I had at my wedding.

"Pry anything out of Bassett?" I asked.

"He was born without handles." He yawned, not bothering to cover it. The memory of acid coffee and stale tobacco clung to the elevator-car-size office. That, and a shower and a change of clothes in the locker room, seemed to be as close as he'd come to a night's rest. "He hung on

118

to that story about finding the commune deserted till it bled. We couldn't keep him, but I've got a man on him while his background is being checked.'' He snorted. ''That ought to read like *The Life and Legend of Wyatt Earp.*''

''He'll shake your man like tissue off his shoe.'' I made my voice casual. ''Any ID yet on the girl?''

''The papers, radio, and TV are running a description of her later this morning. She's Jane Doe until someone comes forward. Forget the neighbors; we barely got out of there yesterday without busting heads. We tracked down the gymnasium's owner up in St. Clair Shores, but he doesn't know anything about the girl. Says he rented the place a year ago to a black dude who gave his name as Woods. Always pays on time and in cash by special messenger. We're looking into that, but I'll lay odds Woods is this year's John Smith.''

''Speaking of Smiths,'' I said.

His face shut down with a bang. ''You've got your car back. Roll.''

I took his advice. On my way through the squad room I met Sergeant Hornet and his maroon jacket. He held up short, leaning backward slightly to counter the forward pull of his paunch.

''That's some new development in the Smith case,'' I observed.

His dishwater-colored eyes drifted past my shoulder to Alderdyce's door, then back to me. He smiled a fat man's smile, tugging the corners of his mouth out a fraction of an inch. ''Tough titty, shamus,'' he said. ''Ain't no fishing allowed up here.''

We parted company. Hornet wasn't that cagey. If there'd been any new developments he'd have tumbled.

At the impound I went around with the attendant about some scratches the lab crew had left on my rear fenders, with results predictable and profane. They hadn't even put gas in the tank. I filled up at a station down the street and continued on to Barry Stackpole's new place on Lafayette, three blocks away from his cubicle at the *News*, after a stop at a liquor store for two fifths of McMaster's.

"Park 'em anywhere," said the columnist from behind his portable typewriter as I entered the apartment on his invitation. The fingers of his left hand flew over the keys. He seldom used its mate, two fingers of which had gone the way of his right leg and part of his skull when his car blew up in his face a few years back. There was also a steel plate under his reconstructed features that gave him fearsome migraines in cold weather. A big Luger lay close-at-hand atop a stack of pages next to the machine, but it wasn't a paperweight. The kind of enemies Barry made didn't forget.

I swept some crumpled sheets off a glass-topped secretary and set down the paper sack containing the two bottles. He was using a folding card table for his work because there wasn't room under the secretary to straighten out his artificial leg. A large suitcase stood next to the door, positioned for swift collection on the way out. "Still on the move, I see."

"Ten minutes later and you'd have missed me entirely." He struck the final key with a flourish and tore the sheet out of the typewriter.

"Another telephone call? Who from this time, blacks or Sicilians?"

"Would you believe the Columbians?" After scooping the Luger into his hip pocket, he got up and shuffled the pages.

"The cocaine connection," I said.

He impaled me with his crystal-blues. We were about the same age, but unlike mine his sandy hair was untouched by gray and he never seemed to tire. "That's the title of my column. Who talked?"

"Nobody had to. Next to Ted Getner at the Freep you're the fastest man with a cliché I know."

"Screw Ted Getner and screw the *Free Press*, and while you're at it, screw you." He closed the typewriter case with the finished pages inside and tossed me a leather folder taken from his breast pocket. "Try not to lose that. I had to eat a carload of Crackerjacks for it."

I looked at his picture on the police pass. "It's a lousy likeness," I said. "I might get away with it at Rouge, except for the eye color."

"Slip the security man a twenty and watch him go colorblind. This isn't World War Two. Sorry I can't offer you a snort, but I've got the rest of my span to try and fill." He juggled the bag with the bottles under one arm and picked up the suitcase with his free hand. Even with that and the typewriter in the other, he didn't limp any more than a man with one tight shoe. "Get the door, will you?"

I got it. "How'll I get the pass back to you?"

"I'll call with my new address. Make an effort not to sell it to anyone."

"Your address—or the pass?"

"My address, jerk. I know of eighty places in town where you can get a card like that printed while you wait. And don't forget, you promised me an exclusive."

"I'll deliver." I accompanied him down a flight to the street and saw him off in a cab he'd had waiting. He told the driver to go where he directed. Barry had a melodramatic streak that was borne out by three attempts on his life. I had him beat numerically, but I still had all the parts I'd come with, give or take a molar and a couple of hundred thousand brain cells. I was young yet, however.

14

THE RIVER ROUGE PLANT. HENRY FORD'S SPRAWLING monument to the Industrial Revolution. One hundred miles of private railroad, a fleet of ships larger than some navies, and enough daily electricity to power two hundred and forty thousand households fire its steel mills, coke ovens, glass plant, paper mill, and assembly operation, all in the name of economic parity with Japan. Cadillac and LaSalle camped on this site two centuries before their names fell to the products of Ford's competitors, but they'd have needed more than a map and a sextant to recognize it the day I visited. Dirty pink smoke leaked from stacks, darkened buildings, obscured sluices, and scudded across piles of tailings, the whole gridded by rails as in a tabletop layout, while rust-streaked ore carriers crawled along the scarlet-tinged waterway like bloated sowbugs down a fissure in a wet rock. Pile drivers grunted and clanged rhythmically against the enraged roar of thousands of engines being block-tested. The air was nine-tenths sulfur. It would have been a fine location for a rest home.

I parked in the visitors' lot and bluffed my way past a bored guard in a booth without having to resort to my wallet. Forty years ago that would have made him a prime subject for government interrogation, but as Barry had pointed out, we weren't at war at the moment.

Here was where the tours I'd taken before the money crunch forced Ford to cancel them came in handy, for without at least a casual knowledge of the setup I could conceivably have wandered around the complex for a week before I found the area I wanted. As it was it took me an hour.

Legend has it that Henry got the idea for the assembly line when he visited a Chicago meat-packing house and watched the efficient manner in which cattle were prodded one by one into a narrow chute and slaughtered. He didn't do much with the process, just reversed it so that the end was creation rather than destruction, and founded a new world order on that one change. I watched a string of auto shells, blue-green in the fluorescent light overhead, roll along a conveyor belt lined with men in safety shields, pause just long enough for torches to splatter blinding white-orange sparks off various portions of the frame, then roll on, like mechanized convicts lockstepping along a prison corridor. There were more robots than on my last visit, but the operation was the same, and had been for over sixty years. It would take more than four wars, a worldwide depression, and a list of political assassinations as long as an unemployment line to interrupt production at Ford.

"Get a good eyeful, bub?"

I turned to face a short chunky construction in white coveralls with the Ford emblem stitched in red script over the breast pocket. The echoing racket in the vast room had strangled whatever noise he might have made approaching on rubber soles. He had a shock of rumpled brown hair going gray, and his puffy features were turquoise in the light reflecting off the steel shells on the conveyor. His desk-sergeant eyes, tired and suspicious in dark sockets, remained on my face as I hauled out Barry's folder, then shifted grudgingly to the ID.

"Stackpole, huh?" He didn't shout, but his flat voice carried over the splash of the torches and the hum and bang of the great belt. "Yeah, you look like this picture. And people are all the time mistaking me for Gregory Peck. Let's go talk to security." A hand closed around my arm.

"Just a second." I put away the folder and produced the wallet with my license photostat. He studied the new picture.

"That's closer. Keep going. We'll get a good likeness yet."

"The police pass was a gag to clear security," I said. "I'm investigating some murders. You the pit boss?"

"I'm the supervisor on this shift. Who's croaked?"

I removed his hand from my bicep. My fingers had gone dead. "Is there someplace we can talk? I'm not used to exchanging confidences at the top of my lungs."

"Who's listening? Robby, here?" He jerked a thumb at one of the robots, a one-armed mass of steel and multicolored spaghetti that looked about as much like the Buck Rogers conception of a mechanical man as I looked like a parking meter. "All right. You walk ahead of me. I'll tell you when to stop."

After a hundred yards or so he directed me into a large room with a linoleum floor and two rows of Formica-topped cafeteria tables and benches folded down from the walls. A row of vending machines stood next to the doorway. At the far end of the room sat a young black man in coveralls, drinking coffee and reading a magazine. We selected a table equi-distant from the door and the lone diner and sat

down facing each other. I offered my companion a cigarette. He shook his head.

"The doc says no. Who's dead?"

I lit up. "A pair of cops named Maxson and Flynn, at
Mt. Hazel Cemetery. Likely you've heard about them. And
a young black girl on McDougall. That one won't be public
until later."

"I know about the cops. What's Alonzo Smith got to do
with Rouge?"

"I was hoping there'd be someone here who could tell
me. Someone named Deak Ridder."

His eyes showed all the expression of screws in a door-
frame. "Ridder's on my shift. What about him?"

"That's what I'm here to find out."

"He didn't show up today."

"That happen very often?"

"Depends on what you call often. He's better than some.
Others, not so good. But what're we gonna do when half
the alphabet threatens to strike if we can one employee?
Don't get me wrong; I'm union all the way. But everything's gotta have its limit."

I smoked. Give me a bellyacher every time. "I guess
the machines will make a big difference."

His face clouded over. Away from the fluorescent lights
his normal color was gray—not as gray as Sturtevant's, but
the gray of someone who worked by artificial illumination
day after dreary day. "The fucking machines. What's not
to like about them? They don't complain about the condi-
tions, they don't call in sick, they don't strike. All they do
is their jobs. A fat lot of use the company'll have for su-
pervisors when robots is all there is on the line. I heard
one of them computer whizzes on the radio the other day.
'Machines don't take away jobs,' he said. 'They create
new ones.' Jobs for college graduates. And if they create

as many jobs as they do away with, I wish someone would show me where the company gains by going to them in the first place. Every time we gripe they throw words at us. My kids can't eat words.''

"There is no gravity," I said.

He grinned lopsidedly. "The earth sucks. Ain't it the truth.''

"Deak Ridder." I tapped ash into a black porcelain tray with a wad of petrified gum in the bottom. "Was he at work Monday?''

"Meaning what?''

"Meaning what I said.''

"What's it worth to you?''

"Not a damn thing. Just proving a little theory of mine.'' Monday was the day Laura Gaye and her two companions sprang Smith. "Where can I find him?''

He took a pencil from a plastic carrier in his breast pocket and poked the eraser end at a live spark in the ashtray. "You pipe them pygmies out there on the line? They get much smaller we'll be wearing them instead of driving them.''

"There's not a lot you approve of about this part of the century, is there?'' I wondered where this was leading and what it had to do with Ridder.

"Nothing since the polio vaccine,'' he said. "When I was a kid, big was the way to go. Maybe that's because this used to be a big country. Now everything's shrinking: Cars, computers, movie screens—hell, even my oldest girl is two inches shorter than her mother was at her age. Maybe a million years from now they'll dig up someone's left shoe and put it in some museum as proof of giants. If there is a million years from now, and there's anyone left to dig.''

"Nice speech. I bet the Kiwanians eat it up.''

"I ain't made my point. Thing is, we're paying more for less all the time. So where do you get off thinking you can pry dope out of me gratis?"

"So far I haven't seen anything worth bidding on."

He shook his head. "It don't work that way. I'm facing layoff in a couple of weeks. My kids need clothes, not promises. I got all of those I need."

"Who do I look like, Mother Waddles? Check out the Perpetual Mission."

"I'm sticking my neck out just talking to you." His tone was as close to a whine as it would ever get. "I'm supposed to report unauthorized visitors."

I sighed. "Twenty bucks."

"Save that green for rabbits. I can have security on your ass in five minutes."

"You'd better cover yours if you do. We've been seen talking when you should have been reporting." I tilted my head toward the guy reading the magazine.

He glanced in that direction, then back to me. "He won't say nothing. I'm his boss."

"Could be if he does say something *he'll* be boss. You never heard of Affirmative Action?"

"I heard of it. I also heard of earthquakes and tornadoes and other natural disasters." He shifted his weight from hip to hip. "Look, I got a family. Dentist bills. My youngest wants to be in the school band, play the saxophone. You know what a sax costs? Can't you do better than twenty? Hell, I spend more than that on a tank of gas."

"Fifteen."

"All right, all right!" He dropped his voice when the man in back looked up. "But don't be surprised if three ghosts visit you Christmas Eve." He consulted a pocket pad and gave me an address and an apartment number on Whittaker. I took both down in my own pad.

"Thanks." I rolled a twenty around my index finger and held it out. He almost amputated the digit taking possession.

"He wasn't, by the way."

I looked up at him stupidly. He'd risen and left the table and I hadn't expected him back.

"Ridder," he said slowly, as if talking to a backward child. "You asked was he at work Monday. He wasn't."

Wordlessly I got out a five-spot and handed it to him. His face lit up like a Chinese lantern. Next I'd be sending Care packages to people I didn't know in Asia.

He left me to finish my cigarette. The racket outside the room seemed to have abated, or maybe I was just growing used to it. The black guy flipped his magazine shut, got up, and started out past me as I was crushing the butt. I stuck out a leg and he went down hard.

Cursing breathlessly, he started to push himself off the floor, but by that time I was up and I kicked his arm out from under him. His teeth snapped together loudly as his chin hit the floor. I leaned down and got hold of the hair at the nape of his neck. He gasped.

"What's your hurry, Big Ears?" I asked. "Looking for someplace to sell what you just heard, or is someone already waiting for it?"

"Let me go, man! My break's over." The words were distorted bouncing off the floor.

"What do you do?"

"Sheet metal work. I'm a tinsmith C'mon, man! That was my boss just left. I need this job."

I let go and stepped back. "Let's see something."

He struggled onto his left side to get at a wallet in the hip pocket of his coveralls. He was built heavy and wore

128

a chin beard as sparse as a mandarin's. His work card looked genuine. Cunning, Walker. What's next, mugging seminarians?

"Sorry." I put out a hand to help him to his feet. He stared at it a moment, then brought up one of his own. There was a barber's straight-razor in it.

"I ought to cut you," he said, getting up. His eyes were nasty. "But I'm late."

I watched him leave, razor in hand, and pondered a new career for when the world finally ran out of victims.

15

By ten-thirty I had a handle on the hangover, and decided that my stomach could do with something to occupy it before the acids dissolved my belt buckle. The something turned out to be sausages and eggs at the counter down the street from my office, served by my favorite waitress, a college girl whose eyes were haunted by the ghosts of a half-dozen busted affairs. But she had a smile for me, even if it had begun to go bad around the edges, and I left a big tip. She swept it up as if it were another crumb on the linoleum.

The telephone started up as I was unlocking the door to my think tank. I grabbed it on the third ring.

"I think the girl at your answering service knows I hook," greeted Iris. "Every time I finish talking to her I get the feeling she sprays the phone."

"That 'girl' is forty-seven and is in electrolysis. What's on your mind, angel?"

"Sex, mostly. Then you, though the two aren't necessarily linked. Where were you all last night? I tried three times to get you at home."

That made two people I'd missed, her and Robert Mitchum. "I didn't hear the bell. Were you worried?"

130

"You're always saying good-bye with bruises on your face and going out to talk to the ones that put them there. Why should I worry?"

Her tone dripped irony. I started to say something flip, but nothing flip came to mind. Instead I said, "I've got an appointment with a certain party later. He doesn't know I've got it, but I'd like you to know." The open line was no place for names.

After a long silence on the other end: "I don't suppose it would do much good to try to talk you out of it again."

"That doesn't mean you won't try."

"Yes, it does. The only words you listen to are spoken by people with guns. Don't go alone, Amos."

"On this one I have to. If I bring the cops in they'll take it away from me. I promised some people I'd see this one through."

"It doesn't have to be cops."

"Who, then? I've got exactly three friends in this town I can count on. One's a cop and one's crippled. You're the third."

"And you won't take me because I'm a woman," she said.

"Don't hang dogma on me, angel. I won't take you because you'd get us both killed. And you know it."

She made no reply to that. I spent some time breathing back some of my own breath off the receiver. Then she spoke again.

"I don't know which is worse, you or the needle."

"I don't leave scars."

"You want to bet?"

I changed the subject, a talent I have. "If I don't call you by one, send the cops to this address."

"Just a second." There was a rustling on her end. "Okay, shoot."

I gave it to her. "One o'clock, remember. Help too early can be hazardous to my health."

"It seems to me we did this once before."

"It worked that time."

"Only because I didn't do exactly what you asked me to. Amos?"

"Be careful?"

"I don't think you know what that means. Stay alive." She clunked off.

I held on long enough for the recording to kick in, then replaced the receiver and squatted to open the safe and withdraw the Smith & Wesson in its holster. After inspecting the chambers I snapped it onto my belt so that the butt snuggled against my right kidney. I hoped I could hold on to this one; I didn't have any others.

THE BUILDING ON WHITTAKER HAD STOOD TOO LONG FOR a city obsessed with the illusion of renaissance. Pigeon splatter iced its brick façade, broken chunks of which littered the cracked sidewalk like flecks of bloody spume at the base of a park bench where an old man sat waiting for his heart to stop. Soot and discoloration had given the windows a senile look. A bill advertising someone's candidacy for an office that hadn't existed in ten years had weathered down to a faded legend on a yellow oval as much a part of the building as the crusted fixture over the door. The bulb was smashed and there were cobwebs and dead moths inside it.

Fourteen noisy-looking steps led almost straight up from the door, but there's a way to get up that kind soundlessly if you've had practice. I crept along the edge nearest the right wall, loosening the revolver in its holster as I neared the landing, just in case I wasn't as lightfooted as I hoped I was.

The hall was narrow and illuminated naturally through a tall window that faced the street. The walls were tobacco-colored above the wainscoting, the floor runner made of ribbed brown rubber and worn through to the boards in some places. The man standing in front of a door at the far end was big enough to tip a truck scale. His ten-gallon Stetson added a foot to his height he hardly needed.

"A little off your range, aren't you, cowboy?"

He stiffened and turned to squint at me against the lighted window. Today he had on a fringed buckskin jacket over a shirt with a smaller check than usual. But it was the same .44 magnum in his huge right hand, and it was pointed at me as usual. Then he recognized me and relaxed just enough. I had drawn mine just before hailing him.

"You set the law on me, hoss," he rumbled. "That wasn't very friendly considering what I done for you."

"In my place you wouldn't have acted any differently, if you're smart. And you must be or you wouldn't be here. What say we put up the hardware?"

He lifted his eight-inch barrel and replaced the hammer without a sound. I did the same and we holstered our respective widowmakers. Every time we met it was *High Noon.* "How'd you tumble to Ridder?"

He smiled in his beard, cracking his face from mouth to eyes. "How'd you?"

"I get it." I jerked my chin in the direction of the door. "He in?"

"I was just fixing to check." He rapped the old varnish with the second knuckle of his little finger. We waited, but no one answered. He rapped again.

We listened for movement. An engine in need of a muffler roared past in the street outside. Bassett tried the door. It gave. He looked at me.

"It was standing open, right?"

I nodded. We moved off to either side and took out our guns again. He finished twisting the knob, pushed, and ducked back behind the jamb. No one shot at us.

"Me first," I whispered.

"How come?"

"I'm a smaller target. Besides, there's a little matter of a debt I owe this big cowboy."

It was his turn to nod. I wound myself up tight, took a heading on a sturdy-looking studio couch five feet beyond the open door, and dived for it. I landed on hands and knees behind the tall back and waited. Again nothing. I gave it a few more seconds, then duckwalked to the other end and peered Kilroy-like around the edge, where the steel frame showed through the worn red fabric.

The apartment was neat but shabby, the furniture sagging and spraddle-legged, the rug trod patternless, the wallpaper bubbled just this side of peeling. A portable black-and-white television set stood on a table piled high with TV magazines and pamphlets I recognized from the hate library at the McDougall commune. From where I squatted I could look straight into the kitchenette, set off from the rest of the room by its linoleum floor and a low counter. I wondered about that counter.

Holding the crouch, I scuttled in that direction, stuck my gun over the top and followed it up. Someone had spilled coffee down the side of the counter onto the linoleum, where it had dried into a yellow-brown stain. Nothing else.

I stood up and called to Bassett. He came in, ducking to

clear the top of the doorway. The magnum looked like a toy in his fist.

"I'll take that one." He waved the barrel toward a door in the wall adjacent to the midget kitchen. I said okay and headed for another opposite that.

In an earlier generation the room had been used for storage, but a toilet and sink had been added to make what realtors today call a half-bath. It wasn't big enough to contain anything else. It was also uninhabited except for a lone cockroach on the wall next to the medicine cabinet.

"Stop looking."

There was a new quality in Bassett's voice I had never heard in anyone else's except maybe half a dozen times. I closed the bathroom door and crossed to where his bulk filled the other doorway. He shifted sideways to give me a hinge at the room and its contents.

The curtains were drawn over the only window, and the light from the living room fell full on the whites of the occupant's eyes, so that they seemed to glow through the gloom. Naked but for a pair of dirty jockey shorts, he lay bound in the shape of a jackknife on his stomach on a bed with a whitepainted metal frame. His eyes had outgrown his lids and his purple tongue seemed longer than a tongue should be. His face was purple too, under the natural brown pigmentation of the skin. The rumpled sheets were soaked and the room smelled like a public toilet.

Out of habit I stepped inside and felt the big artery on the side of his bulging neck. He wouldn't be needing it any longer. The flesh was still warm and moist. I wiped my hand with my handkerchief. He had the fluffed-back hair and the Fu Manchu moustache, but aside from that he bore little resemblance to the mug shot I had studied at police headquarters. I was seeing him at a disadvantage.

It wasn't the classic hogtie. Whoever did it had cut the plastic clothesline after binding the victim's wrists behind his back, looped his ankles to his neck, and drawn the works guitar-string tight, probably bracing a knee against Ridder's spine, before setting the knot. Ridder had tensed his muscles as long as he could, but eventually sheer fatigue had forced him to relax and strangle himself. It would have taken hours.

The bed claimed most of the space in the room. A three-drawer chest at the foot appeared undisturbed, but a small bedside table on casters was tipped against the wall and a white china lamp lay in pieces at its base. Other bedside-table stuff was scattered across the bare floorboards: an unbroken bottle of cough medicine, some Kleenexes, a paperback book with a lurid title and an even more lurid cover illustration, cigarettes and matches, other odds and ends of a cumulative nature. He had put up a fight.

A wallet on the chest held two hundred and forty dollars in tens and twenties, Ridder's work card from Rouge, and three driver's licenses made out to three different names, none of them his but all bearing his picture.

"What you suppose they was after?" Bassett's voice was normal now, which was more than I could say for mine.

"It's a cinch it wasn't money. Maybe revenge." I spoke through my teeth. "You know anything about knots?"

"Do I look like a sailor?"

"Bluto, a little. Ellery Queen would take one look and tell you whether they were tied by a Lascar or a Malay hangman, and whether he was right- or left-handed," I said. "He'd throw in the guy's astrology chart free of charge. He wouldn't stand here like a mongoloid."

He gave me a look I could feel in my shoes. "You all right?"

"I'm just dandy. Finding prime suspects who've had the life choked out of them is the way I like to start every day. How about you?"

He shrugged.

"One more dead nigger, right?" I snapped.

"Did I say that?"

I exhaled. "No. That was just me talking. It's the atmosphere in here. Funeral parlors affect me the same way. Let's get out."

"Out of this room, or out of the apartment?"

"This room," I said. "We'd better holler cop. There's a bare chance no one saw me come up here, but you're about as inconspicuous as a great woolly mammoth."

"Watch that kind of talk, hoss. I'm sensitive."

"You're also extinct." We moved into the living room. "There's a service station around the corner on Green, about five blocks down. Who calls?"

"You done it last time," he pointed out. "I reckon it's my turn."

"I was hoping you'd say that. I'm not sure what effect the combination of my voice and this news will have on Alderdyce."

"You afraid of him?"

"I'm afraid of him. I'm afraid of the Detroit Police Department and the criminal court system and the license review board and unemployment and poverty. There's precious little I'm not afraid of in this town, but those are the top six. Don't forget to come back and help me wait."

After he left I tossed the apartment. All I learned from

it was that Ridder had lived just like Barry Stackpole. He didn't have anything that couldn't be thrown into one suitcase, and I found that in the bedroom closet. It takes a dedicated fanatic to stick with a cause long after the glamor has worn off, and that was as much eulogy as Mrs. Ridder's boy would get from me.

I burned a cigarette and gazed out the living room window, which looked out on Whittaker and my car parked in front of the building. This was where all the half-truths and suppressed evidence got me, looking down the wrong end of a busted license. One of those vans with a sunset painted on the side panel was cruising past and I longed to be on it, or on anything that would take me away from there before the cops arrived.

I got tired of that and turned away. Then the window blew apart.

16

A SHARD OF GLASS FOUR INCHES LONG BRUSHED MY LEFT
cheekbone a half-inch behind the eye, accompanied by a
rapid snapping, like typewriter keys striking a stiff sheet
of paper. I hit the floor rolling and drew the .38 as I
came up on the other side of the reliable studio couch.
Tires cried down in the street, an engine wound up and
then was swallowed by distance. I waited, but there were
no more shots.

Something trickled down my left cheek. The hand I put
up to wipe it away came back with blood on the fingers.
The piece of glass had opened a two-inch cut in my temple.
I pressed my folded handkerchief to it until the bleeding
stopped. My own razor had done worse damage. I was
getting up when Bassett hurtled through the door behind
his big magnum.

"Who's dead?" he demanded. "I heard busting glass
on my way up."

"Not now. I'm having palpitations."

Leathering the Smith & Wesson, I examined the wall
facing the window. They weren't hard to locate. Three
separate dishshaped depressions grouped in a pyramid,
exposing fist-size circles of broken lath beneath the plas-

ter. I'd seen slug holes like those before. I wondered where.

I WATCHED A FLY TAKE OFF FROM THE MOUND OF PAPER in the IN basket on Alderdyce's battleship-gray desk, execute a series of stalls and barrel rolls in the stale air near the ceiling, then light beside another fly on the wall next to the pebbled-glass having failed to strike up a relationship, the newcomer buzzed away when the door opened. Sergeant Hornet paused a beat on the threshold, then came the rest of the way inside, closing the door behind him. The fly escaped into the squad room a quarter of an inch short of being squashed. Oh, to have wings.

"You still here?" Hornet eased his bulk into the chair behind the desk. The springs creaked.

"John said to wait. He let you sit there often, or do you hold off until he's out of the room?"

His eyes were water-colored in folds of fat, but they were cop's eyes just the same. They hand them out in the twelfth week of the training course. He'd smeared something white on his heat rash, making him look like an obese Indian in warpaint. "He's mad as hell at you," he said. "I don't think I ever seen him madder."

"You haven't known him as long as I have."

"That wasn't smart, not telling us the girl on McDougall was Deak Ridder's sister. We'd known that, we could of picked him up for questioning and been on Smith's case right now. Why'd you do it?"

"What is this, relays? I made a statement."

He shook his head. "You never said why. John told me to ask. He don't trust himself to be in the same room with you just now."

I started to tap out a Winston, then decided against it. My throat was raw already. "Ridder was the only lead I had that you didn't. He was my chance to bring Smith in alive, which is what my client ordered."

"You saying we wouldn't?" His tone would cut paper.

"This isn't *The Rookies*, Sergeant. Out of three cop-killers, two are dead. I'll give you Turkel's suicide, if that's what it was. Don't tell me every badge between here and the West Coast isn't hoping to be the one who pulls off the hat trick. If you try I'll throw up all over John's desk."

"I don't know what happened when you were a kid to put you off police, but I don't work that way and neither does John."

"I don't know you. I don't even know John anymore. Do you?"

He looked down at his pudgy hands lying flat atop the desk. When he looked up again we were talking about something else. "Think the guy that threatened you in your office is the one that shot at you?"

I watched the fly on the wall. It hadn't budged from its spot next to the door.

"He could be," I said. "I doubt it. He had his chance. My bluff wasn't that good."

He reached into a side pocket of his goofy jacket and plinked two small brass shells onto my side of the desk. "These were found in the gutter in front of Ridder's building. I guess the other one fell inside the van. Recognize the caliber?"

I picked one up and studied the flanged end. "I ought to. I handled them enough in Nam. It's standard ammunition for the M-16 rifle. The Gun that Lost the East."

"Also the gun Laura Gaye and her friends used to pry Smith out of custody."

"Important bastard, aren't I?" I put down the shell.

"Could be that's the way they see you. Who besides the supervisor at Rouge knew you were going there to talk to Ridder?"

"No one."

He watched me from under his lids. "I sure hope nobody's leg's getting pulled this time through."

"I'm not hopeless." I thought of the tinsmith I'd worked over at the plant.

"Maybe." He picked up the shells. "Kind of puny slugs to do what they done."

"That's because the gun doesn't shoot them, it throws them."

"Huh?"

I made a somersaulting gesture with my index finger. "They tumble through the air, end over end. Makes them useless beyond about sixty yards, but within that range they tear hell out of anything they hit. You saw the wall."

He pressed his lips tight. "Nice people, these militants."

"They're in a nice racket. Who do you like for Ridder?"

"Same as his sister. Bassett looked good for that one at first, but he's aces up with the Oklahoma police and there was no motive. He's been on the hot stick too long to lose control. It looks like Alonzo Smith's good friends chilled her because she was a security risk, then did for her brother for the same reason, or maybe on account of he made a big stink out of her going down. Hell, it could of been Smith himself done it, for that matter."

"Neat," I replied. "For you. Hang Smith and you scrape two murders off the blotter on top of the Mt. Hazel shooting. Except that your theory sucks wind. If Ridder was already dead when I got to him, why try to kill me? If I

142

were any good at interrogating corpses I'd invest in a pointed hat and a crystal ball.''

"So who said these nuts think rationally? Maybe they don't even talk to each other. Organization ain't their strong suit or they wouldn't be fighting against it.''

"Got all the holes plugged, haven't you, Sergeant?''

"Bullshit.'' His irritated cheeks glowed hot pink through the white salve. "I been nineteen years a cop, thirteen with this department. I seen maybe two thousand cases presented to the D.A., and not one of them was airtight. You said it yourself, this ain't TV. We don't get one case at a time and all the time in the world to question every suspect and sift through all the evidence and then make a brilliant deduction resulting in an arrest and immediate conviction, just before the last commercial break. I can spend just so much effort tracing the lost button, the footprint in the zinnia bed, the charred match, knowing that if something does come of it, nine times out of ten a clumsy cop is responsible for its being there in the first place. So don't talk to me about plugging holes.''

"That's my job,'' I said.

"Wrong again. Your job is to take pictures through keyholes and ferret out perjurers to help some shyster whittle down a charge of first-degree homicide to a suspended fine for pissing on the sidewalk. But not much longer, brother. We're recommending they lift your license in Lansing. And that could be just the beginning. Suppression of evidence is a felony in this state, but any charges coming out of that will be up to the D.A.''

"In the meantime, can I go?''

He smiled his fat man's smile, as spare as the décor along Death Row and loaded with secret knowledge. "Aw. And here I was busting my ass to keep you entertained.''

"You were doing okay until you started making speeches at me."

"Your story checks out with Bassett's, so far as it goes. So dangle, wiseass." The smile wasn't even a memory.

I got up. My muscles creaked. Just being close to the wheels of justice had ground me down.

"And tell your friends we're not an answering service," he said to my back. "Someone named Iris called for you a while ago. She wants you to get back to her."

I turned and looked down at him for the first time since he'd entered. The customer's chair was built low on purpose, to intimidate the occupant. "If I can get you a crack at Alonzo Smith, will that make any difference in your report to Lansing?"

"If you're talking, I can't hear you," he said, interesting himself in a paper from the OUT basket. "I'm deaf."

At the door I found out finally why my fly hadn't moved. It was a nailhead in the wall.

THIS TIME THEY'D LET ME DRIVE MY OWN CAR IN. I PULLED out of the police garage under an overcast sky and tried the radio, but the music was too lively for me all over the dial and I turned it off. There should have been organs. I deserved organs. They play them for the dead. I don't know why. There'd be plenty of them playing for the next couple of days, thanks to my clever manipulation of the facts in this case. They ought to play one whenever I enter a room. Amos Walker, the Midnight Man. Watch out for him. His touch is death.

I bought a copy of the *Free Press* on my way to the office, mainly out of habit. The material relating to the Smith hunt was as stale as a tour guide's jokes. Nearing my building, I cruised past a row of parked cars and cranked the Cutlass into a tight space half a block down from the entrance. My mind was so full of the case I didn't react to the van standing across the street until I was in the foyer and the glass door was closing behind me. The painted sunset was distinctive.

17

Get out, Walker.

They were amateurs or they'd have ditched the van before this. That didn't help me any. Assuming they were whom I suspected, they'd helped with the execution of two police officers and the maiming of a third, staged a successful raid on a heavily guarded courtroom, and if Sergeant Hornet was right, murdered two of their own without a qualm. Amateurs like those I didn't need.

Get out, Walker.

That I was still alive was evidence enough that no one was in the van. So they were in the building. On the flip side, they might have planted the vehicle there just to give me heart failure, and split. Maybe they were miles away laughing at the petrified hoojie. But I didn't figure them for a sense of humor.

Get out, Walker. Call the cops and have them send a riot team down to flush out the building. Don't be a graveyard hero. Who'll care a week from today?

It was good advice, except that they might have thought of it themselves and stationed a shooter in the van after all to close the trap. After the first attempt they might be leery of an execution on another public street, but that didn't mean they'd chance a second escape.

A guy could stand there figuring all the twists and turns and end up chewing off his tail. The steel fire door to the stairs was propped open as usual, exposing the first of three narrow flights to my floor. I'd long thought it a prime spot for an ambush. This was my chance to prove it. Drawing the revolver, I took the folded newspaper from under my arm and underhanded it up the shaft. The pages exploded outward like frightened bats.

The waiting M-16 stuttered too fast to count, riddling the flying newsprint and knocking large chunks of brown plaster off the wall. The shots rang deafeningly in the echoing stairwell. Brittle blue smoke glazed the air.

Silence crackled at the end of the burst. Shaking myself loose, I ran noisily to the front door and heaved it open. While it drifted shut against the pressure of the pneumatic closer I lightfooted back the other way and withdrew behind the open stairwell door. It had received a fresh coat of thick green paint recently; turpentine filled my nostrils.

The front door settled into the frame with a barely audible click. A beat, and he came pounding down the steps, cradling the fat, sausage-shaped carbine along his left forearm. The broad vented tails of an unseasonably long overcoat billowed out behind him.

I waited until he had a hand on the door handle, then cocked the Smith & Wesson. The crunch was loud in the silence following the shots. He hunched his shoulders and started to turn.

"Uh-uh," I said. "Unless you want that hot coat ventilated."

His shoulders went slack. He was black, not very tall, with a short thick neck and close-cropped hair on a bullet head. His back was mounded conspicuously with muscle. The barbells knew they'd had a workout when he was through with them. I thought I knew him from somewhere, but maybe that was prejudice.

"Put the chattergun on safety, squat down, and slide it this way," I directed. "If you can do all that without turning around I would be ever so appreciative."

"I can't. It's on a sling."

He had a very deep voice.

"Aren't you the clever one. Do your shoes explode too? Peel off the coat and climb out. Slow, like striptease."

He obeyed, dropping the coat to the floor with a clunk that coats don't usually make. The harness was fashioned crudely from belts, and fixed over one shoulder so that the carbine could be swung out from under his arm. Willie Lee Gross had worn a similar rig the day he was killed.

"Bad idea," I told him. "This time of year the coat's a dead giveaway."

He undid the sling without comment. His white T-shirt clung wet and transparent to his lumpy back. Finishing, he sank to his haunches and prepared to propel the carbine backward. The scaly green door to my right opened and the building superintendent stepped through, climbing into his suspenders. He stopped when he saw what was going on. A toilet whispered and gurgled behind him.

"Something, Mr. Rosecranz?" I kept my attention on the gunman, still squatting with one hand on the M-16.

"I heard a noise. Shots, maybe." The super's eyes were large in his tattered face.

"Firecrackers, Mr. Rosecranz."

"I don't think firecrackers was it," he said.

"Sure, firecrackers. Left over from the Fourth. You know kids."

'No kids in this building.''

"Of course not. If you were a kid, would you set off fireworks in your own building?''

He looked from me to the crouching figure, and from him to the stairwell. "What about them holes? Who's going to pay to replaster?''

"Send me a bill, Mr. Rosecranz.''

"Suppose the other tenants complain about the noise?'' he persisted. "I should tell them firecrackers?''

"What tenants, Mr. Rosecranz? There are only four at the moment. I'm one, and two are off on vacation.''

"There's Mr. Styles on the fourth floor.''

"Styles is in numbers, Mr. Rosecranz. The telephones alone would have drowned out the noise. You don't see him down here, do you?''

He spent some more small change looking from one of us to the other. Then he blew his large nose into a red handkerchief that crackled when he stuffed it back into his hip pocket, and grasped the doorknob. "I hope this don't become a habit.''

"It won't, Mr. Rosecranz. See you later, Mr. Rosecranz. Mr. Rosecranz?''

He almost had the door shut. He paused.

I poked a twenty through the gap. "Firecrackers, right?''

"Happy Fourth.'' The door closed with the bill on his side.

I smiled at the back of the black man's head. "Mr. Rosecranz.''

"Who gives a fuck?'' The carbine slid my way, its receiver and stock scraping loudly on the linoleum. I stopped it with my foot and told him to face the wall across from the super's door. Bracing him, I bent and picked up the M-16. A lot of stamped metal with a cheap wooden stock, shaped like a grease gun. I broke loose the straight clip and inspected the load. Four gone, enough for the brief burst that had made confetti out of today's *Free Press*. He would have reloaded after the attempt on Whittaker.

I leaned the gun against the wall behind the propped-open door to the stairs and went over to find out what had clunked in his coat. I knew what it was the second my hand closed on it in the right pocket. The Luger's clip was full. It was nice having it back. I stuck it under my waistband and frisked my captive. He was practically defenseless. I put a set of brass knuckles in one side pocket of my jacket and a switchblade and jackknife in the other. He didn't have any hand grenades or rocket launchers.

"White motherfucker," he muttered.

I backed up a step. "Say again."

He said it again.

"Just wanted to make sure I recognized the voice." I reached out and slammed his forehead into the wall. He groaned. I brought a knee up hard between his spread legs, and as he was doubling over I grasped his belt, planted my feet wide, and whirled him clear across the room into the opposite wall. He struck on his back and began to slide. I walked over and hoisted him up by his damp shirtfront. Holding him with one hand, I started batting his large face with the other, left to right, right to left, left to right, in rhythm. Blood spurted from his nose onto the T-shirt.

At this point a fat guy carrying a briefcase entered by the main door. I paused, hand raised in mid-bat. He stopped long enough to take in the spectacle, then mounted the stairs and passed from sight. If he was an associate of Styles's he'd seen it before. I went back to work.

I lost my victim a few cuffs later. His eyes rolled over

white and he got too heavy to hold. Still hanging on to the shirt, I dragged him over to the super's door and dumped him into a heap to free a hand for knocking. When it opened:

"Bucket of water, please, Mr. Rosecranz."

His creaky old eyes lowered to the mass of humanity almost at his feet. He nodded and moved away, allowing me a view of two unmatched overstuffed chairs with floral-print slipcovers, a swaybacked sofa, and a console TV on a square of brown rug on a gray concrete floor. He hadn't changed a thing in the seven years I'd been a tenant. Water roared against metal beyond sight of the doorway. A minute later he reappeared lugging a galvanized pail three-quarters full.

"Thank you."

"For what? I'm not even here."

The door shut, I swung the bucket back in both hands and dashed its contents over the unconscious black. It made a noise like wet laundry slapping a board fence. He coughed and spluttered and sat up, scooping water from his eyes. His features were starting to discolor and swell.

"White motherfucking son of a bitch!" he gasped.

"Your record's stuck, parrot. Get a new writer." I was breathing hard from the exercise. "How many you got stashed in the van?"

He thought about that. He had a brutal face, the lower half pushed out like a baboon's muzzle. I remembered it vaguely from the locker room in the defunct gymnasium on McDougall. "Three," he said finally. "All armed. I was you, I'd duck out the back way before they come looking to see what happened."

"You would if you were me, but you're not so I won't.

You took too long answering. That means you're alone.
See how it works? Now, where's Alonzo Smith?''

"Go fuck yourself."

I swept the empty bucket backhand against the side of
his head. The impact made a satisfying gong and left a big
dent in the vessel.

"Again. Where is he?"

He was still reeling from the blow, but he managed to
make an obscene gesture. I put a matching dent in the other
side of the pail and set it down. The lobby was beginning
to sound like the bell tower at Notre Dame.

"You owe Mr. Rosecranz a new bucket. Where's
Smith?''

He spat at me, missing by six feet. This was sizing up
to be a large job. I changed my tack.

"What's your name?"

"Go fuck yourself."

"Imagine that," I said. "Señor Wences is alive and well
and smarting off in the foyer of my building." I aired the
Luger. "Who killed Deak Ridder and how come?"

He leered, his upper lip a smear of red mud from his
smashed nose. "You won't shoot."

I moved the barrel a little and shot the heel off his left
hobnail boot. The explosion filled the room and shattered
a tile. He grabbed his foot as if he'd been hit.

"Son of a *bitch!*" It was a shriek.

"Watch your language in my building. Ridder. Who
punched his ticket? Next one goes in the foot." I pointed
the gun at it.

"Man, save that jive for some dumb J. D. Deak ain't
dead no more'n me or you." He picked up the broken
heel.

"You're left-handed, correct?"

"What the hell's that got to do with nothing?"

"From the way you were strapped into that harness I'd say you're left-handed. That means you favor the left foot. So I'll shoot the other one first. I'm not unreasonable." I shifted my aim accordingly.

He stared at me. "If Deak's dead, you done it."

I sighed. You can't argue with a fanatic. "Okay, we'll park that for now. Who told you I was on my way to talk to Ridder? The tinsmith on his shift at Rouge?"

Again he said nothing.

"I'll take that for a yes," I said. "The cops will want to question him too. Not that he's a militant, but groups like yours stand or fall on the sympathy of brothers. So you thought I might get something out of Deak and tried to take me out at his apartment. Who did the job on his kid sister?"

"I figure you know that better than me," he snarled.

"Grow wise and prosper. If I'd wanted to get back at someone for that beating I took, it wouldn't be her I'd pick." I paused, not for lack of another question to ask. I was sorting them out. "Who helped Laura Gaye crack Smith out of court, you and Ridder?"

"Pretty slick, huh?" There was pride in his voice.

"Slick as spit. Why?"

"It was just our little way of telling the motherfucking white system where it can stick its motherfucking judges and lawyers."

His Oedipus complex was getting on my nerves.

"Not good enough," I said. "We'll come back to that. Where's Smith?"

He clamped his mouth shut. I raised the gun a little higher.

"You're going to shoot me anyway," he said then. "Why not now?"

"A martyr yet. You know why your movement is going

153

to die out? You don't trust anyone. No one. That's one of the two Great Mistakes. The other is trusting everyone."

He shrugged. I rapped on Rosecranz's door.

"More noise," said the super, opening up. "I'm quitting, maybe."

"Before you do, I want you to make a telephone call."

Watching the prisoner, I gave Rosecranz the number and Alderdyce's extension and told him what to say. It might not have been in my client's best interest, but it was fourth and four and time for the first string.

18

Iris was mad as hell when I finally got around to calling. Nearly six hours had elapsed since she'd telephoned police headquarters as I'd requested, and I was two sheets to the wind to boot. She held on just long enough to determine that I was healthy and then hung up in the middle of my apology.

I put the receiver back on its hook and threaded my way between tables to the back booth, where Alderdyce sat nursing a beer. The saloon, operated by an old county horse patrolman, was located a few blocks over from headquarters and served as a watering-hole for cops between shifts. A blowup of the manager's class at the Academy—rows of visored adolescent faces in sepia ovals—occupied the place of honor behind the bar, surrounded by prints of great steeds. Police patches from all over the country plastered one whole wall. At a nearby table, a boisterous party of six was comparing hair-raising episodes from the annals of the department, punctuated by whoops and obscenities. "I Shot the Sheriff" blared from the juke. Police humor.

My Scotch had gone flat. I signaled for a fresh slug and touched off a weed. I didn't catch fire, which meant I hadn't exceeded my drinking limit. John saw things differently.

"What's that, your fourth?"

"I'm anesthetizing myself. Is that the beer you started with?"

"I'm on duty." He was sitting with his forearms resting on the table and his head sunk between his shoulders, glaring into the amber liquid in his glass. Bar lighting brought out the blue in his roughed-out features.

"So you went and bartered back your license," he said. "How long you figure to keep all the balls in the air?"

"I sometimes wonder." I swapped glasses with an over-ripe barmatron who had black eyebrows to go with her platinum hair, paid, and put down half of the replacement. The ache in my ribs had spread to my back. I'd stood two hours in an interrogation cell watching the sniper I caught exercise his right to remain silent. Even the man's name remained a mystery. His prints drew a shrug from the computer and the cops were waiting for an answer on their Telex to Washington.

I said, "I think I fell asleep on my feet for a space there. What came of sending those uniforms to the tinsmith's place?"

"Zilch. Landlady said he packed up and got missing this afternoon right after he got home from work."

"Advice from our friend in the lockup, no doubt."

"He'll turn up. There's an APB out on him all over the state."

"He might know our sniper's name," I said. "I doubt he's one of them. Some of them are pretty clumsy, but he's a neon sign."

The conversation faltered. We soaked up some atmosphere.

"Hornet told me what you said about me in the office." John's words were brittle. "You and I used to be friendly."

"It was a pretty good relationship."

He shook his head. It was the first time he'd moved except to lift his glass in almost an hour. "When birds start hanging out with bats someone's going to get bit."

I wasn't quite sure what that meant, but I was drunk. "You're too close to this investigation, John. You ought to ask off it."

"My wife said the same thing night before last. I'll give you the answer I gave her. No."

A burly cop at the big table was imitating a machine gun, complete with sound effects. His companions didn't seem to mind being sprayed with saliva.

"It's a no-win situation," I said, watching the panto-mime. "If you don't break it, the commissioner hangs you out to dry. If you do, the blacks on the east side brand you traitor. Either way you stink."

"There's no going back to the deck in this business. You play what they deal."

"The hell with that. You're doing this because you want to. Check that. It's because you think you have to. You've got Alonzo Smith's name taped on your bathroom mirror and it won't come down till they tag his toe."

He turned hot eyes on me. "What makes you so different?"

"I'm not out for blood. That wouldn't fit my client's conception of justice. Smith made him a prisoner of his body, he wants to make Smith a prisoner, period. Or she does. Sometimes I have trouble peeling them apart. Remember the opening scene in *The Godfather?* A guy comes to Don Vito asking him to kill the two punks who raped and beat up his daughter. The Don says that wouldn't be justice, because the girl was still alive. But he agrees to make them suffer as she did."

"That's vengeance, not justice. Eye for an eye. We're not even talking about the same thing."

"Sometimes it's hard to figure out where one leaves off and the other starts up. Isn't it, John?" I watched him over the lip of my glass.

He looked at me. "I'm a police officer, not a samurai warrior."

"Next you're going to tell me a healthy percentage of the contract killings done in this country aren't done by police officers."

There was silence at the big table. I could feel six pairs of cops' eyes on me. It seemed a long time before the various conversations resumed.

"Smart, Walker," John said. "What else do you do for fun, flash the peace sign at John Birch Society meetings?"

"I have a death wish. That's why I'm in the business I'm in.

"It isn't so much that they killed two cops." He revolved his glass slowly between his palms. "It's the way they did it, with that specific end in mind. I can understand blowing down an officer while making a getaway from another crime. I'd want their heads, but I can understand it. This execution stuff gives me chills. The only way to stop that kind of thing is to stop it cold." He finished his beer in a swallow.

"The hell with that too. If you won't face up to the fact that it's revenge you're after, if you keep backing your play by claiming the greater good, you're going to start losing pieces fast."

"You're drunk."

"Glad to hear it. I'd hate to think I've been sitting here wasting my time and money. Anyway, did you ever know me to talk this way when I wasn't drunk? Stop trying to change the subject."

The party was beginning to break up. The cop with the machine gun impression scraped back his chair and took a heading on the men's room. He didn't jostle any more than six or seven imbibers on the way. Two of his friends paid for their drinks and left.

"Then there's the race thing," I said. "You don't even have the release of calling Smith a nigger, because you're black too. It was like that in Nam. The brass kept telling us to waste gooks, but they forgot it was gooks we were over there fighting for."

"Nam, Nam, Nam." It sounded like a mantra. "I'm sick of hearing about it every time we talk. You're back now, so forget it."

"I'd like to. I'm sicker of talking about it, but I find myself doing it more and more the longer I'm away. I hope it's not nostalgia."

He picked up his empty glass, set it down, and picked it up again, arranging the wet rings on the table into the Olympic symbol. "There could be some truth in what you said before. But if you don't want to stop me from killing Smith, why is it I haven't made a move in this case without tripping over you?"

"I didn't say I didn't want to stop you. My client wants me to, and I want what my clients want. That doesn't mean I don't agree with you."

"I must be drunk too," he said. "I haven't understood one word of this conversation."

"Me neither. How about a refill?"

WHEN I GOT IN THAT EVENING I GAVE THE STURTEVANTS' number a whirl and reached a busy signal. Nadine was on duty. I wondered how many lawyers an invalid cop's wife has to keep her from home. Then I decided I was being unfair. Too much Scotch on an empty stomach brings out the detective in me. Resisting the urge to flop, I lowered me and my injured rib cage carefully onto the bed without undoing even my tie, after which I don't remember much of anything except the dream.

I was seated alone in a dimly lit room. Someone knocked at the door, but when I tried to get up to answer it I could move only my left arm and leg, and those feebly, as if they had each gained a hundred pounds overnight. I was in a wheelchair.

Cadaverous Nadine appeared from another room and opened the door to admit Van Sturtevant, upright in full uniform and looking as he had the day we'd met on the Edsel Ford Freeway. He came forward to greet me and my eyes went past him to a figure standing in the shadows just beyond the threshold. The figure showed no weapons, made no attempt to enter, and yet the sight of it filled me with hollow dread. I couldn't even summon strength to lift my good hand to clasp Sturtevant's. I felt the dread's icy breath on my face. Then Nadine closed the door, separating me from the faceless apparition, and the feeling evaporated.

Not for long. She turned up the lights and I saw that we were in the bedroom of Deak Ridder's apartment. His corpse lay trussed like a rodeo calf on the bed, sticking its purple tongue out at me. I looked away quickly—right into the shadowy face of the Figure, now looking at me from outside the window. It held Tallulah Ridder's body in its arms, curled in the fetal position in which I'd found her, her head twisted nearly all the way around so that her sightless eyes fell on me. I started screaming for help, in that strangled, tongueless voice that tells you even in the midst of a dream that it can be heard in waking life. But no one in the room could hear me for the organ music that swelled and swelled until I couldn't even hear myself. I screamed not because of the corpse, but because the shadows had lifted and I recognized the face of my Figure,

160

grinning at me like a demented gargoyle, and it wasn't the face I'd expected, not at all . . .

The door buzzer ended the nightmare, though I sat up for a moment separating illusion from reality. The face was gone. I couldn't summon it back. It seemed important that I try. Then I couldn't remember why it was important, and I ended up thinking that maybe it wasn't so important after all. The other details were already fading. I got up.

The buzzing droned on as I stumbled through the living room, turning on lights as I went. The wall clock read 12:06. The kids in my neighborhood weren't above jamming the button with a safety pin and running, but I went back for the .38 just in case. At the door I called for my visitor to identify himself.

There was a long stretch of nothing but buzzing. Then came the words, distorted by the panel.

"My wife in Oklahoma calls me Munnis, but mostly I'm just plain Bum."

It took him a long time to say. It sounded like him; it didn't sound like him at all. Gripping the gun tightly, I snatched open the door and stepped back.

The giant cowboy smiled wearily at me from the side of the tiny porch, where he was leaning on the buzzer. He was hatless and there was a sheen of perspiration on his broad red brow. Then he rolled off the button, the buzzing ceased, and I went down beneath three hundred pounds of dead weight.

19

DON WARDLAW FINISHED CLEANING AND DRESSING THE
wound in Bassett's thigh, swished his surgical probe around
in the bowl of alcohol on the table next to the bed, wiped
it off, and laid everything away carefully in the bottom of
his scuffed black bag. He was a scrawny rooster with no
chin and a mop of curly brown hair that came off when he
took a shower. He'd once had a license to practice medicine but he didn't anymore, and still doesn't. His name
isn't Wardlaw either, but I owe him too much to blow any
whistles.

He picked up an object the size of a pencil eraser from
a piece of stained gauze on the table and handed it to me.
"A souvenir."

It was made of dull gray metal with a copper jacket and
retained its conical shape. "Twenty-five," I said. "Kind
of small for so much blood." Some of it had come off on
my clothes when I broke Bassett's fall.

"There could have been a lot more. It entered the fleshy
part of his thigh, just missing the main artery. A hair to
the left and he wouldn't have needed me. He'd have read
empty before he was halfway here. He might still have, if
you hadn't applied that tourniquet when you did."

162

"I owe it all to Ho Chi Minh and the local draft board. Thanks, Don." I handed him a C-note. "Another session with the cops tonight would have been five too much. Just helping me get Godzilla into bed was worth the century."

"I ought to soak you more, considering the hour. But you're good for business." He folded the bill lengthwise and sidewise and poked it into the watch pocket of his vest. He always took the trouble to put one on, even when summoned in the middle of the night. When it came to clothes, he and Alderdyce were soulmates.

Suddenly he asked, "Are you in pain?"

"I've got a cracked rib, maybe two, and three hundred yards of adhesive tape around my middle. I didn't know it was that obvious."

"It isn't. With you I stand a fifty-fifty chance of asking that question and getting a yes. Let's see it." He indicated a kitchen chair in the corner.

I stripped off my shirt and sat down. He whistled.

"Nice work. Who did it?"

"You just met him."

"Where's the pain?"

I circled the area with a forefinger. He pushed against it lightly with the heels of his hands. "That hurt?"

"A little."

He moved his hands. "How about that?"

"A lot." I bit my lip.

He straightened. "You can take off the tape. If it's cracked I'm the President's personal physician."

"What've you got, x-ray eyes?"

"You're not Gary Cooper," he said. "If that rib were anything worse than bruised they'd have heard you yelling in Toronto when I leaned on it. That's one ex-doctor's opinion. Get it x-rayed."

I stood and climbed back into the shirt, leaving it un-

163

buttoned. "The way I feel it ought to be broken. At least cracked. It's not fair."

"Could be you tore a muscle. I wouldn't try busting any broncos for the next month or so."

I escorted him to the front door. "Any instructions?"

"Find another line of work." He smiled thinly.

"I mean about Bassett."

"Change the dressing daily. Keep the wound clean. If his temperature goes up, call me. And don't let him out of that bed for at least two days, except to go to the toilet."

"I never talk about letting or not letting where anyone over two hundred and fifty pounds is concerned. But I heard you." I started to open the door and paused. "By the way, I saw Iris the other day. She says she took your cure." Don ran a drug rehabilitation clinic in Hazel Park and was a former user himself.

He nodded grimly. "I hope it takes."

"Why wouldn't it?"

"If she were anything but a hooker I might be more optimistic. Too many of the people she hangs out with are addicts. It distorts your judgment. You get to thinking that everyone else is turning on and you're outside looking in. Peer pressure isn't restricted to teenagers."

"She's pretty level-headed," I said.

"If she were level-headed she wouldn't have needed me in the first place." He opened the door himself and went out without saying good-bye. He never said it. We all have our own demons to fight. But Don never asked questions, which was another mark on his side of the board.

His heap started with a clatter in the street out front and plowed away, bringing me around to my demon of the moment. I went out in the dark to find a GMC four-wheel-drive pickup parked at a crazy angle at the end of my driveway. The key was in the ignition and there was a lot of blood dried brown on the seat. Knobs, dials, and speakers studded the dash, few of them standard equipment. The glove compartment contained a road atlas and an Oklahoma registration made out to Munnis Bassett, under a .357 magnum revolver that looked like the one from his trailer. It hadn't been fired recently and the cylinder was full.

But for mine, none of the windows in the neighborhood was lit. I opened the garage door as quietly as possible and pulled my Cutlass out onto the lawn. Leaving it idling, I got out and climbed up into the driver's seat of the pickup. My foot kicked something on the floor. I picked up Bum's .44 magnum, reeking of cordite. All but one chamber had been fired. I stuck the gun under my belt, ground the big engine into life, and drove it into the garage. From inside I tugged down the door and rummaged through some junk on the workbench until I found an aerosol can of blue paint I'd bought to touch up my car. It took only a minute to spray over the garage's only window. Finally I went back out through the house and put the Cutlass in the driveway. The perfect coverup, provided none of my neighbors had witnessed the game of musical parking spaces.

Bassett was still unconscious when I checked on him. He would be for a while. He was pale under the sunburn but his breathing seemed normal. I unloaded the magnum and laid it atop the dresser. I wondered what the hell I was getting into this time.

The clock in the living room struck two. I peeled off my bloodstained clothes, leaving them in a heap on the floor, and started unwinding tape. There was enough of it to line a football field. I put on my robe and slippers, gathered up the debris, and carried it into the kitchen, where I dumped it into the wastebasket. Cleaners get curious about things like bloodstains. Then I filled a bucket with water and scrubbed the blood from the linoleum at the front door and the boards of the porch. I felt like Macbeth's maid.

I was hungry as the devil when I finished. There was a period in my life, not so long ago, when the sight of blood would have slaughtered my appetite. But I was growing a shell. The time would come when I'd be able to crack jokes in the presence of death, like some cops, because I'd be dead inside, deader than the stiff. In the cupboard I found a box of cornflakes I'd missed on my last search. I poured some into a bowl and added milk. When that was gone I felt like going out and belting a baseball over the back fence. I settled for a smoke.

The buzzer razzed. I was getting not to like that sound a lot. I slid out of the nook and opened the door to John Alderdyce. He was dressed as he had been hours earlier, in dark slacks and a sport jacket with a tiny check. He hadn't been home.

"You're up late," he observed.

"I'm up early. How about you?"

"*I* didn't kill half a bottle of Scotch just a few hours ago. Do I get invited in or what?"

"Like you said, John, it's late."

His eyes roamed the living room beyond my shoulder. "Seen anything of Bum Bassett this A.M.?"

"What's he done?"

"I didn't say he did anything." He spoke offhandedly. Never trust a casual cop.

"Yes, you did."

He met my gaze. "I talk better sitting."

I hesitated, then stepped aside. He came in and I closed the door. When I turned I found him staring down at the rug. It was buckled where Don and I had dragged Bassett's heels across it.

"I was doing some cleaning." I straightened it out with a foot.

"At this hour? In your bathrobe?"

"Some people play solitaire. I clean. And my wardrobe is none of your business."

He held up his palms in a sign of surrender. "I see you're not parking your car in the garage these days."

"Too much junk. You know how it is."

"Yeah. Did you know someone's painted over your garage window? From the inside. It looks fresh."

"I'm building a birdhouse. The sun hits me square in the eye when I'm working. Can I get you a drink?" The moment I asked it I wished I hadn't. I didn't want him snooping around while I was in the kitchen.

"I'm still on duty." He pulled up the knees of his trousers and sat down on the sofa. "Couple of officers answered a disturbance call about eleven last night at a house on Bagley. They found three corpses in the living room and a guy on his knees in the back yard coughing blood. He was DOA at Detroit Receiving twenty minutes later. Only one of the victims was white, a woman."

"I'm listening."

"Prints match Laura Gaye's."

I lowered myself into the easy chair, feeling vulnerable in robe and slippers and practically nothing else. "I take it food poisoning was not involved."

"Not hardly. The M.E.'s still working, but we dug a forty-four slug out of a wall. Ballistics has it right now. We also found a cowboy hat on the floor, which checks out with the DOA's babble about John Wayne before he threw it in. Where is he, Walker?"

"What makes you think I know?" I fumbled cigarettes and matches out of the robe pocket.

"We followed a trail of blood out the front door and

across the lawn to the street, where it stopped. Someone got into a car and drove away, someone who was hurt and needed help. Someone who knows only one person in town who's not a cop. That person is you."

I trotted out the routine—striking, lighting, drawing, shaking out, and discarding, all those things that smoking gives you to do while waiting for your brain to warm up. The Surgeon General hasn't come up with any ammunition against that yet. "Just because I euchred you once doesn't mean I plan to make a career of it." I laid down a smoke-screen between us. "Have you tried his trailer?"

"It wasn't in the K-Mart lot in Warren," he said. "We called the manager at home and he says he told Bassett yesterday to move it or he'd have the police come and tow it away. I've got men running down all the courts and free parking lots in the area. Then I thought of you. Is he here?"

"That would make me an accessory after the fact, if there is a fact. I'd be taking a whale of a chance with my license."

"That's hardly unfamiliar territory for you. You won't mind if I take a look around." He started to get up.

"Not if you have a warrant."

He paused with his hands braced on the cushions. "I can get one without any trouble."

"That's a TV line, John. First you'll need the ballistics report linking the slug you found to Bassett's magnum, and then you'll have to convince the judge we're close enough for me to risk my ticket and my freedom hiding him. Even then he may want to wait until you've scoured all the trailer courts and lots. But I'll be here when you get it, if you get it."

He leaned forward, resting his forearms on his knees with his hands dangling in front.

"It's taken me years, but I've finally got you figured

out.'' His eyes were bright under the shelf of his brows.
''When you're doing a number on me you never answer
my questions directly. A lie's a lie, Walker. Are you harboring Bum Bassett?''

I matched his level stare. ''No.''

The wall clock click-clunked five times while we dared
each other to blink. Then he stood up with an oath.

''Well, it seemed like a good idea when I had it.''

I filled my lungs with smoke and let some of it curl back
out on its own. ''Alonzo Smith wasn't among the dear
departed, I take it.''

''That would be too neat. I want you at the morgue to
view the cargo, by the way.''

''How come?''

''If you pipe any faces from that reception you got on
McDougall, we'll at least have a link between Ridder and
Smith, for whatever that's worth.''

''I'll be down later, if that's all right. I'm still not quite
sober. What was it, an ambush?''

''We're still sorting it out. Right now it looks like everyone pulled off at the same time. One of the stiffs was
stretched belly-down across an M-sixteen, we found a
thirty-two revolver in the back yard near the DOA, and
there were two automatic pistols on the living room floor,
a thirty-eight and a twenty-five. Upstairs we found a Winchester thirty-ought-six with scope, a sniper's piece. Of the
rest only the M-sixteen was unfired. It's my guess Bassett
got him first. The woodwork looks like beavers gnawed
it.''

''He did all right for himself.''

''Not good enough, or he wouldn't have taken that bullet.'' He yawned bitterly. ''Hornet got the owner out of
bed. He says he rented the house to the woman last week.
She wore dark glasses during the transaction and a scarf

over her head, so he didn't recognize her picture in the papers after the courtroom raid Monday. Stupid son of a bitch didn't even ask for references. It made a good hideout for Smith as long as he didn't poke his nose outdoors. The others were there to make sure of that.''

"You think he was a prisoner?"

"Maybe not quite. Maybe they just felt he needed reassurance to keep him from changing his mind."

"Changing his mind about what?"

"Hell, I don't know." He dropped back onto the sofa amid a general protesting of springs. His shoulders were slumped and he had bags under his eyes you could pack for an overnight trip. "They busted him out for a reason, but I'm damned if I can put a name to it."

"What's he got that the others haven't?"

He stared down at his hands clasped between his knees. "He's an experienced killer. The others are amateurs."

"He's something else too," I added. "Condemned."

He looked at me. "He hadn't even stood trial when they sprang him. Even then he had a better-than-even chance of beating jail on a plea of insanity. Then the shrinks would look him over and give him a clean bill of health and he'd be back on the street in time for church Sunday. It's happened a hundred times. At worst he'd have pulled life and been out in six or seven years with good behavior. His hair wouldn't even be gray."

"That's not the way his friends saw it. Their entire philosophy is based on distrust of the system. As far as they were concerned he was dead meat from the time the warrant was issued for his arrest. So he's a man with nothing to lose, and if whatever they've got planned for him backfires, he's a martyr. Better and better."

"I don't know. It sounds too much like a Ludlum novel."

"Life imitates art," I said. "Question is, what's the plan?"

"That's not the question." He got up again. "It hasn't changed from the start. Where is Smith?"

I ditched the butt in the ashtray on the scratched coffee table. "Maybe Bassett took him with him. Maybe it was Smith's blood you saw."

"I thought of that. If so, he'll be turning him in for the reward any time, and there's no course of action for us. I'm proceeding on the assumption that Smith got away in the confusion and the cowboy went looking for medical aid. That way all bases are covered." He studied me. "Incidentally, Washington got back to us on those prints we Telexed. Your sniper's name is Felix Treadaway. Know him?"

"Should I?"

"He's a fellow vet. Sharpshooter in Cambodia, no rap sheet stateside. Medals from here to next week, including two Purple Hearts. He was a solid citizen until he fell in with this crew."

"I'd remember someone named Felix Treadaway. He's your key." I stood up, straight into the path of another dull headache. It was time to think about lowering my intake. "What about my friend from the office?"

"We've got copies of the Identikit picture you put together all over town. Don't get your hopes up, though. If he wasn't in the mug books he's not local. He's probably back home, counting his money."

"You agree he was hired."

"You said he was a pro. Would a pro hang out with this set if he wasn't being paid?"

"Depends on what set he's with. Thanks, John." I got the door for him. "Seven early enough for the morgue?"

"Make it six-thirty." Halfway through he stopped and

171

looked back. "I really hope you don't know where Bassett is."

It was an opening. He waited, but I didn't step through. Then he got going and I closed the door on my oldest friend.

20

My patient continued to rest comfortably, one massive arm flung across his forehead. After a quick shower I swallowed a couple of aspirins, fixed up the sofa with bedding from the closet, and stretched out raw under a sheet. Bruised or torn or broken, my side was giving me trouble. For a long time I lay listening to the antique clock knocking out the minutes. I couldn't make up my mind whether it was going tick-tock or tock-tick. It struck three, then the half hour, and I was still wondering. I reached up and switched on the lamp on the end table.

The headache had settled in for a long stay. I got into the robe and slippers and peeked in on Bassett. He was starting to stir and groan. The bedsprings creaked like a gallows in use. I retreated to the kitchen and splashed some Bourbon into a tumbler along with some tap water. When he came to in the glare of the bedside lamp I was sitting in a chair close by holding the glass.

His bright blue eyes flicked around the room and lighted on me. He braced an elbow on the mattress, started to lever himself up, gasped, and settled back. He stroked his injured leg under the covers.

"Drink this here," I said, mimicking his Southwestern

drawl. I got a hand under his head to lift it, and thrust the glass under his nose. He sniffed.

"Where's the chicken soup?" Rust flaked off his vocal cords.

"I'm out. Sue me for malpractice."

He drank long and deep, longer and deeper than I could match healthy. I took away the glass and set it down on the table.

"That'll do for now. Alcohol thins the blood, and you've got little enough as it stands. Welcome to the Chateau Walker. We never close. It's quarter to four A.M., you've been here since midnight, and a friend of mine who isn't a doctor anymore plucked that out of your estimable thigh." I showed him the .25 slug. "What happened?"

"You don't give a fellow a hell of a lot of time to catch his breath, hoss," he said.

"We don't have a hell of a lot of time to work with. The cops are quartering the city looking for you and they'll have a warrant to search here soon enough. One's been around already. Where's your trailer?"

"I made a deal with a guy sells them on Schoolcraft. He's hiding it out amongst his new models. Figured there'd come a time when I'd want to play button-button with the law. You in trouble on my account?"

"Purely on mine. Bagley. How'd it happen and in what order?"

He climbed into a sitting position with my help and bunched the pillow behind his back as a prop. The movement made him curse. "I been shot before," he said, massaging the bandaged thigh. "It don't get no easier. Anyhow, I was chasing down some information—"

"Information from who?"

"None of your friggin' business, like the injun said. I got folks to protect same as you. Where was I? Oh, yeah."

He shook his leonine head. "The good thing about not being a public servant is I don't got to worry about warrants. The bad thing is I get shot at a lot. I took down the front door and it was the Lincoln County War all over again. All five of them was in the one room. This nigger with a auto-rifle—"

"Back up," I interrupted. "*How* many?"

"Five. So this nigger—"

"Cops found only four."

"I'm coming to that. This here nigger makes a grab for a auto-rifle on a table and I put one through him. I never made a better shot; he was dead standing. Then something stings my leg and I pull the trigger twice on this white woman who had a little pistol. I got another nigger while he was aiming a bigger automatic. I think he forgot to take off the safety or he'd of nailed me. That was when Smith lit a shuck out the back."

"You're sure it was Smith?"

"I carry his picture around with me everyplace I go, like I'm Judge Bean and he's the Jersey Lily. I fanned one at him, but this here leg buckled on me and maybe he wasn't hit. A bullet just misses my ear then, and this fourth nigger with a revolver ducks out behind Smith. I fired at him too. Don't know what come of that."

"You hit him. He's dead."

He nodded absently. "Hell's fire, that's a new record."

"Congratulations. Feed me some more."

"I tried following Smith, but it was a big house and I was commencing to feel dizzy. I got turned around and ended up back in the front room. You ever been shot?"

"Once."

"Then you know what it's like. You always think you're dying. When I got to my truck I remembered your address from your wallet and come here. I didn't feel like facing any law just then."

"Quite a story," I said. "I wouldn't buy it in a movie."

"Hell, I been in worse. One time I braced seven, but only three of them was armed and I had a partner. Even then we didn't kill but one, and *he* wasn't the one we was after. That was before I knew about magnums."

"You like this work, don't you?"

"I must. I sure as hell ain't in it for the money. I figure to clear fifty bucks on this job. *If* I get Smith."

"Alive, naturally."

He looked at me. "Sure, alive. I don't make nothing otherwise."

"How does a guy get started bounty hunting?"

He laughed explosively, then caught his breath, gripping the leg. "Christ, that's easy. First you got to fail at everything else you try. Then you got to get into bail-bonding and wind up getting stuck for fifteen thousand. Then you bounce all the private detectives and go into business for yourself. Line up some bail bondsmen who like living and don't mind getting back a client dead now and then and you're all set. It worked for me. Damn!" His hand moved up and down the injured area.

I handed him the tumbler. He drained it and handed it back. A healthy flush crept up from his collar into his hairline. "Ever see a picture called *Shane*?"

"Produced and directed by George Stevens, starring Alan Ladd, Jean Arthur, Van Heflin, Brandon de Wilde, and Jack Palance?"

"I reckon."

"Heard of it."

"There's this big scene," he said, eyeing me strangely. "Shane faces down the killer and says, 'You're a lowdown Yankee liar.' That was a big insult back then. So the killer draws one of these two hoglegs he packs. He gets off a round, but Shane wounds him and he drops the gun. He goes for the other and Shane shoots him again. He dies. Then Shane mounts up and rides out of town, and no one realizes until he's almost gone that he's been hit."

"It wasn't the killer's bullet that hit him," I corrected. "It came from upstairs. Shane and the bushwhacker fired at the same time. The bushwhacker died."

"Whatever."

"So?"

"So it don't work that way. When you got a forty-five slug in you, everybody's gonna know it because you can't stand up. Even that little twenty-five near done for me. When are them movie people going to wise up to what getting wounded is all about?"

"When one of them gets wounded, I suppose."

He scowled and combed his fingers irritably through his red beard. His eyes moved around the room. "Not married, huh?"

"How'd you know?"

"No mirror on the dresser. Ever been?"

"Once."

He grinned. "That's what you said about being shot."

"Yeah."

"Tough row to hoe. So they tell me." He switched tracks, "Reckon I'm wanted myself, now. Maybe I'll have a bounty man on my own back."

"My sympathies to his widow. What were they doing when you broke into the place on Bagley?"

"Sitting around talking." He snorted. "That was a sucker move on my side. If I'd thought to peek in through a window I'd of known they had all their hardware out on the table. I'm damn lucky they weren't heavyweights or they wouldn't of been so slow to react. I guess I'm getting old.''

"You didn't happen to overhear any of the conversation."

He started to shake his head, then looked at me. He was sweating. Talking had taken a lot out of him. "I reckon you and me are about even now."

"I reckon."

"Not really, though. I wasn't taking chances with the law when I took you in. That puts you one up on me."

"Maybe. I flunked math."

"I pay my debts," he said solemnly.

"It's not that much. Laura Gaye was wanted, which made her friends guilty of harboring her even if you can't prove Smith was there. You have quasi-official status built up over a period of years. Then there's a little matter of self-defense. Technically you're not wanted at all, except for questioning. Alderdyce wants to see me later this morning; I'll tell him you showed up after he left. He won't believe me, but that will square things between us. I wanted to hear your story first. Besides, I like you."

He squirmed. "Where the hell are my pants?"

Don Wardlaw and I had removed everything but his shirt.

"In a trash can out back. We had to cut them off you. I'll fetch clothes from your trailer when you're ready for them. There's a cane in the living room closet left over from the time I sprained my back. I'll make you a present of it, but you won't be leaving for a while. The cops can just as well pump you here. You lost enough blood to power a rabbit and it needs time to replace itself."

"It's my wallet I want."

"Forget it," I said. "It's on the house."

"I ain't talking about money. You ain't been through it?"

"Why should I? I know who you are." I got his wallet from the dresser and handed it to him.

"I been doing this a long time," he said, fingering the papers inside. "I wasn't so silly from that bullet I didn't think to scoop up what evidence I could from the table and stuff it in here." He drew out a couple of things, glanced at them, and extended them to me. "Like I said, I owe you."

I examined the two items. One was a detailed street map of the downtown area. The other was a photographer's contact sheet with four rows of 35-millimeter positives exposed on a black background. The mayor of Detroit was featured in every frame.

21

"WHEN WERE THESE TAKEN?" THE LIEUTENANT frowned over the contact sheet on his desk. Sergeant Hornet stood behind Alderdyce, looking over his shoulder.

I was standing at the window, admiring the cityscape by early-morning darkness through the iron-mesh grille. Lighted windows were scattered like yellow diamonds on black velvet. Dawn was a sliver of lead over Windsor.

"Pretty recently," I said without turning. "That's his new limousine he's getting into. The trees in the sidewalk plots are fully leafed out. Sometime this summer or late last spring. The shots were taken with a telephoto lens, probably from across the street."

"How can you tell?" asked Hornet.

"I take a lot of pictures through keyholes, remember?"

Alderdyce said, "This is getting to sound more and more like a bad Movie of the Week."

I turned. "Stop talking as if I wrote it. I got it from Bassett and came running to you with it right away like a good little citizen. It explains a lot. The sniper rifle you found on Bagley, for one. Why Smith was pried out of custody, for another."

"It also bolsters their motive for getting rid of Deak and his sister," the sergeant pointed out. "Too much talk."

His superior tapped the edge of the sheet against his palm. "Shut the door."

It had been left partly open to allow a cross-draft between the open window and the almost empty squad room. The humidity was thick for this time of the morning, even for Michigan, even for summer. I went over and secured it.

"The mayor's black," John said. "What do they stand to gain by *his* death?"

"Pandemonium. These groups thrive on it." I poked what was left of my cigarette through the grille. The glowing tip fell and fell and was extinguished in darkness. "Remember the riots after Martin Luther King was killed? The Black Panthers doubled their ranks that night. Why do you think the PLO and the IRA and the rest of the alphabet plant bombs in public places? Out of hate, sure, but also because they like to see authority crumble and the bureaucrats scrambling like ants. Then there's publicity, and the applause of their peers. One thing all terrorists have in common is vanity. This is their chance to put their cause on the map."

"Which is?" Alderdyce waited.

"Anarchy, pure and simple. The total breakdown of the white capitalist system, if only for a night."

"Regular answer man, aren't you?"

"It's a gift," I snarled. "All I need is someone to tell me where to go and what to look for when I get there."

"So why Smith? Why not someone who's not wanted, with more freedom to move around?"

"That's easy," said the sergeant. "Of all of them, he's the only one with nothing to lose."

I nodded. "We had this conversation before, remember?

Keep in mind that they view established authority as a stacked deck. The way they see it, Smith has the choice of life imprisonment or running and hiding for the rest of his days, which are numbered at best. All the successful assassinations of the past hundred years have ended in the assassin's death or capture. He might as well do it as not.''

"Okay, let's say I buy it." John tapped the sheet some more. "Why should he go ahead with it now, with the rest of them dead? I'm going on the assumption this whole thing was their idea, not his. He didn't look all that happy when they busted him out. Maybe he'll just powder.''

"Good point, except that they're not all dead," I reminded him. "Even if the three who died with Laura Gaye turned out to be part of the bunch that walked all over me at the commune, that leaves at least two unaccounted for, with Treadaway in custody. Ridder and the woman weren't with them that night.''

"You're sure there were six?''

"At least. I can take five.''

Hornet made a rude noise. I rose above it.

"I'm not saying the whole thing doesn't leak," I admitted.

"Even you wouldn't try to get away with that." Alderdyce glanced at his subordinate. "You got anything to contribute?''

"I think it stinks.''

I said, "That's just that white gunk on your face.''

"How'd you like me to spoil yours?" The rash ointment stood out starkly against his flush.

"I'm not sure. What's it like?''

He jacked himself up to his full height, his fists down at his sides. "Anytime, brother. Any time.''

"Ding ding," John said. "Back to your neutral corners.''

The room fell silent. Alderdyce scowled at the pictures some more. His face and bearing betrayed none of the exhaustion I'd noted back at my place, but I couldn't decide if that was iron determination or the lousy light in the office. He turned to the sergeant.

"Call the jail. Get Felix Treadaway up here now."

THE CONTACT SHEET DIDN'T BREAK HIM RIGHT AWAY. That never happens outside of Perry Mason reruns. Alderdyce produced it after a quarter-hour of reconnaissance over old ground, and though it jarred him visibly, Treadaway clung to his stoic silence until Hornet, the bad guy, threatened to stick him with the murders of Deak and Tallulah Ridder. It wasn't the first time that had been suggested, but coming on top of charges of attempted murder *and* conspiracy to commit, it opened a fissure wide enough for the two dicks to leap in with both feet and crowbars.

"When's it going down, Felix?" probed the lieutenant.

The suspect avoided his gaze. The lumps and bruises I'd lent him stuck out in the harsh light of the interrogation room and made him look deformed. The Elephant Man, squirming on the grill. Sweat rolled off the end of his smashed nose and darkened the blue cotton shirt of his jail uniform. That in itself meant nothing. We were all in our shirtsleeves and sweating freely. The room had no window and the door was closed. There were a long yellow oak table scalloped around the edges with cigarette burns, and one chair, in which Treadaway was sitting. Nothing else, not even a lawyer. He didn't trust them.

"Speak up, schmuck! I'm hard of hearing." In contrast to his superior's soothing tones, Hornet's words rang off the walls like cherry bombs hurled at an oil tank. Treadaway flinched before them. So did I, and they weren't even directed at me.

It went on like that for a while. I watched, fascinated. Not that I hadn't seen it more times than I cared to record in my diary. It had even been used on me. But I was always amazed when it appeared to be working. It was older than all of us put together, and I guessed that was why.

At length a signal passed between the cops, unseen by their guest. As he approached the man in the chair, Hornet appeared to inflate himself, and I understood then his choice as heavy, no pun intended. Without the maroon coat he looked enormous, a garage door in a white shirt with the cuffs turned back and size 52 trousers. His loosened tie barely reached his sternum after the hike around his neck. He filled the room.

"They're all dead, sucker." His voice was harsh but not loud. His face was so close to Treadaway's that spittle flecked the latter's features. "Laura Gaye. Deak Ridder. Quincey Flagg. Tommy Jack Dupuis. Earl Southwaite. The whole fucking Bagley bunch, dead. They're barking in hell and you're left up here, smeared with their shit. They're shitting on you all the way from the Great Beyond. Ain't that a hoot?"

Treadaway jerked in his seat as if struck. He goggled at the sergeant. Then his puffed lips spread in a nasty grin. "Sure, they're all dead," he said slowly. "And I'm Pat fucking Boone. What you want me to sing, 'April Love'?" But the reference to the house on Bagley had shaken him, as had the roll call.

"You'll sing, monkey-face. Where you think we got those pictures of the mayor, wiseass?"

"Some carnival booth, I expect."

Alderdyce said, "Get it."

Reluctantly, Hornet took his face away from the suspect's and went out through the soundproofed door. The room seemed a lot larger without him. We listened to ourselves breathing and admired the walls. They were soaked deep in sweat and old fear and by now must have been accustomed to being stared at.

He came back carrying a drab green folder under one arm. From it he drew a thick sheaf of color snapshots, removed the rubber band from around it, and scattered them across the table in front of Treadaway. "I suppose those came from the same booth."

I came away from the wall for a better look. They had been taken with a cheap instant camera, the kind some cops carry around so that they have something to refer to later while waiting for the official photos to be processed. The green from the emulsion had seeped into the faces as in a Renaissance painting, but it didn't make them look any less dead. Each body had been photographed several times from different angles: sitting in a chair with head tilted back; slumped over a table in the middle of a brown stain; stretched out on a buckled carpet with one arm flung up in a flamenco-like gesture. The flash obliterated the shadows and spared nothing.

It didn't look like Shakespearean tragedy. The blood was brackish brown, not scarlet, and the wounds looked big enough to drop a bucket through. The woman on the floor didn't have a lower jaw. It wasn't dramatic. It was just real. Treadaway stared at the pictures a long time without expression. Then without warning he threw up all over them.

"Son of a bitch!" snarled the sergeant, as the acrid odor filled the close room. He tore open the door and leaned out. "Somebody get a towel!"

Five minutes later, Hornet folded the mess, pictures and all, into a frayed rag, stepped out into the squad room, and came back after ten seconds empty-handed. His face was frozen in an expression of disgust.

"Anyone ever tell you you'd make a hell of a nurse's aide?" I asked him.

"Fuck off, wiseass."

"Just cheering you up."

He stood over the suspect, who despite his build had managed to look wan. His face was gray and he was perspiring more than ever.

"That ain't all of them either," Hornet pointed out. "Tommy Jack made a stop at the hospital on his way to the morgue."

"Smith?" The depth was gone from Treadaway's voice. He was still gaping at the table where the photographs had lain. It was shiny where the sergeant had wiped it clean of vomit, leaving the original dust everywhere else.

"He's still kicking, but not for long. We got you." He thumped a finger against the suspect's chest hard enough to hurt.

"The conspiracy charge alone can get you life," said Alderdyce, leaning against the door with his hands in his pockets. "The two murders will sink any chance of parole for a long, long time. We don't want that, Felix. Your war record by itself separates you from these scuzzes you've been hanging out with. They're dry bones. What do you owe Alonzo Smith? What've you got against the mayor?"

"You offering a deal?" It was barely audible. He seemed too weak to lift even his eyes.

"No fix, if that's what you mean. But we'll tell the judge you went along. That swings a certain amount of weight in this kind of case."

"Pretty thin."

"You want a guarantee, buy a toaster."

There was a long stretch of nothing. The room was a steambath. My eyes stung from the salt, but I didn't want to upset things by mopping my forehead. We were at the eighteenth hole, waiting for the putt to sink.

"The Afro-American festival," Treadaway said then. "Hart Plaza."

The detectives looked at each other.

"The mayor's due there Saturday," said Hornet.

Outside, Thursday's sun was just breaking the horizon.

"DON'T THINK YOU GOT AWAY WITH IT," ALDERDYCE said as we emerged from the Wayne County Morgue an hour and a half later. The sun was pounding the sidewalks on Brush, a welcome sight after the artificial lighting on the waxed floors and waxy corpses inside.

I stared at him innocently. He broke up.

"You do the worst Freddie Bartholomew I ever saw." He laughed again. An elderly couple hobbling past looked at him strangely and went on, watching their feet. God knows what they thought. Not a lot of mirth is heard in the vicinity.

"Feel better?" I asked, when it was over.

"You don't know." He massaged his eyes vigorously with thumb and forefinger.

"I just got through placing two of your D.B.'s at that gymnasium on McDougall, on top of helping expose the kind of plot a promotion-happy cop dreams of. I didn't expect thanks, but I wasn't counting on a kick in the pockets either."

"Poor Amos," he said. "Got his feelings hurt."

"You son of a bitch." I put out a hand.

He grasped it, grinning. "Let's go over to your place and talk to Bassett."

"Thanks, I've seen your act." I got out my ring and worked off the house key. "Here. Leave it under the mat when you're through. And I'm not giving you permission to search the place, so keep your hands out of my underwear drawer. I've got errands to run.''

For a moment he looked as if he wanted his handshake back. "You're not still sitting on something.''

"I'm tired of sitting, John.''

"Nix on the mayor," he warned. "He's our only chance of flushing out Smith.''

"Just because I've got a lot of smart mouth doesn't mean I can't control it.''

It must have come out pretty sharp, because he backed off. He rubbed his eyes again. The bright sunlight found the sags and creases in his face. We were about the same age, which worried me. "I know, I know. I'm getting so I can't tell the good guys from the bad guys anymore.''

"You didn't seem to have any trouble in the interrogation room," I said.

"Go build a birdhouse." We parted.

22

THE LOBBY OF THE DETROIT *News* building, erected at a time when edifices were designed to impress, not intimidate, was cool and almost deserted at that time of the morning. I felt a physical shock passing from the blinding heat of West Lafayette into the muted interior, where a female security guard or something asked me to wait while she called up Barry Stackpole's office to make sure I wasn't an anarchist and was therefore to be trusted with the elevator. That done, she handed me a visitor's tag to hang on the outside of my pocket. I stuck it inside. I'm not luggage.

Barry's floor was a rabbit warren of partitioned cubicles like the toilet stalls in a public lavatory, with men and women scurrying along twisting aisles paved with discarded newsprint. Typewriters rattled. Video terminals peeped. Somewhere an air conditioner hummed discreetly. A radio droned last night's baseball scores to the accompaniment of an amateur gambler's cursing. Nobody seemed bothered by the fact that I wasn't wearing my tag.

I found Barry seated behind the desk in his cubbyhole with his bogus leg elevated on a bale of copy paper, taking sucker shots at a steel wastebasket in the corner with crumpled sheets and missing every third time. The desk, filing

189

cabinet, and visitor's chair were stacked high with papers and file folders stuffed with clippings. Books on organized crime were jammed every which way onto shelves among unpublished manuscripts on the same subject, some of them his own. The back wall was plastered over with official police photos taken on the scene of notable gangland slayings. Office wags had added arch inscriptions to a number of them, complete with the victims' forged signatures. The *News* boiled with wit.

"Sorry to bother you during your busy period," I said, flipping his police pass onto the heap atop his desk. I transferred debris from the chair to an antique wooden whiskey crate he used for a magazine rack and sat down.

"I'm waiting for a call." He took careful aim at the basket and lobbed a fresh crumple clear over it into the cubicle across the way. A stout party with a gray beard looked daggers back.

"New York or L.A.?" I asked, tapping out a Winston.

"Boston." He flatted the first *o*, mimicking a New England twang. "I'm bouncing a book idea off a publisher there."

"Exposé?"

"Cook. *Favorite Recipes of La Cosa Nostra*. A killer."

I didn't pursue it. Several grand juries had already learned the folly of asking him a question he didn't want to answer. "If you're still sore over that crack I made about clichés," I said, "I'm sorry."

The next one rimmed the basket and plopped out onto the linoleum. He scowled and gave up.

"I had it coming. What brings you to *Pravda* West?"

"I promised you an exclusive, remember?"

He drew his peg down to the floor and sliced a gloved finger across his Adam's apple, rapping the flimsy material of the partition at the same time with his good hand.

"Anywhere you suggest," I said.

"Had breakfast yet?"

"What's breakfast?"

He got on the telephone and asked the switchboard to refer his calls to the Detroit Press Club.

"I'm buying," he announced, climbing into his jacket.

Over pancakes and eggs I recounted the whole thing, starting with why I was hired, tying in the two murders with my beating, describing the sniping attack on Whittaker, and finishing with Bum Bassett's shoot-out on Bagley. I left out two things: the assassination plot, because I'd promised Alderdyce, and the guy who threatened me in my office, because I still wasn't sure where to hang him. I came to the end of it just as the waiter showed up with more coffee. We waited until he finished pouring and withdrew.

"It's dynamite," Barry said, blowing steam off his cup. "Our cophouse scribbler got the scoop on the shooting, but the dicks played it close to the vest. If we'd known Laura Gaye was one of the victims—well, that's the city editor's headache. The Bassett angle shines. He was born good copy. I wasn't expecting this much return on the loan of some moldy press credentials."

"I'm glad you brought that up."

"Uh-oh, I hear a cash register."

"How are your street connections?" I asked.

"Depends on the connection."

"I want to get a message to Alonzo Smith."

"They're not that good."

"It's harder to get information about a fugitive than it is to get it to him," I persisted. "I'd hate to have to call your editor and tell him your story's phony."

"Hey, I thought we were friends."

I said, "I'm in a bind. The cops have all my cards and

my job isn't finished. You've twisted the screws on me once or twice. I still eat with you."

"That's because I'm picking up the tab." He made a face. "What's the message, Iago?" He made no move for a pad or pencil. Barry was one of those people who can repeat word for word a three-way conversation overheard months earlier. On the flip side, he could never remember to put the cap back on the toothpaste tube. We'd shared a bungalow in the army, in case you're worried about the relationship.

"Smith doesn't trust the law," I began. "He thinks because he's wanted for killing two officers the police won't give him a chance to surrender."

"He's right."

I made a gesture of assent. "I'm not connected with any authority. If he wants to talk I'll meet him anyplace he chooses, alone. I'm in the book."

"That's it?"

I said that was it.

"What makes you think he'll go for it?" He etched designs with the edge of his spoon in the egg yolk left on his plate.

"I'm offering him life. That's pretty strong incentive."

"Life in stir."

"Death is longer."

He put down the spoon. "It's barely possible you're setting yourself up as a target."

"Yeah. It'll look nifty in my autobiography."

"You'd better write it now."

I left that one drift.

"I suppose your client's name is off the record," he said.

"I didn't think I had to tell you that. I gave it to you because I know you'll sit on it till it hatches."

"Too bad. It's a honey of a scenario. Intrepid P.I. fills in as crippled cop's arms and legs. I could center a book around it and sell it to the movies like that." He snapped his fingers loudly. A couple seated at the next table looked up.

"Who'd you get to play me?" I asked.

He thought. "Dreyfuss?"

"Too short. Eastwood?"

"Too tall. How about Allen?"

"Steve?"

"Woody."

I got up. "Pay for the food, Stackpole."

I MADE TWO STOPS ON THE WAY BACK TO MY PLACE, ONE at a party store to put something in the larder besides dust, the other at Bassett's trailer in the lot on Schoolcraft for a change of clothing for my patient. He'd lent me his keys for the task. By the time I opened my own front door Alderdyce and Hornet had been there and gone. The toilet flushed and the cowboy came stumping out of the bathroom leaning on the cane I'd left beside the bed. In just his shirt, shorts, and boots he looked like a Viking.

"I hope that's food." He was looking at the paper bag I was carrying.

"If I'd known you were that hungry I'd have come sooner." I set down the package on the kitchen counter. "Eating is usually the last thing you think about when you've been shot."

"When you're my size it takes a lot of fuel to keep going. Those my pants? Gimme." He reached for the bundle I had under one arm.

"First, sit down. I want to look at that wound."

"Hell, I clean forgot about the little thing. It's probably all healed up by now."

"Uh-huh. Sit." I indicated the easy chair behind him.

He obeyed, muttering. I had him prop the leg up on the footstool and bent to examine the bandage, placing the bundle on the floor. Blood had soaked through the gauze, leaving a brown ring on the outside.

"Nice going. You managed to open it up again."

"A man's got to go to the can."

I started unwinding the stained material. "Cops give you a hard time?"

"I'm used to it. I signed a statement and got a lecture about leaving the driving to them. They tried to get me to give up my gun, but I said I lost it. I had it under the blankets. Last time I gave one up I never saw it again."

"They're a little more honest here."

He said nothing. His thigh was as hard as a tree trunk and almost as big around. There wasn't a hair on it. "I forgot to ask you if you wanted me to call your wife," I ventured.

"I'll call her my own self. She don't have to know about this."

"I take it she doesn't favor your occupation." The stain got redder as I unwound.

"The bills get paid. She don't complain none about that."

"She's your second wife, isn't she?"

Every muscle in his body bunched. "You been checking up on me?" His voice sounded strained, but that could have been because I was peeling the last of the bandage away from the wound and it stuck.

"Not really. Hold that." I placed one of his enormous hands on the blood-soaked pad to maintain pressure on the wound, and rose. "I saw some pictures in your trailer. One looked like a family shot, but the woman standing next to you wasn't the one you were with in the later pictures. It's none of my business. I just have trouble turning off the detective when I'm not working.''

As I spoke I went into the bathroom for the extra roll of bandage Don Wardlaw had given me, and a bottle of alcohol. When I came back Bassett's magnum was looking at me. I stopped in the doorway.

"I bet I hold the record for the number of times that same gun has been pointed at one person.''

"You come close." Grunting, he pushed himself upright with the aid of the cane. The big muzzle hovered at chest level. "This pains me after all your hospitality, hoss, but I figure I evened things up by giving you that stuff I found on Bagley, so nobody owes nobody nothing. I got business needs tending.''

"I unloaded it, cowboy.''

"Look again.''

I looked again. No light showed through the chambers.

"I keep an extra loaded cylinder under my truck seat,'' he explained. "Can't remember when was the last time I was more than two feet from a usable weapon. It don't feel good.''

"Quite a trek to the garage and back for a man in your condition. No wonder you're bleeding again.'' The pad had dropped to the floor when he stood, and blood was running down his leg into his boot. His eyes flicked down and up, too quickly to do me any good.

"Fix it.''

He sat down again, holding the big revolver on his good thigh. I used alcohol and some clean cotton to cleanse off the blood, placed a fresh pad on the wound, and reached for the new bandage I'd laid atop the bundle of clothing on the floor. I put out a hand to steady my balance and it closed on the gun, my thumb jamming itself between the hammer and the firing pin. It was a neat maneuver, right out of the textbook, but I forgot about the cane.

The hickory crook caught me right on the meaty part of the temple and I saw stars, just like in the comic books. My head dumped empty. My hand slipped off the end of the gun and I sat down. Then metal flashed and something a lot harder than a hickory crook found the big muscle on the side of my neck. That time I didn't see stars. I didn't see anything but Bum Bassett's bearded face, surrounded by purple-black and growing rapidly smaller as I hurtled down a long dark shaft. There was no pain, just that shrinking face and the sensation of falling.

"Sorry about that, hoss." The voice echoed hollowly down the walls of the shaft. Then the darkness closed in.

23

HERE I WAS AGAIN, STRETCHED OUT ON MY BACK ON A hard surface, staring up. I was thinking of having my suits tailored with padding in back to spare myself unnecessary discomfort. I couldn't swallow and the whole front of my skull ached as if the brain were trying to push through. Sunlight dazzled me streaming through the east window. Somewhere in the stratosphere a jet shattered the sound barrier with a throbbing explosion that shook the house. At least I wasn't blind or deaf.

I got up, managing not to toss my breakfast, and lurched to the bathroom, where I filled the sink with cold water and stuck my head in as far as it could go. Drowning was better than this. Spluttering, I buried my face in a towel and held it there until my stomach stopped galloping. Then I rubbed my hair gingerly with the towel. Sparks leaped between my temples like a special effect in Colin Clive's laboratory. Finally I ran a comb through my damp locks and sneered at the bruised face in the mirror.

"Hello, Zero."

I returned to the living room, where the clock read 9:45. I hadn't been out more than fifteen minutes. The old dressing and the stuff I had used to clean Bassett's wound were on the floor where I had left them, but the new roll was missing. He had finished the job himself. The fresh shirt and jeans I had brought were gone too. The shirt he'd been wearing was left in their place, folded neatly. I recognized the fold. Why not? I'd seen it in Laura Gaye's living quarters at the commune the second time I searched the place.

The door leading into the garage from the kitchen hung open. I stepped through it. The big door was up. There were marks on the front lawn where he'd cranked the big pickup around my car in the driveway. I wasn't going after him with anything smaller than a panzer.

My big mistake hadn't been in trying to get his gun, although that ranked right up there. It went back further. I thought about it while I was changing shirts and selecting a new tie, but all that did was make my head hurt worse. Still, it gnawed at me all the way across town and even as I passed through the entrance to the main branch of the Detroit Public Library on Woodward.

I found Tulsa, Oklahoma, among the out-of-town directories, looked up the private investigation agency that had the biggest Yellow Pages display, and jotted down the number in my pocket pad. Then I drove to my office to make the call. Karen Sturtevant was sitting in the reception room.

She stood up when I entered, clutching her purse in front of her. It was blue today: tailored serge suit with a calf-length skirt, no slit, matching flat-heeled shoes, and a darker Robin Hood hat with a feather no larger than the kind they used to stuff pillows with before foam rubber came along. It was obviously an attempt to dress down, and it was just as obviously not working. Sex won't be overcome so easily.

"I—I was beginning to think you weren't coming." She didn't sound elated that I had.

"Did you wait long?" I left the door to the hallway open. Silly thing. The sofa wasn't even long enough for successful seduction.

She shook her head quickly. The feather bobbed. "No, I just—when someone isn't in his office by—I assumed you were out working." She closed her mouth before her tongue could tangle itself further.

"Well, I was out. Are you in a hurry, Mrs. Sturtevant?"

"I—no. Not particularly. Nadine's with Van, and—"

"I have a telephone call to make. I'd appreciate your waiting in here while I make it."

"Certainly."

"Read a magazine if you like. I'm proud of my new magazines.

"They're not really so new," she said abashedly.

"You haven't spent a great deal of time in waiting rooms. Be with you in a few minutes." I went into the tank and closed the connecting door.

It was more like twenty, with most of the discussion tacked to professional courtesy rates. I believed in them, the guy on the other end didn't. As we jousted I went through the mail I'd found under the slot. Three advertising circulars, a second notice, and a newsletter from the Christian Anti-Communism Crusade in Long Beach, California. How I got on their list I'll never know. Tulsa and I finally struck compromise: He'd charge the regular rate and I'd stop bothering him about it. But I wheedled a promise from him to get back to me in forty-eight hours with what he'd learned. He'd wanted three days.

She sat demurely on the edge of the customer's chair, knees together, purse in her lap. I got out my pack and pushed it across the desk, but she declined. The antique fan rattled and squawked as it shoved the same hot moist air around the room.

"I tried to get hold of you all day yesterday," she said. "When I couldn't reach you here I tried your home, but there was no answer there either."

"I did a lot of moving around yesterday. I tried to call you once too and got a busy signal for my trouble. What was it you wanted to talk to me about?"

She looked down at her purse. Her knuckles were white on the edge of it. Then she looked back at me. In that light her eyes were like jade. "I wanted to apologize for my behavior the night before last. And to explain. I know what you must think of me."

"We've been all over that, Mrs. Sturtevant. Like you said, you weren't alone. Stress brings out sides of our personalities few people ever see."

"You sounded just like Joyce Brothers then." She laughed, a little too gaily.

"Excuse it, please. Once you've been in this business a while you get to be either a vest-pocket Freud or a saltine. How are things between you and Florence Nightingale, if it's any of my concern, which of course it isn't?"

She shrugged. "They were never warm; that hasn't changed. She didn't say anything to Van. I can tell, even if he can't talk. She knows her boundaries and she stays within them. In a way, that's much worse than anything she could have done or said."

"That's guilt. Forget it. I think you have. That isn't the real reason you've come, is it?"

"It's one of them. Mainly I'm here as a client." Her gaze was level. All the awkwardness had evaporated. She was a cop's wife, all right.

I started to pluck out a cigarette, then pushed it back in. It wasn't dignified enough or businesslike enough. I'd thought from time to time about taking up the pipe, but it involves an entirely different set of mannerisms, none of them honest. "I know where Smith was last night. When the evening *News* hits the street, so will everyone else. Where he is now I couldn't say."

Her fingers whitened further on the edge of the purse as I related the details of the police discovery on Bagley, leaving out the mayor. As I wound down her eyes took on an emerald hardness.

"It looks as if I hired the wrong man," she said stiffly. "Perhaps I should have gone to this Bassett person."

"In the first place," I sighed, "you hired me because the price was right. In the second place, Bassett's not the kind of man anyone hires, and in the third place, you came to me in the first place. I didn't go looking for this job. But due in no small measure to my courage and sagacity, the police have a man in custody right now who holds the key to this whole case. Now, I know that's not what we agreed on, but I have to work in this town and a certain amount of cooperation with the local constabulary is the price I pay to go on practicing."

She started to speak. I held up a hand. "As you recall, I gave you an out night before last, and you chose not to take it. I'm offering it again. There are some good men in this city whose services I can recommend, though I can't guarantee they'll come as cheap. If you accept I'll consider my obligation to your husband discharged."

"My," she said, after a beat. "Aren't we testy."

"I have a headache. I'm not at my most disarming when I hurt."

She leaned forward over the desk. The mole came into view just above the second button of her blouse. "I'm sorry for what I said. Straight thinking doesn't come easily to me these days. Please go on doing what you've been doing.'' She lowered her eyes for an instant. Her long thick lashes were natural. When she raised them I saw tiny gold flecks floating in the deep green, like phosphor in an aquarium. ''I wish you'd known me before—all this. I wasn't always a bad-tempered whore.''

That presented thorns no matter where I took hold of it, so I didn't. That was just as bad. We were still looking at each other when the telephone rang.

I speared it halfway through the first jangle. Bell's invention has done more for celibacy than all the saltpeter produced over the past two centuries. ''Walker.''

''Don't bother tracing this, pig. I'll be smoke by the time anyone shows up.''

An even voice, young, masculine, slightly drawled, a little out of breath. Traffic noises in the background. Karen Sturtevant saw my reaction and leaned closer.

''Is this Mr. Jones?'' I asked. Simple association. Even my client caught it. Her eyes widened, then returned to normal. Unattractive lines appeared under her eyes and from her nose to her mouth. Her nostrils went white.

''That's right. Stupefyin' Jones. Like in *Li'l Abner*, get it?''

I said I had it. ''I didn't expect my message to reach you so soon.''

''I got lots of friends. What you got to sell?''

''Same as in the message. Your life.''

He laughed nastily. ''Damaged goods, pig. Sell me something I can use.''

''That's my point. I'm not a pig.''

''You roll in their mud, honk.''

''That doesn't make me one of them. You want to keep breathing or what?''

''I hear you talking.''

''Here's the script. We meet someplace, your choice.

202

You turn yourself over. I make a call to the press, have them at police headquarters when we arrive. TV cameras, the works. That way you don't get picked off on the way up the steps. The idea is to get you into police custody alive. After that you're on your own.''

"Why can't I just walk in by myself like I done before?"

"You know the answer to that or you wouldn't have called." An automobile horn blasted wherever he was. I wondered what sort of disguise he was wearing to call from a public booth in broad daylight. "How does this make you rich?" he asked.

"Publicity. When you do what I do, a little free advertising never hurts. Also the people I work for want you brought in kicking. Who they are doesn't matter." I met Karen Sturtevant's gaze. "Thing is, I've nothing to gain from your untimely death."

"Words. Why'd you say I want to do this again? I'm flappin' free right now."

"What are you wearing?"

"Huh?"

"Your clothes. I'll take a guess. Big hat, long coat with a standing collar."

"Pretty close, pig. So what?"

"It's eighty-nine in the shade. You call that free?"

He said nothing. I pressed on.

"A lot of otherwise tolerant people want to stuff you and stand you out by the airport as a monument to safe streets. They've saved a spot for you next to Laura Gaye and the rest."

"You know about that, huh?" I thought he sounded subdued. Then I thought he didn't. You can't tell over the telephone.

"It was pretty tight," I said. "Your odds of squeaking through the next time are that much smaller."

"Call you back in ten." The line went dead.

"He's afraid of a trace," I told Mrs. Sturtevant, pegging the receiver.

"I heard. I think I'll have that cigarette now," she said.

I reached one over. This time she let me light it. She tilted back her head and expelled smoke, showing off the long line of her neck.

"Do you think he'll agree to it?"

"We'll know in ten minutes."

"It's an eerie feeling, listening to you talk to the man who shot Van. Like going back over what's left of your house after it burned down. You can almost convince yourself it didn't happen until you're faced with the evidence. But of course I face it every day, so maybe it's not the same at all. Still, it's strange."

There was nothing in that for me. I lit one up too. We sat and smoked and took turns using the ashtray on the desk. Streetside a big truck took off from the light with a loud mashing of gears. The sound reminded me of Dooley Bass and his Kenworth. I hadn't read anything of him in the papers, so I assumed Transcontinental Transport had elected not to press charges. He was probably driving for another company under somebody else's license. Keeping his nose clean until the climate cooled down enough to attempt another boost. People don't change, don't change, don't change.

The telephone beckoned again and I took time squashing out the butt, letting it go three times before answering.

"Where the hell was you, in the can?" He sounded agitated, maybe. There were no traffic noises this time. He'd found another instrument.

"Where'll we meet?" I asked.

"Pretty sure of yourself, ain't you, pig?"

"You dropped the dimes, not me. And if you keep calling me that we can consider this conversation terminated."

"Okay, okay. Don't get hot on me, man." He paused. "There's an old brownstone on Antietam. You can't miss it. It's got a great big CONDEMNED sign on the front door." He gave the address.

"I know the area," I said, scribbling the number on the calendar pad.

"Not as good as me. I grew up there. Midnight. Come in the Antietam side. No weapons. Wait for me in the lobby. I'll be watching good and close, so don't get cute."

"Is it all right if I come alone?"

"You're a riot, Walker."

"That's almost twelve hours," I said. "Think you can hold out that long?"

"Just worry about your own self. My face might just be the last thing you ever see." On that blinding note he hung up.

"Are you going?" Mrs. Sturtevant was studying me.

"It's my party. Can I call you a cab?" I got up from behind the desk.

She rose. "I drove. Be careful, Mr. Walker. I suppose you've been told that before."

"Not as often as I'd like. This conversation doesn't leave this room, okay? Wait till after midnight to tell your husband. Neighborhoods like yours are full of ears."

"You have my word. You won't forget to call once you have him?"

I said I wouldn't forget and put a hand on her elbow to turn her toward the door. She didn't budge.

"He'd have nothing to lose by killing you, you know,"

she said. "What I'm saying is if worst comes to worst, don't feel bound by my request to bring him in alive."

"That dedicated I'm not. Thanks for dropping by, Mrs. Sturtevant. I'll call you, one way or the other." I went over to get the door for her, and here was one woman who let me.

24

My NEXT CALL WAS TO BARRY STACKPOLE, ASKING HIM to be available around midnight and to be prepared to share the event with colleagues. He was too good a reporter not to press me on the details, but when I didn't comply he was too good a friend not to back off. We ended the conversation on a note best described as amiably obscene.

The rest of the day passed routinely, which is to say soporifically. After lunch I came back to the office and started spelling my name across the pad with pencils taken from the cup on the desk, but I ran out before finishing the *K*. I turned on the radio in time for the news. The manhunt for Smith had dropped to third place behind the mayor's address to council and the Bagley shooting. Bassett's name wasn't mentioned and no connection was made between the bloodbath and Smith. The victims remained unidentified. When it comes to aggressive reporting, broadcast journalism ranks next to blue cheese.

A patch of Venetian-blind-striped sunlight had by this time shifted from the right wall to the floor. I made a bet with myself on how long it would take to reach the desk and won on points.

At half-past two a fortyish woman came in and sat in

the customer's chair and dangled a ten percent finder's fee under my nose for the return of a hundred-dollar bracelet she swore had been ripped off by a co-worker at the office where she was employed as a secretary. She named the co-worker. I told her that although the ten bucks was tempting I was involved with something else at present, and gave her the name of a fellow P.I. I had never liked. She was the only visitor I had all afternoon.

I played six games of solitaire and lost every one. Then I played a seventh under my own rules. I lost that one too.

The telephone rang twice. The first caller tried to sell me wall-to-wall carpeting for next to nothing if I agreed to let his company use my office as a model, and the second was a drunk looking for somebody named Madeleine. I tried to strike up a conversation with each of them, but they lost interest when they found I didn't have what they were after. My practice, always at low ebb, all but dried up during the vacation season. When the clock hand finally crept around to five I locked up and went home.

I fixed supper and ate it in front of the television set, where John Wayne was fighting Indians in *Hondo*, a favorite. When that was over I set the alarm for ten and stretched out fully clothed on the bed. For a change I slept without dreaming.

At quarter-past eleven I left the house with my .38 snapped to my belt under the jacket. Instructions to the contrary, people who keep late-night appointments with killers on streets like Antietam without arming themselves first don't deserve to come back.

25

THERE WAS A NEW MOON THAT NIGHT. THE STARS GLIT-
tered like steel bearings on a black cloth. To the south a
lone jet crawled silently westward between winking red and
green lights, separated from the hollow whooshing of its
engines by an entire sky.

The building was a slightly denser mass than the black-
ness that surrounded it, sensed rather than seen, blank,
silent. The beam from my flash picked out six concrete
steps leading up to the entrance, worn hollow by the pas-
sage of feet that no longer trod anywhere, steps as old as
the battle for which the street was named. Even the CON-
DEMNED notice tacked to the door looked mature enough
to vote. At the top of the steps I snapped off the flash and
pocketed it.

It was the drying perspiration of a long day, and not a
premonition of death, that chilled me as I pulled open the
door on crusted hinges. But I unholstered the Smith &
Wesson just the same and kept my hand on it in the side
pocket of my jacket. The ruins of a padlock and chain
jingled from the scaly iron door handle.

I stepped across a crumbling threshold—and was instantly whisked back to the alley next to the gymnasium

on McDougall. Suffocating darkness wrapped itself around me, smelling sourly of urine and old garbage and rats. The pain of that earlier awakening raked my rib cage and arms and legs and head, the last still suffering from Bum Bassett's symphony for cane and gun. I moved sideways quickly to avoid being outlined against the lighter rectangle of the doorway and stood without moving, my back against the wall, breathing shallowly between parted lips while waiting for my eyes to adjust.

They did, with the gradual coming-to-realization of the sun rising or a clock hand moving. The minimal starlight sifting through the open door—not at all through the windows, which I assumed were boarded over—touched litter on the floor, curlicues of old spray paint on part of a naked wall, the indistinct looming solidity of a standing staircase. Beyond here were dragons. I fingered my gun and breathed and waited. I could have heard my watch ticking if I were wearing one. I was a figure in an unfinished charcoal sketch, crowded into one corner with the whole brooding emptiness of the canvas before me. I was at the mercy of the artist, and of whatever dark thing he chose to place in that emptiness. Portrait of a sleuth beyond his depth.

Hard fingers clamped themselves around my right wrist. I pulled back instinctively, and a point of cold fire found the pulse beneath the left corner of my jaw. I sucked air.

"Move just one hair and I'll carve you up like a Halloween punkin."

The voice was the same in person as over the wire, only sharper, more electric. His face was a dark steaming reality two inches from mine. I smelled chicken on his breath.

"I'm carrying," I told him. "I stand a fair chance of hitting something vital by firing through my pocket."

"You better move fast after you pull the trigger, 'cause

your jugular goes next." He was breathing raggedly. "You ever see arterial blood? It's orange."

He was commando wise and suicide smart. I relaxed my grip on the .38. "You've got the wheel."

"I do like a man with a clear sense of his own mort— mortality." He worked his hand down my wrist and into my pocket, where he got his thumb behind the trigger and tugged out the gun, hand and all. He pried it out of my grasp.

The blade was withdrawn. His hands probed my whole length, even patting my hair for a hideout shiv. He relieved me of my wallet and flash.

I knew what was coming next and rolled with it. The gunsight raked stingingly across my cheek without drawing blood. I made a noise as if it had.

"I ought to make you eat it," he spat. "Didn't you hear me when I said no weapons?"

"Would you, in my place?"

That time I wasn't ready for it. A cut that was just starting to heal split open and a warm trickle coursed down my cheek into my mouth. I was getting used to that salt-and-iron taste.

He backed away then, out of my reach. He wasn't stupid or he wouldn't have remained at large this long. The flash snapped on and he studied the cards and papers in my wallet. The yellow light reflecting off the celluloid windows glowed dimly on even, ginger-colored features recognizable from an early mug shot used again and again in the papers and on television. He sported a week's growth of beard, and his hair frazzled out untidily from under a worn cloth cap with a creased peak. His eyebrows slanted away from the bridge of his nose, giving him a surprised look. He removed some bills and turned out the light.

"Getaway stake?" I said.

He came forward and thrust the wallet back inside my jacket, keeping the flash. "Let's call it a deposit in case you don't turn out to be everything you said."

He retreated again. I could make out some highlights on his face now, but nothing else. He was wearing dark clothes.

"I got you white folks all figured out. You're full of brotherly love long as you got the gun. But when one of us gets it you holler 'nigger' and go for a rope."

I grunted. "*Roots*, right?"

"So you heard it before. This time listen to the words."

"There's a little more to it than that," I said. "There's a matter of two cops killed and another paralyzed from the waist down."

"I didn't invite them out there, man."

"Didn't you?"

He breathed some air. "Keep talking, whitey. Make sense."

"It wasn't like you to leave evidence linking your group to the arson that brought those cops out to Mt. Hazel. You weren't as dumb as the others. Like the fisherman said, if you expect to catch trout you got to dangle bait."

"For someone who says he ain't a pig, you sure talk like one."

"Sometimes it pays to think like one. You know that. That's what you were doing that night at Willie Lee Gross's place."

"Who's paying your way, flapjaw?"

"Does it matter?"

"It does if it's John Blue. Maybe you're their judas goat. Get me out in the open so's they can do for me just like they done for the others."

"Would I have come alone if that were the case?"

"You tell me. I'm the original endangered species."

"All broke up over your woman, aren't you?" Easy, Walker. He's got the hammer.

He laughed nastily. "She was my woman like she was Deak's woman like she was Felix's woman like she was everyone else's woman. She'd ball anything in pants and then she'd go to church to save her soul and then she'd ball anything in pants again. I didn't ask her to come get me out of the slam. If she didn't I wouldn't be here. I'd be in a nice cozy cell dictating my mem—memoirs."

"Speaking of here, why'd you pick this spot?" Keep him talking.

"Why not? I was born in this building. Like it?"

"I can't see much of it."

"You ain't missing nothing." His feet scuffed the worn linoleum, the sound echoing. "I know this place better than anywhere. We used to pitch pennies against that wall. Kids don't do that no more, I guess. When I was nine I fell down them stairs. Landed right there and busted my arm. Ma took me to this old white doctor with onions on his breath. I can smell them onions now. He set the bone but he didn't do a good enough job and it had to be busted again later and reset. Sometimes, when it's cold out and that arm starts hurting, I dream about finding that son-of-a-bitch doctor and busting *his* arm. Stupid kid stuff."

He stopped walking, and sniffed loudly. "Smell that? Cabbage and piss and puke. I grew up with that stink. It's in my nose and I can't get rid of it. I joined the marines and they sent me to Germany, but it followed me. Guess I'll die smelling it. That and the onions on that white doctor's breath."

"Tallulah Ridder didn't smell much better."

Something creaked. He was leaning on the staircase bannister. "Everything dies, man."

"Not at fourteen, man," I said. "Not stuffed into a hot trunk with a broken neck."

The building settled in the silence that followed.

"My father took off when I was little," he said then. "So did the fathers of most of my friends. Where do all the fathers go, man? Tell me that." He didn't wait for me to tell him. "There was hookers in the lobby when it rained. They used perfume instead of soap. First time I had the bread I took one in a doorway two blocks down from here. I was thirteen. It was all over in two minutes. She took my money and my cherry and gave me the clap. Some trade."

I wasn't there. He'd been on the run so long he was talking to himself. I'd mentioned Tallulah to flush him out from behind the Selma-to-Montgomery rhetoric, hoping for a glimpse of his true face. I was just starting to realize he didn't have one. Corpses were only broken parts in his vengeance machine. He bored the hell out of me. My skull ached. I needed air. I got more words.

"My mother scrubbed white folks' toilets and hooked a little on the side. She drank. I didn't think nothing of it; all my friends' mothers was drunks and I thought that was the way it was supposed to be. They found her on her face in a mud puddle on Sherman five years ago. She drowned in less water than they used to cut the drinks in her favorite bar. She was too drunk to lift up her head."

I breathed some of the fetid atmosphere. "Sorry to hear it. But you were already pretty far gone by then."

Floorboards shifted. He was standing upright again. I'd reminded him I was there. I pressed on.

"Is that why you knocked down those cops? Because you got a dose from a working girl and your mother died breathing dirty water?"

He let loose a string of curses. I caught a dull flash of teeth. "Man, you wouldn't understand if I tattooed it on your lilywhite chest. You think juicing folks is all we stand for? I been years working up to this. I even went into the service just to learn all you motherfuckers could teach. That's what the Indians done toward the end. Sent the young braves east to study in the white man's schools so they'd know how to deal with him. But it was too late. Well, it ain't too late for us."

"Working up to what?"

"Say what?"

"You said you've spent years working up to this. What's 'this'?"

The building groaned like an old man lowering himself to a bench.

"Nothing," he said finally. He sounded played out. "Just the cause, man. Just the cause."

I almost brought up the mayor. But I was too far away from having him bagged to slam that door. "So what's the punch line? Do we go to police headquarters or what?"

More silence. An ambulance siren started up many blocks away and climbed fast, as thin as an exposed nerve. Someone's always bleeding somewhere. Smith sighed.

"Davey said it would come out like this. I told him to be more positive.

"Davey?"

"Luke David Turkel." Rhythmically, like a tired instructor prompting a difficult pupil. "He said going in we'd all end up in the slam or dead. I said he shouldn't talk like that. By this time I expected the brothers and sisters to be rioting in the streets, torching and trashing and dumping over cars. I figured the revolution would be *on*. Willie Lee agreed with me."

"That should've tipped you off. Never go with a nineteen-year-old kid's hunch."

He wasn't listening. "Bet 'I told you so' was the last

215

thing Davey was thinking when the bastards spilled him in Carolina.''

I said, "You were as late as the Indians. Ten years too late. Too many of the brothers and sisters are making steady wages to riot. They got sucked into that white system you hate so much. Pancho Villa's defunct."

"That's e. e. cummings." He responded wearily. "Only he said it about Buffalo Bill. 'Buffalo Bill's defunct.' I finished school in the marines. See, we ain't all illiterate."

Something struck the floor with a tapping sound and rolled to a stop. The noise was repeated five times. Boards sighed under the linoleum as he came toward me.

"Hold out your hands."

When I obeyed, he slapped a heavy steel something into my right palm and a lighter something into my left.

"Careful with that blade," he said. "I oil it a lot and it slips out if you breathe on it."

I put it away in a pocket and poked the empty revolver into its holster. "What about the flash?"

He handed it over. I turned it on and frisked him, making a chiding noise with my tongue against my teeth when I found a .32 Remington pocket pistol in his right sock.

"Man's got to have an edge," he said.

I dropped the little automatic into the pocket containing the knife, retrieved the bills he'd taken from me, and stuck them back into my wallet. "My car's down the street this side. We'll stop on the way to the cophouse to call the press. You first, Spartacus."

The street looked a little less dark than it had going in. I gave Smith plenty of time to descend the steps before I followed. On my way down, the night exploded in a brilliant flash of blinding white light.

The headlamps of a car parked facing us in a driveway across the street bleached out the shadows, impaling Smith to the sidewalk in front of me like a bug on a card. The engine caught with a shriek. I hurled myself from the steps, tackling my charge around the waist and forcing him face first into the gutter. I suppose he'd consider that symbolic. He woofed when we struck.

The first bullet whacked one of the boarded-up windows from the sound of it, like a wooden bat breaking on a fastball. The second went somewhere into space, and a third twanged off the curb a few inches short of my face. Concrete dust pelted my cheek. There may have been others. I wasn't counting.

Rubber chirped on asphalt. The engine noise swelled. I pushed myself up onto my knees, straddling Smith as I clawed for the little Remington in my pocket. The world filled with naked light. I thrust the automatic straight out in front of me in both hands and fired three times. Glass fell apart with a noise like coins falling. I was breathing hot metal when the light raked past me. Tires screeched, a wheel bumped over the curb on the other side. The car accelerated. I leaped up and sprayed bullets after it until the gun snapped empty. By that time even the exhaust was fading. Tires squealed around corners farther and farther away. I'd had as much chance of getting the license number as I had of being named Miss Black America.

Another thing I didn't have was Alonzo Smith. When I looked around I was alone.

217

26

I spent the next half hour cruising the neighbor-hood, stopping here and there to train the powerful beam of the foot-long police flashlight into the shadows behind trash cans and between buildings. No Smith. If he had the smarts I gave him credit for he'd stashed a vehicle near our rendezvous for just such an emergency as this and was moondust by now.

Bright boy, Walker. Talk them into going with you and then nail it down by leading them into a trap. The Midnight Man rides. I took out my frustration on the accelerator getting out of there. I had no doubts about my destination. I was on my way to meet an attempted murderer.

I made the driveway on the fly, cutting across the front lawn and braking to a jarring, screeching, bouncing stop two feet short of the garage door. Leaving the lights on and the engine running, I piled out without bothering to slam the door and leaned my face close to the garage's oval window with my hands cupped around my eyes. It was too dark to see if a car was parked inside, let alone if its windshield was smashed.

She had the front door open by the time I got to it. In

blue chiffon robe and backless slippers she looked small enough to wrap up and carry home in a pocket.

"Mr. Walker," she said, clutching the neck of the robe. "What—"

I tore loose the robe's belt and tugged it open before she could stop me. She caught her breath. She was fully dressed underneath. I seized her right wrist and sniffed the palm of her tiny hand. Maybe I smelled cordite, maybe not. She might have worn gloves.

"Let's go inside, Mrs. Sturtevant." I rode her in past the entrance, leaving the door gaping.

"You must be drunk, thinking you can burst in here and—" Fury distorted her features, painting fever spots high on her cheeks. She wasn't wearing make-up.

"Save it. Where's your husband?"

"In his bedroom, sleeping. Or he was before you—"

"Nadine?"

"Home. She doesn't live here." The gold specks in her eyes threw off angry light.

"Where'd you ditch the gun?"

"I don't know what you're talking about. Let go of me!"

I was still grasping her wrist. I held on and towed her into the kitchen, where with my free hand I swung open cupboard doors and pulled out drawers and shoved curtains aside and lifted the lids off canisters and moved things around on the work shelf. I even tried the oven and broiler. Nothing.

"Wives like to hide things in kitchens, but I guess you're too smart for that," I said. "You might as well help me. I don't need it to place you on Antietam. You were the only one who knew I was meeting Smith there at midnight. He was speaking loud enough for you to overhear. The car you used is missing a windshield, and even if you wore gloves a nitrate test of your clothes will prove you fired a gun."

We glared at each other. Finally her chest rose and fell. "If you'll let go of me I'll get it for you."

I let go. She shook circulation back into her fingers and went into the living room with me on her heels. There she lifted the smoked-glass cover off a stereo turntable on a built-in shelf. A .38 Police Special stood upright with the record spindle threaded into the two-inch barrel. I reached past her and unspiked it.

"Lousy hiding place," I said, inspecting the piece. "That 'Purloined Letter' stuff doesn't stand up to modern police search methods."

"It wasn't meant to be permanent. I was planning to dump it into the river tomorrow." She paused. "It was Van's."

"What if they came tonight?"

No reply. The fever spots still burned on her cheeks.

The muzzle reeked. I rotated the cylinder, thumbing out shells. Five were empty. I transferred the gun to my left side pocket. That made three on my person, with one usable cartridge among them.

"You didn't get him, you know."

"I thought not. You moved too fast. I didn't want to hit you.

"If you wanted him dead in the first place, why hire me? The cops would have obliged soon enough."

"Come with me," she said stiffly.

I followed her into the bedroom. With the door open the light from the living room stretched across the floor and scaled the bed, falling dimly upon the motionless figure lying on its back under the blanket. Sturtevant's eyes were open. They moved slowly from the ceiling to us. One arm, the good one, lay twitching in a loose pajama sleeve atop the cover. The wheelchair stood empty at the foot of the bed. Its owner didn't look as if our entrance had awakened him. Unless his hearing was seriously impaired he'd heard every word we'd said, door or no door.

The room smelled of medicine and sweet decay. I wanted out of there, bad. But Karen Sturtevant was standing in the doorway.

"Thursday used to be his bowling night," she said quietly. "He'd stay out too late and stagger home stinking of beer, and half those nights when we tried to make love he couldn't. I hated him those nights. It was the one time we could be together, when he wasn't working a double shift or sitting on stakeout days at a stretch. Sometimes he didn't even take his bowling ball. I'm stupid. It took me months to figure out that he was whoring around. After that I prayed that something would happen to make him stay home. That was the only one of my prayers that was ever answered."

Her voice broke on the last part. Then she straightened her back, ushered me out, and drew the door shut. It was like leaving the chamber where they lay out the corpse. She turned to me. Her eyes were dry.

"Who knows what would have come of our marriage if Van hadn't answered that assistance call? But I can't leave him now. I'm as much a prisoner as he is, only it's worse in my case because I'm healthy. I can live with that if the one to blame pays for what he did. I can't knowing that someday he'll be free. Sure, he might be killed. But what if he isn't? It's a chance I don't care to take."

"That still doesn't explain why I was brought in."

"Doesn't it?" Her complexion was even now, the red spots gone. "He got a crafty lawyer once. He might again if he's captured alive. With all the publicity his case has been getting it's an easy matter to claim press prejudice and win acquittal. Van always said if you want something done right, do it yourself. That's why I asked you to call me before anyone else when you had Smith in custody. I didn't want him wriggling out from under this one. Since I'm going to be stuck in one spot for the rest of Van's life, the prospect of imprisonment was no risk at all.''

''Smith accused me of being a Judas goat,'' I said. ''I was too close to the case to realize he was right.''

She did up the belt of her robe haughtily. ''You have nothing to complain about. You were repaying your precious debt. As for being lied to, I'm sure you're used to that by now.''

''Being used to it and liking it aren't even cousins. I promised Smith safe conduct to police headquarters. I may not have had much going in, but I had my word. You'll excuse me if I don't fall all over myself thanking you for taking it away.''

She laughed. The laugh climbed too high too fast.

''Listen to the cut-rate Lone Ranger. You're just a back-door peeper, and a cheap one at that. A roll on the couch buys you.'' She stopped laughing abruptly. ''I suppose you go to the police from here.''

''No chance, sister. As much as I'd like to pipe your performance on the witness stand I'm not in the business of casting daytime dramas.'' I patted the pocket in which nestled the abbreviated .38. ''I'll just hang on to this for now. In my line, a little leverage goes a long way.''

''You're dropping out?''

I looked back at her from the front door. The one lamp burning in the living room cast a golden halo around her hair and placed shadows just where they belonged on her body. Her face was in darkness.

''I can't afford to, Mrs. Sturtevant,'' I said. ''Your husband is still holding my marker.''

"You're cheap *and* stupid. If this whole thing hadn't happened he wouldn't recognize you on the street."

Having the last word in an argument can get to be an obsession. I left without indulging myself.

AFTER SIX BLOCKS MY HANDS STARTED PULLING AGAINST each other on the wheel and I parked, killing the engine and lights. It was a quiet night. A grim face I didn't know glared at me from the windshield. It didn't look as if it belonged to someone I'd get along with. Just to be sociable, though, I got the pint out of the glove compartment and toasted the welfare of my new acquaintance. He drank, but he didn't return the gesture. The hell with him. I upended it again.

A scout car came cruising in the opposite direction a few minutes later. It slowed down as it drew alongside. The spot mounted outside the driver's window sprang to life, cooking my eyeballs. I made as if to hurl the half-full bottle at it. The car took off with a squirt of rubber. I watched its lights in the rearview mirror as it spun into a composition driveway, backed out, and swung up behind me, springs squeaking. Powerful headlamps whited out the mirror and threw a solid black shadow twenty feet beyond the Cutlass's hood.

I gathered the guns from my pockets along with my own piece and holster, reached down and shoved them as far under the seat as they'd go. When I straightened back up there was a uniform on either side of the car.

"Good evening," said the cop at my window, leaning down to peer inside. He had a clean jawline, and amber-tinted Polaroids gave him that impersonal look cops love for some reason. "What are we celebrating?"

"The sight of your blue backside going away," I growled. "If I'm lucky."

"Didn't anyone ever tell you that failure to show proper respect to a police officer is a misdemeanor?" He still sounded pleasant.

I gave him a loud raspberry.

His amiable expression slipped. "License and registration, Mack."

I got the wallet out carefully, handed him the license and reached across for the vehicle registration in the glove compartment. His partner was a lowslung belt and a thick midriff framed by the passenger's window with a hand resting on the butt of his gun.

"What's that other card there?" asked Polaroids.

I took the photostat of my investigator's license out of its window and gave him that too. He read it swiftly. His eyes flicked across the roof of the car to his partner.

"P.I."

I said, "That a misdemeanor too?"

"Not yet. D.U.I.L. is. Get out of the car."

I got out of the car. He told me to close my eyes and touch my nose. I closed my eyes and touched my nose. He scraped a line with his heel in the gravel beside the road and told me to walk it. I walked it. He fetched the breatholator from the scout car and told me to blow up the balloon. I blew up the balloon. It smelled of cheap rubber and stale liquor and foul breath. He squinted at the gauge.

"A little on the shallow side," he said, taking back the contraption. "That leaves driving while drinking."

"Who's driving?"

He frowned at that. Meanwhile his partner reached through the window of my car and scooped the flat bottle off the seat. He brought it over.

Polaroids grinned then, flintily. "Open intoxicants. That's good for a night in the can and maybe a hundred dollars, depending on which judge gets it."

"It isn't open," I pointed out. "Okay, it's enough to haul me in as a suspicious person. I get a lawyer, you climb into a suit and testify, he makes you look like a baboon with arrested development, the judge tosses it out, and your watch commander makes that little notation in your record. And all because you don't like me."

He was chewing on that when a garbled call came over the radio, which they'd left on full volume. "That's us," he told the partner. To me: "You're no Darrow. Robbery-rape comes a little higher than open intox, that's all." He handed back my papers.

"What about the bottle?"

"That goes with us."

"I get it."

"No, you don't." He stabbed a finger at me. "I don't give a damn about you, but just because something's got you sore is no reason we should have to scrape someone else off the highway tonight." He started for the blue-and-white.

"Dilute it with water," I called after him. "It's eighty-six proof."

He didn't hear me, maybe, as he pulled shut his door and screwed the car around in a neat three-point turn. It didn't matter. I felt better for having said it. I felt better for the whole confrontation, in fact. Then I remembered something and reached into my pocket and felt the switchblade I'd taken off Alonzo Smith. That was good for ninety days if they'd searched me. I laughed at that. We Midnight Men thrive on adversity.

IRIS HAD LEFT THE HOOK SHOP ON JOHN R WHERE I'D first met her for an apartment of her own downtown, in a building still considered respectable by people who were considered less than respectable themselves. A piece of paper taped over the bell button told me it was broken. I used my knuckles.

After a minute the door opened. She was barefoot, in a piece of cobweb that hung to her ankles, through which the lines of her long tawny form showed with no little assistance from the lamp at her back. She was getting conservative. The first time I'd ever seen her she was naked.

"Alone?" I asked, and got a faceful of door.

I rapped again. She tore it open, her face furious. I spoke fast, before she could start in.

"Sorry, but I had to ask. I had Smith tonight and lost him. Someone I thought I knew squirted lead and he melted. Maybe I wasn't thinking straight on account of someone else I was sure I had pegged played Ping-Pong with my skull this morning. To cap it off I just this minute squeezed out of an invitation to spend three months at the county's expense. I guess you could call this a shameless play for sympathy."

"You smell like a distillery." Her spine was straight, her head tilted back to look at me from under her eyelashes. I knew that pose.

I said, "Liquor's losing its appeal. I'm thinking of giving it up for a uniform and a big bass drum. Sing hymns and collect donations in a tambourine."

She smiled sourly. Her head came down. "That straight dope about you losing Smith?"

"I had him wrapped and stamped."

"You got blood on your face again."

I touched the crusted thread on my cheek, which I'd forgotten about. "I did that. I wasn't sure you'd recognize me otherwise."

She laughed and stepped aside, opening the door wider. "Let's see what's in the medicine cabinet."

27

"YOU SNORE."

I was half-leaning over the bed when I said it, buttoning my shirt in the damp gray light of dawn, watching Iris stretch. She pushed two small fists toward the ceiling, cuffed me on the chin with one of them, then snuggled back under the covers and looked up at me sweetly. "Self-defense," she said. "You punch things in your sleep."

"That's what makes me such a lamb when I'm awake." I stuck my head through the loop in the necktie and did up the knot, which I hadn't bothered to untie when I took it off earlier.

The bedroom smelled of lovemaking. The flimsy garment she'd greeted me in hung over the footboard, the hem stirring in a slight breeze drifting through the screened window.

"I'm sorry again about calling you so late the other day," I told her. "A lot of things happened and I forgot."

She sat up, propping a pillow behind her, and, holding the sheet over her breasts, reached for cigarettes and matches on the lamp table next to the bed. She offered me one, but I turned it down. She smoked one of those feminine brands with a filter tip you couldn't suck oxygen through. I wondered why she bothered to light them.

"We've talked about this before," she said, shaking out the match and puffing. "I'm not some canary in a covered cage you can uncover when you want to hear me chirp and cover up again when you don't. I've never complained about your work, stupid as it is. We ain't exactly star-crossed lovers. I expect some sort of consideration in return."

"You've been reading *Cosmopolitan*." I grinned, but she didn't respond. I wondered why I'd brought this up.

"I don't need a Goddamn magazine to tell me my time's too valuable to waste sitting by the telephone."

"You're right. I said you were right before. You're still right. I was wrong before and I'm still wrong. I'm wrong and you're right. Let's see, have I forgotten anything? Oh, yeah. You're right."

She giggled. "Okay, so maybe I overdid it. But at least we both know where I stand." She watched me through the smoke. "You know what's wrong with you?"

"Everyone seems to have a theory about that. I must be pretty screwed up."

"That's it. You joke too much. Every time I get near what makes you run you crack wise. Ask a question, get a joke. Make an observation, get a joke. I know you were married once, that you went to Vietnam, and that you had a partner in the detective business who got killed. Nothing else. When I try to find out more you make a funny and change the subject. Must be a cop thing. Some kind of built-in protective device, like a smoke alarm."

"Scratch *Cosmopolitan*," I said. "Substitute *Psychology Today*."

' 'There you go again. Who the hell are you, Walker?''

"Nobody knows. I'm an enduring mystery, like the Riddle of the Sphinx and where the yellow went."

She burlesqued a scream. "I give up!"

Traffic swished by down below. It was nearing the early rush hour.

"I saw Don Wardlaw yesterday," I said.

"Oh?" She sucked on the cigarette.

"He's worried about you."

"Sweet of him."

"He thinks there's a chance you'll start shooting up again."

"He should talk. Didn't you tell me he went cold turkey twice?"

"He's not the subject of this conversation. You are."

She tapped ash into a tray shaped like the state of Florida. Whatever happened to plain old ashtrays? "I'm off it, Amos. I don't plan to go back on. What else do you want?" Her chocolate brown eyes were steady.

I exhaled. "When I start caring, stop me. It's a bad habit in my profession. It can get you killed."

"If you stopped caring you'd be just another cop." She blew smoke out her nostrils. "So don't go playing the perfect reasoning machine with me. I may not know you as well as I should, but I know you better than that."

"I've got to go." I hooked my jacket off the back of a chair.

"Where? After Smith?"

"Not today. Tomorrow. By then I'll have a whole police force behind me. But other things need taking care of first."

"I'd feel better if they were in front of you."

I bent down to kiss her. "Thanks for the sympathy."

She got back at me. She bit my lip.

THE TEMPERATURE WAS DOWN SOME THAT MORNING, AND with the humidity still up there and a little wind blowing, the walk to my car was like a stroll along the south shore of Lake Superior. A light haze softened the edges of buildings and obscured flaws on their faces. I kicked on the wipers to sweep condensed moisture off the windshield. The seat felt cool.

Alonzo Smith was all over the radio. In the wake of Barry Stackpole's scoop in last night's *News*, the cops had released the suppressed information on the Bagley shooting, with the exception of the plot against the mayor. A spokesman for the NAACP denounced Bum Bassett's "storm-trooper tactics" in dealing with a delicate civil rights issue and called for a thorough investigation of the incident. A Detroit Police Officers Association rep said that if it were up to him he'd award Bassett a medal. The police commissioner, still smarting from the reaction to his earlier statement that the Mt. Hazel killers deserved no more consideration than a pack of mad dogs, regretted the violence. The mayor was on his way back from a panhandling trip to Washington and was unavailable for comment. Editorials for and against gun control abounded.

I swung by my place for a shower, shave, and change into my last suit, bolted toast and coffee, and headed back downtown to police headquarters. A double phalanx of hyper patrolmen in riot gear stood between a swelling mob of black men and women and the entrance. A camera truck belonging to one of the local TV stations was parked across the street, the crew standing by while a male model in blow-dried hair and blue blazer counted into a mobile microphone. Nobody seemed in a hurry. Nothing much was going to happen until the tape started rolling.

A uniform I had seen with Alderdyce from time to time recognized me and let me through, to a chorus of mutters from the crowd. As I entered the squad room all conversation stopped. I was used to that, but this time there was an electricity in the silence that had more to do with the scene down in the street than my reverse charisma where authority was concerned. A big dick with terminal five-o'clock shadow announced me to Alderdyce and I went past him into the office.

John and Sergeant Hornet were bent over a large-scale map of the riverfront area spread out on the desk, with another pair of plainclothes men I didn't know following the lieutenant's gestures across the maze of streets and freeways. He was using a compass and protractor to seal off possible escape routes.

"What's going to stop Smith from crossing your pencil lines?" I asked.

"Hold it down!" snapped Alderdyce. "Let's keep this between you, me, and the fifty or sixty cops on the grapevine. What do you want?"

"How come you're on security?"

"I'm not. Thankfully, there are enough homicides in the City of Champions to keep me from having to wet-nurse politicians. Protecting the mayor is someone else's headache. Nabbing Smith is mine. But since they happen to come together in this case I'm working with security. I work here, they work downstairs. See how we cooperate? What do you want, Walker?"

"Early retirement, if I can swing it. For now I'll settle for an update. It's my case too."

"Funny, the commissioner didn't mention you when he gave me this assignment." His eyes took in Hornet and the others. "Beat it."

The two strange detectives glanced at me curiously on their way out. The look I got from Hornet would melt zinc. When the door was shut:

"Who tipped Stackpole the details of the Bagley shooting?" demanded the lieutenant.

"You have an idea or you wouldn't be asking me," I said.

"You as much as promised me yesterday you'd keep it under wraps.

"I said I'd sit on the plot angle, which I did. You were going to release most of it by this morning anyway. I owed Barry a favor, so he got it first. You know how that works, John. We've used it on each other often enough."

His fist smacked the map. "Damn it, I'm trying to catch a killer! Will you at least tell me what you're going to do before you go off and do it?"

"How am I supposed to follow all of your rules if you keep making them up to cover something I already did? I don't like dance charts. Sometimes I have to invent my own steps, and when I do I don't always have time to send you a Xerox copy."

"The courts keep changing the rules on me. Why should you be any different? Oh, to hell with it." He tossed me a laminated card with the Seal of Detroit stamped on one side.

"What's this?" I fingered it.

"That'll get you through the cordon tomorrow. You're a royal pain in the ass, Walker, but you've got good eyes. Keep them open."

It took me a moment to adjust to the about-face. Then I pocketed the pass. "Where will you be?"

"Never mind about me. Smith's the one you want to look for."

"Has Hizzoner been notified?"

"He'll be met at the airport today by someone I trust, don't bother asking who. He'll still want to put in an appearance, of course, and even if he doesn't his PR people will talk him into it. One act of bravery is worth a thousand baby-kissings at the polls."

"Is that good or bad? For your purposes, I mean."

"Bad. But we'll handle it."

"Handle it how?"

He smiled secretly. I hated him when he did that. There was no trace of his earlier anger. "Let's just say I know enough about him to predict his reaction to certain suggestions my man will make."

"You're being cagey, John," I said. "You know you're not good at it."

The smile was stuck on his face. He was wearing a tawny jacket over a yellow shirt and matching tie, and the color scheme together with his self-satisfied expression gave him the look of a hunting cat.

"There was some shooting early this morning on Antietam," he said then. "Hear about it?"

"Should I have?"

"You tell me."

"I haven't heard a thing." That much was true.

He played with his protractor and frowned. "It's probably nothing. Blue-and-white answered the call. They found a slughole in one of the boards nailed over a window. The building's coming down next year. It's one of the old addresses we have for Alonzo Smith."

"Anyone see anything?"

"If they did they aren't talking. It's that kind of neighborhood."

"How many of those has the department investigated down there in the past year?"

This time his smile was bitter. "You made your point. I guess I've got Smith on the brain like you said. When this thing is finished, you know what I'm going to do? I'm going to grab the wife, drop the kids off at her sister's, and head west. I'll pin my badge on my shirt and keep going until someone asks me what that thing is I'm wearing, and

233

that's where we'll stay until I've used up every minute of vacation time I've got coming.''

''Ulysses did that,'' I said. ''He used an oar. When they asked him what he was carrying on his shoulder, he pitched his tent on that spot.''

''I remember. Was it before or after the voyage?''

''After.''

He nodded. ''Smart man, Ulysses.''

I said, ''Tomorrow's going to be sticky, if what's going on out front is a clue.''

''Forget about that. I keep seeing the same faces at all these demonstrations. They'd protest lower taxes and higher wages if they thought it would draw a crowd. A cop can't take a leak in this city without someone seeing something sinister in it.''

''I bet someone told Mussolini the same thing. Just before they shot him and strung him up by his heels.''

That bothered him for all of two seconds. Then he returned his attention to the map. ''Send in Hornet and the others on your way out, will you?''

THE SHOUTING WAS STILL GOING ON AS I LEFT THE BUILD-ing. Someone made a grab for my shoulder but I ducked it and kept moving, forcing my way through the press of sweating bodies while trying my best not to look like a cop. The cameras whirred. By the time I got clear I was wringing wet and my heart was rattling like a loose rod. Getting torn to pieces by an enraged mob does not rank high on my list of enviable demises.

I was in the car and office-bound when I remembered the guns under the front seat. I had no idea how many pickup sheets the little Remington I had taken from Smith might be on, and if the cops retrieved any of the slugs Karen Sturtevant had fired on Antietam and traced them to her husband's gun I didn't want them making the jump to me. Together the two pieces of evidence formed an indigestible lump in the pit of my conscience.

In a city as crowded as Detroit, ditching hot iron is only a little less troublesome than getting rid of a body. The river was out, at least from the bank—too many windows by day, too well patrolled after dark. "Well, officer, I had this client, see, and she hired me to catch this wanted fugitive, but when I got him she tried to kill him with this gun and I took it away from her, and, well, I already have one of my own, and—what's that? The other gun? No, that's not mine either, actually. You see . . ." But there was Belle Isle.

Sunlight was sparkling off the gunmetal-colored surface of the Detroit River as I turned off East Jefferson, my tires whistling on the MacArthur Bridge, and approached the thousand-acre playground located halfway between Detroit and Windsor. Two hundred years ago it had been called *Isle des Cochons*, or Hog Island, because pigs were pastured there to protect them from wolves. But in 1763 it offered feeble security against Chief Pontiac's braves, who swam across to massacre the family that looked after Fort Detroit's vegetable garden. Today a greasy fountain marks the gravesite of the family's two small boys.

There weren't many people milling around this early on a Friday. After parking in the almost empty lot I took off my jacket and tie, thrust the guns and the switchblade into my pants with my shirt hanging out over the butts, and got out to walk along the beach. I stopped a couple of times to pick up stones and examine them before casting them away. To anyone watching I was just another rockhound. I flipped odd items of debris idly into the river. One of them was the knife. A hundred yards farther on I squatted near the water's edge where part of the beach had been scooped out to launch a boat and looked at some more stones. While I was doing that I tugged out the revolver and automatic and slid them into the water one after the other. They made a few bubbles going down.

THE REST OF THE DAY WAS A WRITE-OFF. I CALLED IRIS from work and talked about nothing at all, read the mail, swept out both offices, had lunch, and waited until five for the telephone to ring or the door to open. They didn't. After dinner I caught a movie solo, went home not liking it, and cleaned and oiled the Smith & Wesson and the Luger. I hit the sheets at ten. The night was warm and I dreamed of death and dying.

28

AFTER AUTOMOBILES AND MURDERS, DETROIT IS MOST FA-
mous for its riverfront ethnic festivals, which take place
every weekend of the summer, rain or shine, at Hart Plaza.
Polish, German, Italian, Ukrainian, Greek, Hispanic—each
group gets a weekend. In an area where more than twelve
percent of the population spoke no English only eighty
years ago, the emphasis on its motley heritage is understandable. Just as understandable, in view of the city's
changing complexion, is the fact that many of the celebra-
tions grow less crowded and rowdy each year. But not the
Afro-American festival. It just keeps getting bigger.

This year's was no exception. Under a sky so blue it
hurt to look at it, the parade ground was jammed with
people carrying Thermos jugs and picnic baskets, screaming children in shorts and bare feet thundering around and
between and occasionally into them amid twangy curses
and flying chicken sandwiches. A skinny sweating brown
girl with cornrowed hair and African jewelry that clanked
and rattled like a scrap truck when she moved stood on the
bandstand, wailing soul into a microphone while an amplified combo behind her made the earth tremble. The

greasy-sweet smell of ribs roasting on portable grills was everywhere.

There were very few white faces. You had to be white to notice the undercurrent of bitterness beyond scattered shoving matches and the rabble-rousing of street orators desperately trying to attract an audience. Conversations stopped as I drew near isolated knots of people. The jostling I got when I penetrated the main stem seemed rougher than necessary. I was wearing a Windbreaker over a short-sleeved shirt and jeans, and I was constantly reaching back as if to tug down the elastic band and brushing the butt of my concealed .38 just to reassure myself that it was still in its holster. The hunt for Alonzo Smith had set back race relations ten years locally.

I didn't see John Alderdyce anywhere, but I did recognize three or four plainclothes men from police headquarters sprinkled among the celebrants, all black; and there were likely many more from the precincts and uniform division in mufti. You could pick some of them out by the fact that they were wearing jackets. With the temperature in the low nineties, the only good reason for having one was to hide a gun.

I circled back to the parking area for some fresh air, and saw Bum Bassett's big silver pickup standing near the entrance. He had the driver's door open and was sitting on the seat facing out. His huge raw face broke into a thousand wrinkles when he saw me.

"Howdy there, hoss," he said, pumping my hand with his meat grinder. He was wearing a white T-shirt and his biceps were as big as grapefruits. An old tattoo on his right had faded or been obliterated to a blue blur. "I been meaning to call. I'm right sorry about cold-cocking you that way. I wanted to get out of there and I wasn't in no mood for arguments."

I worked circulation back into the hand. "I thought maybe it was because you didn't want to talk about your first wife."

"Well, there's some things a man don't like to get into. No hard feelings, I hope." His grin was anxious.

"I don't use all my brain cells anyway. What's a few hundred thousand more or less? No objections outstanding. How's the leg?"

"Sore as hell, but I'm used to that. Just a matter of keeping her clean and not climbing any mountains for a spell. I'll get this here back to you soon as I can meander without it." He patted the cane, hooked on the steering column.

"I'd appreciate it. I consider it good luck. As long as I have it, maybe I'll never need it. Knock wood." I reached up to rap the cane. In a twinkling he had the .44 magnum out of the frontier-type holster on his right hip and pointing at me. I froze.

He smiled shamefacedly and replaced the gun. "Sorry. You don't do what I do and get to be my age by liking quick movements."

"No apology needed." A drop of sweat rolled down my rib cage. "That's some draw. You practice?"

"Every day in front of a mirror. Ain't had to use it but once. That once made it all worthwhile."

"How'd you get that hogleg past security?"

"I got police credentials from three states. Also, I'm famous. You'd be surprised how much red tape just being known cuts through."

"I'll bet. And you do all you can to stay known, don't you? Like dressing up like John Wayne, and the way you talk, all those "I reckons' and 'hosses' and such. You really put the myth of the American cowboy to work for you."

He winked broadly. "Okay, so you flushed me out. Do

me a favor, hoss? Don't tell nobody. I need all the weapons I got.''

"I'm not writing my autobiography this year," I assured him.

A small group of young black men and women was gathered on the other side of a battered Pontiac parked next to the pickup, conversing in low tones punctuated by sharp laughter. A strong scent of marijuana drifted our way. I moved closer to Bassett and dropped my voice.

"Assuming he decides to go ahead with it, how do you figure to beat the entire Detroit Police Department to Smith?"

Teeth flashed in his red beard. "I was just fixing to ask you the same thing."

"My situation's changed. I'm just here for the festival."

"Funny, you don't look it."

"You didn't answer my question, Bum."

"Didn't know I had to," he said. "But I like you, so here it is. When something happens I like to be there. I couldn't see staying home changing bandages when the one I come a thousand miles to get is here. Maybe I don't get him, but I figure I paid to see him get got. Answer enough?"

I watched him. "No, but I know when to settle." I paused. "What did you expect to find when you went through Laura Gaye's things at the commune?"

"What makes you think I did at all?"

"There are things everyone does the same way every time, and that no one else does quite the same. One is folding clothes. You shouldn't have bothered, Bum. They weren't that neat when you found them."

"Doggone. The rest of the place was so neat I guess I just got carried away when it come time to put everything back. You got me there, slick. I was inside the place. I

240

didn't want the law to know that, with murder done there and all. I didn't find nothing anyway.''

"That's your main fault, overdoing things. Sending that trigger around to scare me off the case, for instance. That was too much."

He scraped nonexistent mud off his bootsole on the edge of the rocker panel. "I hope you'll take that as a compliment, hoss."

"Compliment how?"

"You just had too much on the ball and I had enough competition from the law. That fellow used to pack iron for a numbers man I picked up in St. Louis two years back. I could of run him in too, but I didn't, so he owed me. You didn't figure to be the type to rabbit, though. He was just a hunk of ripe meat I drug across the trail to throw you off. Reckon his plane fare was wasted. I don't know now how you tied him to me."

"Simple deduction. You were the only one left."

"Well, I didn't know you so well then. I wouldn't do it now, and that's a fact."

"I think it is. Anyway, your giving me that stuff you found on Bagley cleans that slate, so let's forget it. It's always bothered me why you thought Smith was worth the trip up here, though. Five thousand would barely pay your expenses."

He glanced across the Pontiac at the teenagers and caught one staring at him. I couldn't think why. He was just another Mack truck in a cowboy suit. The youngster looked away quickly.

"I wouldn't be in this here business if I didn't like it," said Bassett. "Call it a working vacation. Hell, you know what I'm talking about. From some of the things you said I got the feeling you was in this before there was a reward."

"I owed someone something," I said.

He studied me through clear blue eyes. "We got lots in common, hoss. That we do."

I moved off. It was 11:18 by my new watch. The mayor was due at noon. I was stopped twice by plainclothes detectives and forced to show my pass. They weren't questioning any of the blacks, Smith or no Smith. I could have saved myself a lot of hassle by spreading burnt cork on my face.

"He's okay," said a familiar voice behind me the second time I was stopped. Sergeant Hornet flashed the black cop his credentials. The latter nodded and walked away, adjusting his shoulder holster under a Pistons warm-up jacket.

"Where's the neon blazer?" I asked Hornet. He was wearing a blue nylon jogger's top with a zip front and no tie. The white racing stripe made him look like a weather balloon.

His expression was sour. "The idea's to be inconspicuous."

"You didn't make it."

"You're a hoot, Walker. I see your pal Buffalo Bob is here. You two wouldn't be working together."

"Like Moscow and Pittsburgh." I listened to the dark canary on the bandstand moaning a new tune. "John's with the mayor, isn't he?"

"You know so much, why ask me?"

"You're a fountain, Sergeant. Who's your voice coach, Marcel Marceau?"

"I'm considered a real motor-mouth when I'm with someone I got use for," he said. "I guess you noticed I don't do flipflops whenever you come in sight."

"Too bad. I'd like to see that."

He'd been standing sideways to me, watching the crowd.

Now he turned to face me. He wasn't like most fat men, with all their features crowded into the center of their faces. His eyes were a hand-span apart and his mouth was as broad as a six-lane highway. He wouldn't have looked right skinny. His rash had dried to pink crusts on his cheeks. "That's another thing, your bright patter. You don't hear that from cops. It cooks out early. John and I do this because we got to. It's our job, and if we wind up in a bag like Maxson and Flynn or a wheelchair like Sturtevant, that's just the way milk turns. With you it's like slumming. If things get hairy you can walk away, tell your client you came up dry and still get paid. We don't have that option. So excuse me if I don't find your sense of humor ingratiating."

"Sometimes a sense of humor is what's left after everything else is gone," I told him. "Sometimes it's the only thing keeping you from spraying your brains all over the ceiling."

"That's something else," he snarled. "You got this picture of yourself nobody else sees. Tragic hero, fighting the good fight all alone. One of these mornings you're going to wake up married to yourself."

"I guess that means I'm living in sin now."

"I like brains on the ceiling better."

"What about it?" I asked. "Is Smith coming?"

"Not this year. Why should he? Everyone else is dead and he's squirreled away in some hole hundreds of miles from here."

"That might have been true last night." I mumbled the words.

He nailed me. "You got reason to think he's changed his mind?"

"Gut feeling. You know how it is."

"I'd like to." He was still looking at me. "Maybe someday I will."

He left me, a graceful hippo of a man swaying from side to side as he shifted his bulk from one incongruously small foot to the other.

The crowd was surging in the direction of the parking area, where uniformed officers had set up sawhorses and were standing around sweating in their summer blues, their guns and handcuffs obvious on their webbed belts. Portable radios with antennae fully extended rode crackling and sputtering in special pockets, topping off the military look. It was almost twelve o'clock.

A big black cop with a thick moustache touched a hand to my chest as I started between sawhorses. I displayed the pass. He looked at it, nodded, let me through, and stepped in to block someone trying to come in behind me. If I live to be forty I'll never understand the faith people put in credentials you can order from any catalogue.

The asphalt was tacky. This part of the lot wasn't shaded. The sun nailed directly overhead drew shimmering waves of heat from the composition surface. The officers smelled of leather and perspiration, and when they shifted weight their feet creaked in their boots. I made the mistake of resting a hand on the fender of a parked scout car and jerked it away with a first-degree burn. Forget about eggs; you could roast a fourteen-pound turkey with all the trimmings on the sidewalk and keep it warm for a week.

They came with a blue-and-white before and behind and enough motorcycles to remake *The Wild One*, sirens strung out long and thin and warped by the sodden air, the riders in glistening black leather from neck to foot and looking as alike in their mirrored glasses as cartridges in a belt. Two blocks of shiny black automobile—the object of the procession—slid around the corner and into the area enclosed by the sawhorses, with the haughty look of the *Queen Mary* docking among tugs. It cruised to a stop without a sound. The engine cut out and there was still no sound. You could power a fleet of Honda Civics all week on what it took to get the chief exec here from his office. But the mayor of Detroit doesn't ride around in Japanese automobiles.

The cops in the enclosure snapped to life—forcing spectators back from the sawhorses, growling over portable radios, lining up to form a protective cordon of blue around the limo. They could have saved themselves the trouble. Most of the people there were fighting to get on camera as crews from the local TV stations unlimbered their equipment in the area reserved for the press. Politicians come and go, but how often do you get the chance to wave hello to your friends over the airwaves?

In the middle of all this confusion, a chauffeur in a powder-blue uniform got out, circled the car, and opened the right rear door. One of the mayor's eight-hundred-dollar suits alighted with John Alderdyce inside. He raised his hand in the characteristic bent-arm wave. At that moment something thumped his chest, kicking him back against the open door so hard a hinge snapped. Then we heard the report.

29

IT CRASHED OVER THE ROOFTOPS, ECHOING ON THE WINDsor side and finishing with a roaring hiss somewhere between Lakes Michigan and Huron. You just can't place a highpowered rifle by its report.

There were shouts of "Oh, my God!" and "Not again!" but most were unintelligible, deteriorating into shrieks as the realization spread that a sniper was loose and that the mayor might not be the only target. Sawhorses splintered and fell over with a crash. A television cameraman was shoved off balance; losing his grip on his camera. It exploded against the pavement, feeding the panic. Cops bellowed obscenities at the crowd, the sniper, and each other, their guns out and gleaming greasily in the bright sunlight. Screams tore the air.

Uniforms and plainclothes men had closed in a protective huddle around the fallen detective, cutting off my view. I started shoving my way through to the car. It was a moment before I realized I had my gun in my hand.

My legs went out from under me suddenly and I came down hard on my back on the sticky asphalt. When I opened my eyes I was looking up the black bore of a Police .38. Beyond that was a bare arm covered with fine red hairs protruding from a short blue sleeve. Beyond that was a freckled face under a shiny black visor.

I tried to sit up but couldn't. A black brogan was pinning my right wrist to the pavement. I was still holding the gun in that hand.

"Don't move, you son of a bitch," the cop was saying. "Try to kill the mayor, will you?"

His voice shook. People were still running around screaming. I had to shout to make myself heard. "Easy, son. We're on the same side." I inched my free hand toward the pocket containing the pass. The gun leaped closer.

"Don't move, I said!"

I stopped. "Check my gun, for chrissake! It hasn't been fired. Don't you know a rifle when you hear one?"

"I heard the rifle. Maybe you're the back-up." His mouth stayed open when he wasn't talking and his breath moved in and out in shudders. But the gun didn't wobble.

"Let him up."

The command came out in a grunt from behind the cop. He didn't move. "Who says?"

"Your bread and butter, sonny."

The cop shifted his weight and turned slightly to take in both me and the speaker. John Alderdyce was sitting on the pavement with his legs spread out stiffly, his back resting against the limousine's doorsill. His chest heaved as if he'd been running. His jacket and shirt were open, exposing a shiny black surface that was distinctly nonorganic. There was a dent where his heart should be. Hornet was bent over him, undoing the straps that held the bulletproof vest in place.

"He's got a gun, Lieutenant," said the youngster. "He don't look like a cop."

"That's because he isn't one. But as much as I'd like

you to pull the trigger, you better give him some slack. It'd be just like him to haunt me."

Reluctantly the rookie holstered his revolver and removed his foot from my wrist. I got up and put away my own gun. By this time Hornet had the vest off Alderdyce and was vigorously rubbing the heel of his hand over a discoloration the size of a saucer on the lieutenant's chest, which was nearly as dark and glossy as the shield itself.

"That's one hell of a bruise, John," the sergeant was saying. "You sure you're okay? We got a doc here someplace. Where the hell's that croaker?" He bellowed the last over his shoulder.

"I'm fine, except for a burning on my chest," John told him.

"Burning? Oh." He stopped rubbing.

Alderdyce climbed to his feet with the aid of the detectives gathered around him. He was streaming wet. "Get those fucking cameras out of here."

There was a general hubbub of grunts and curses as a flying wedge of uniforms shoved two technicians out of the enclosure, their cameras bobbing.

I said, "Bright move. There aren't a lot of vests that will stop a bullet fired from a deer rifle."

"It's a new design, effective past a hundred yards. Inside of that there's no reason for so much firepower." He worked his left arm, wincing.

"What if he'd aimed at your head?"

He said nothing.

"I can't figure where he got the gun," put in Hornet. "We confiscated that thirty-ought-six on Bagley."

"There are gunshops all over this town," Alderdyce said. "Robbery can tell us if any were broken into recently. Any line yet on where the shot came from?"

"We just got the squeal. Cop down on Shelby. He was

securing a rooftop when someone hit him from behind. Investigating officers found a Winchester ditched on the stairs." Hornet ran out of breath.

"Roadblocks up where I said?"

"Far as I know."

"Jesus H. Christ. I bet you don't even check your fly." He shoved a path through to the scout car in front, leaned in through the open driver's door, and snatched out the mike. At that moment Central Dispatch came on the air. The female operator sounded as if she were talking in her sleep.

"Suspect seen in blue nineteen-seventy-four Buick Riviera license number Tom-Edward-Robert-six-two-seven heading west on West Fort Street between Shelby and Washington."

Even as she spoke we heard the gulping sirens. I met Alderdyce's gaze. The whites of his eyes were brilliant against his blue-tinged skin.

"Officers engaged suspect at roadblock between Second and Third. Suspect now heading north on Second."

"That's the wrong way," said Hornet.

"We'll be sure and issue him a citation when we catch him. Get this thing turned around." The lieutenant scrambled into the front seat of the scout car and slid to the passenger's side. A uniformed officer detached himself from the cluster of officialdom standing nearby and got in under the wheel. I dived for the back seat, shouldering aside a plainclothes man. Hornet was already in back. We were moving by the time I got the door shut.

We were starting to pick up individual reports from officers on the scene, crackling and indistinct.

". . . identified myself. When he didn't slow down I opened fire. Windshield smashed. I put one in the block too, but I don't . . ." The signal faded out.

Another cut in. "This is Sergeant Morrison at Third and Howard. I think I just spotted that blue 'seventy-four Riviera turning east on Howard from Second. He was going the wrong way till he turned."

"Full circle," said Alderdyce, hanging onto the dash as our car swung in a tight turn inside the sawhorses. "Go right on Jefferson. Come on, come on."

We knocked over a sawhorse and shot out into traffic. We were barely clear of the service drive when a tall silver pickup flamed past on our right.

"Was that who I think it was?" demanded the lieutenant.

I said, "There can't be two men that size driving a truck that color and wearing a cowboy hat."

"He got a scanner in that rig?" Hornet asked me.

"Could be. There's a lot of Buck Rogers stuff in the dash."

"Why don't you climb on the air, John? Order him to pull over."

"Yeah, I'd like to hear his answer," I said.

"Forget him."

"Forget him!" echoed the sergeant, incredulously. "He's interfering in police business."

"I said forget him and forget him is what I meant. Stop at Randolph."

The driver braked at the intersection. Bassett's truck hurtled across without slowing and pulled away from us at a rate I wouldn't have thought possible. I wished I'd taken a look under the hood when I'd had the chance.

"What we stopping here for?" Hornet peered up and down Randolph.

"We're waiting for Smith," said Alderdyce.

"What makes you think he'll come this way?"

"Twelve years with the department, that's what."

"I got nineteen years says how come?"

"I get it," I said.

The lieutenant twisted around in his seat to glare at me. "What the hell are you doing here anyway? No civilians allowed. Get out."

I opened my mouth to reply. Central Dispatch cut me off.

"Suspect turned south on Randolph. Cars one-six and three-four-two in pursuit."

"I'll be damned," said Hornet. "But I still don't get it."

"That's why they gave me my own office and you're lucky to have a desk."

"There he is!" The driver pointed out his open window.

We saw the blinking red and blue lights first, and then, well out in front, a blue bullet skidding along barely on four wheels as it wound through the slowing traffic. Half the windshield was gone, the jagged edges glittering brilliantly. The Buick roared past within arm's reach of our radiator. Its slipstream rocked the blue-and-white on its springs.

"Pull out!" John bellowed.

Invisible hands pushed me back against the seat. The slot between Smith's car and the bubblegum machine behind wasn't big enough for us but we made it. We went into overdrive, and then we weren't on the pavement anymore. We weren't earthbound at all. Cars and buildings streamed past in a blur of color.

The blue back of Smith's car slewed in and out of sight among the traffic ahead. Tires wailed, horns blared. We were shifting lanes constantly, taking advantage of every opening. Cars drifted right, left, any direction that would put distance between them and the godawful racket our sirens were making. I looked at the sergeant. His eyes were bright and when he shifted his considerable bulk on the seat his movements were hyper.

"I get it now," he said.

"Wish I did," put in the driver.

"Don't you see it? John's figuring to bottle him up in the tunnel. Catch him between bases with the Canadian authorities on the other side. What I don't see is how he knew Smith was going to go for it." He looked at the lieutenant.

"You know how tough it is to extradite a prisoner from Canada?" He kept his attention on the road ahead.

"Hang on." The driver spun the wheel and we tore down the circular, spiraling ramp that led down to the Detroit–Windsor Tunnel, that mile-long air-conditioned umbilical cord linking the United States and Canada. We came in sight of the well-marked entrance just as the rear of a blue car shot into its depths, leaving a trail of black exhaust behind. I wondered if he'd taken a bullet through a cylinder wall.

"Bet he ducked the toll," Hornet commented.

Our driver eased back on the throttle. "Well, he's meat for the Canucks if our guys don't take him. You want to pull off and wait?"

"We've stuck this long." John's voice was tight.

One of the uniformed toll collectors was standing outside the booth, looking down the tunnel, when we sped past and hurtled down the decline, our tires singing on the steel ribs. His partner was inside on the telephone, probably to the Windsor end. Our sirens boomed deafeningly off the tiles inside the two-lane tube. The driver flicked off the switch. I felt a tightness in my chest beneath all those tons of water in the river and realized for the first time that I was claustrophobic.

It took a moment, I think, for the sound to reach us. A

hard bang, louder than a gunshot, that left behind a roaring in the ears as if they'd been boxed. Hornet sat bolt upright.

"What the hell was *that?*"

"Better slow down," Alderdyce told the driver.

A line is painted across the walls and floor of the tunnel where the boundaries of the two nations meet, with crossed American flags decaled on the tiles on our side and crossed Canadian flags on the other. A hundred feet short of the line, Alonzo Smith's Buick was stalled diagonally across both lanes, its left front fender and that half of the grille twisted into a fist of crumpled metal. The driver's door hung open. A tour bus from Canada was stopped in the other lane. There might have been a dent in its left front fender. The driver was just climbing down when we got there.

"It wasn't my fault!" he shouted. He was a tall white with a seamed face and gray hair and his uniform jacket was too short in the sleeves. "He was going way too fast. Skidded across the line. I didn't have no place to go. Ask the passengers."

"Where's the driver?" Alderdyce shot.

"He jumped out and took off down the tunnel. That's illegal, ain't it?"

John turned to the cop in uniform. "Stay here. Make sure no one leaves the bus." To me: "You too. I don't have to tell you why."

"You don't," I agreed.

The two detectives started down the tunnel, one on each side. They had their guns out. The bus driver started to follow. The uniform took hold of his arm.

"John!"

Hornet was on the other side of the bus, out of sight. The lieutenant spun in that direction, bringing his revolver up in both hands. "Police! Drop it!"

He fired.

The report rang along the tiles in two directions, giving each country its share. There was a short silence, and then a dark-clad figure staggered out from behind the bus, clutching its stomach. In the pale artificial light it was hard to tell if he had a weapon. He picked up his pace and ran with faltering steps toward the Canadian end. I could hear him gasping.

"Stop!" commanded Alderdyce.

Smith kept running. John took aim. I don't remember hearing his second shot. I saw fire leap from the barrel. I saw the gun jump in his outstretched hands. I saw Smith stiffen, run two more steps, then collapse like a tent when the pole is kicked out from under it. His face ended up on the other side of the line.

Time hesitated a beat. Then Sergeant Hornet appeared beyond the end of the bus and walked over to where the fugitive lay. For a long moment he was bent over him. Then he turned and approached the lieutenant, who hadn't left his spot.

"It was a good shoot, John. He had a Saturday night special and he was going to use it on you. I saw the whole thing."

Alderdyce remained unmoving. "Dead?"

"He won't be ambushing any more police officers."

His superior nodded. Then he grasped his stomach with his free hand, supporting himself with his gun hand against the wall. His face had lost some of its dark coloring. I started toward him. Hornet stopped me.

"Twelve years with the department," said the sergeant. "That's his first one."

The noise of John's retching echoed off the tiles.

30

It was a little after two when I reached the office. It should have been later. It felt later. The waiting room was as crowded as an asteroid. I looked for mail under the slot, then remembered that it was Saturday and that they held it until Monday. I left the connecting door open and threw up the window in case the air felt like circulating. It didn't.

There was plaster dust on the desk, which meant that the Korean who ran the martial arts class upstairs was back from vacation. Bump, bang, wham. Now you throw me. Wham, bang, bump. So sorry about the cracks in your ceiling, Mr. Walker. Would you like to talk about the bulletholes in the foyer? The new wallpaper looked more and more as if it were slumming.

Creaking into the tired swivel, I broke out a fresh pack from the top drawer and lit one and blew smoke at the door. Thinking. I'd made the case a lot tougher than it had to be by trying to shield everyone and everything from the cops, running around in tighter and tighter circles like a scorpion on a hot rock. It was no wonder I ended up at a standstill while the cops brought it to a close. They didn't owe anyone anything beyond a full day's work.

255

I stopped pitying myself long enough to dial my answering service for messages. I had a message. Next I got Tulsa on the line. We spoke for ten minutes. I said I'd get the check off Monday and hung up. For a time afterward I sat and scowled at the telephone. Ivan the Terrible once skewered a messenger's foot to the floor for bearing bad tidings. Me, I paid for it once a month. I closed the window and connecting door, locked all the locks, and hurried downstairs to my car.

Part of Bassett's pickup stuck out from behind the maze of trailers and camper shells in the lot on Schoolcraft. I cruised past to a service station on the next corner, called police headquarters, and went back. I parked in the driveway so that he'd have to drive around me to get out, cut off a beaming salesman on his way over, and walked up to the bounty hunter's battered Airstream. He had the truck backed up to it and was stooped over the hitch. He straightened as I approached. His T-shirt was big enough to cover the infield at Tiger Stadium, but it was just barely big enough for him. With the cane hooked on his pants pocket, its rubber tip dangled nearly twelve inches off the ground. They don't make them in his size. He was wearing his gun.

"Good to see you, hoss. I was afeared we'd miss each other." He wiped his hands on a stained rag, biceps straining the material of his shirt as he worked the fingers.

"I wanted to apologize for leaving you dangling today," I said. "It wasn't my idea."

"Well, you never know which way the spit's going to fly." He kneaded the rag some more. "I got to admit, I had him pegged for the Chrysler. That was damn good figuring, crowding him into that there tunnel. Like treeing a possum."

"That was Alderdyce, not me. I was just along for the scenery.

"I guess you got to be one to think like one."

"They're talking promotion," I said, ignoring the slur. "For setting himself up as a decoy, not for killing Smith. He'll be lucky if he gets a letter of commendation. It would look too much like they were rewarding him for the other thing. The civil rights people are already screaming execution. Could be they're right."

"You know him better than me."

"That's not what I mean. I think John saw a gun when he spotted Smith hiding behind that bus. After all the publicity his case got I don't think it was possible for an angry, exhausted cop to look at him without seeing one, whether he had one or not. But we'll never know for sure, because Hornet got to the body first. I wouldn't put it past his type to plant a throwaway piece on Smith just to protect his superior. A lot of cops carry one for just such an emergency."

"It don't really matter," he said. "Some men need killing."

"Especially this one. Right?"

Something in my voice alerted him. "Hold on there, hoss. I told you that dead or alive stuff was just for the rubes. He wasn't worth an iron penny to me cold."

"You didn't care about the bounty," I countered. "This one was on the house."

The sun was shining full on his big red face. He reached up and tugged down the curled brim of his hat, then unhooked the cane from his pocket and stood fiddling with the crook. Not leaning on it. "Let me know when you start making sense, hoss."

It was beginning to grate, that *hoss*. I jumped in swinging. "It's all in the way you look at things. In your case, bounty hunting was the perfect disguise, like hiding something in the most obvious place. It's such a bizarre occupation I couldn't see around it. Mysteries like your sources of information seemed explained by your larger-than-life image. The wardrobe, the John Ford dialogue, the chewing tobacco no one actually saw you chew—they were all camouflage to keep guys like me from asking too many questions. It was when I stopped thinking of you as a bounty hunter that things started figuring. Am I boring you?''

He was frowning down at the cane. "Not so far. I got a long attention span.''

"Deak Ridder held the key to Alonzo Smith's whereabouts," I continued. "He planned the raid on the Frank Murphy Hall of Justice. That much I got from his kid sister Tallulah. When she turned up dead—police thought at the hands of the other militants—he got sick enough of the whole business to talk. Some of us thought that was why he died. It wasn't, though it *was* why he died the way he did, strangling himself with his own bonds. There are only two reasons for killing a man slowly like that. Revenge is one. The other's information.

"If there was any reason to doubt that you're a master of misdirection, Bum, you proved me wrong on that one. When I got to Ridder's apartment and saw you lurking outside the door I assumed you were going in. I didn't suspect that you'd been on your way *out* and just reversed directions when you heard me coming up the stairs. As tricks go that one dates back to the last ice age, but I bought it because of that subliminal cowboy ethic you carry around with you." I paused. "What did you do, promise to cut the ropes if he told you where to find Smith?"

"You're telling the story. Did I?"

I said, "It didn't come to me in a blinding flash of inspiration. The suspicion was there all the time. I just didn't want to entertain it, because it didn't work. There are plenty of ways to obtain information without committing murder.

Ridder's death had a ritual nature, like a sentence pronounced and carried out. I couldn't fit you to that. Besides, I'd made up my mind by this time that whoever cooled him was also his sister's murderer, and *that* was an act of pure passion. I couldn't see you getting that het up over a five-thousand-dollar bounty. I kept spinning my wheels on that notion. It took a good jolt to get me loose. A whack on the head with a cane was what it took."

He looked down at it again and smiled, but said nothing. "We were talking about your first wife when you let me have it. I'm a nosy person or I'd pursue a more rewarding line of work, like raising chinchillas. After I came to and remembered who I was I got hold of a firm of investigators in Tulsa and asked them to look up that part of your life. They got back to me a little while ago.

"You had two sons by that marriage, Thomas and William. I imagine they were the boys I saw in those pictures the day I frisked your trailer. They were eight and six, respectively, when you were divorced. Irreconcilable differences. Your wife got custody. She remarried soon after and her new husband adopted the boys. The report gets sketchy after that. I don't know what became of Thomas."

"He sells real estate in Texas," Bassett said. "Got a wife and three kids, and he don't know a revolver from a shotgun or which end to point."

"Bully for him. I do know what happened to William. I didn't, until I found out his stepfather's name, the name your younger son took when he was adopted. He was known as William Flynn from the age of seven until almost three weeks ago, when he was shot to death near Mt. Hazel Cemetery in the same ambush that killed his senior partner and crippled Van Sturtevant for life. You were on your way here to kill Alonzo Smith before there ever was a bounty, to avenge your son's murder."

"I was hoping to kill all three."

His voice was strained. The fingers on the crook of the cane were cramped and white.

"The law moved too fast," he continued jerkily. "I was still packing when they got Gross. Then Turkel went down, and then when I was on the road Smith turned himself in. But he was alive, hoss. That was the main thing. He was alive.

"Billy was the one that wanted most to be like me. But too many folks back home knew he was my son, so he come up here to make his own reputation as a police officer. He'd of done it, too, if anyone had gave him half a chance. If he wasn't murdered while he was still learning."

"From the standpoint of justice," I told him, "Smith and Ridder deserved what they got. But you shouldn't have killed the girl, Bum. She never hurt anybody. She just happened to be Deak's sister, and she couldn't help that any more than Billy could help being your son."

"She was doped up to the eyes. I got Ridder's address out of her but I didn't know who he was. I wanted to know where Smith was hiding. She kept drifting in and out. I shook her. I slapped her. I reckon I slapped her too hard. I didn't mean to. I was blind crazy."

He was teetering. I lowered my voice. "You slipped this morning, when you said you lied about going into the commune because you didn't want to get involved with a murder investigation. At the time you told me you didn't go in no one knew there had been a murder. No one but the murderer. You.

"You'd cooled off by the time you came out of the place and saw me staggering up that alley. I must have been there a while by then. After I passed out at your feet you went through my wallet, and when you found out I was an investigator you had a good idea what I was doing there.

You took my keys and loaded Tallulah's body into the trunk of my car and locked it and threw away the keys so I'd think I lost them in the fight. I was a prime candidate for a frame."

"Not you," he corrected. "It was too weak. When the law heard your story I knew they'd think the niggers done it to keep her quiet and tried to pin it on you. The double-double cross, we call it."

"You could have left me in that alley, but I'd seen you, so you took me to your place for doctoring. Why'd you call Iris?"

"I wanted someone to hold you there while I checked out Ridder's place. Not for long—I just wanted time to follow up my lead before you found the girl in your trunk and we all went in for questioning. Only Ridder wasn't there."

"He was working down at Rouge," I said. "But you didn't know that, any more than I knew where he lived. We came at him from opposite ends and met in the middle. It must have taken him a long time to die or you wouldn't still have been there when I showed up."

"Seven hours." He was watching the salesman extolling the virtues of mobile-home living to a young couple on the other side of the lot. The cane's crook rotated rhythmically between Bum's calloused palms. "A man can hold out longer than you'd think when he knows if he relaxes he'll choke. I stood watching him the whole time, after I got him to tell me about the place on Bagley."

"Was it worth it?"

He looked at me. His marblelike eyes were startling in the ruddy-tan face. "It would of been, if I got to Smith first."

I heard sirens in the distance. They might have been going anyplace. I kept him talking.

"You're pretty open about all this."

"So far we're just two guys talking. There's no proof."

"Proof enough to hold you. The cops don't need me to make the connection between you and your son; they'd have done that eventually after the confusion died down. That's motive. Means and opportunity they've got. Most convictions in this country are obtained on circumstantial evidence alone."

"I can't see your percentage in this," he said. "Still sore about that knock on the head?"

"It's not my head. It's the girl. You can justify wanting to kill Alonzo Smith till the cows come home, but you can't explain away her death. That one you'll have to go down for."

"I got to go in before I go down." He choked up on the cane until he was holding it in the middle, the tip foremost.

"You've been playing cowboy too long, Bum. These days you can't just ride out to the Territories and duck the law. They'll come after you. You won't like being on the other end of a manhunt."

"They don't build cells to fit me, hoss."

"Do me a favor," I said. "Don't say, 'They'll never take me alive.' Spare me that."

He grinned. "The good lines have all been took, hoss. So I reckon I just won't say anything."

He threw the cane at me, but I'd seen that coming and sidestepped it, drawing the Smith & Wesson at the same time. He already had his .44 out. Death measured me. But he hesitated with his finger on the trigger.

I didn't. I shot him in the right arm. He grunted, fell back a step, and switched hands in a neat border shift. I shot him again, in the chest this time. He coughed. A little cough for such a big man, as if to get someone's attention.

But there was blood on his lips. His teeth still showed in a grin, but he wasn't looking at me anymore, or at anything else. He wasn't there to look.

He toppled forward, all of a piece like a great tree until his knees touched the trailer hitch and he jackknifed. His muscles bunched twice and relaxed. The big gun slithered out of his grasp onto the ground.

The corners of my mouth ached. I realized then that I was grinning too, grinning like a demented gargoyle. The sirens, louder now, sounded like something on the dark end of a terrifying dream.

From where I stood they might have been organs.

About the Author

Loren D. Estleman is a graduate of Eastern Michigan University and a veteran police-court journalist. Since the publication of his first novel in 1976, he has established himself as a leading writer of both mystery and western fiction. His western novels include Golden Spur Award winner ACES AND EIGHTS, MISTER ST. JOHN and THE STRANGLERS. THE MIDNIGHT MAN is the third book in the series, following MOTOR CITY BLUE and ANGEL EYES. SUGARTOWN, the fifth book in the series, was presented the Shamus Award for Best Private Eye Novel of the year by Private Eye Writers of America. Estleman lives in Whitmore Lake, Michigan.